GAMES

GAMES

WANDA B. CAMPBELL

MICAH 6:8 BOOKS

Games
Copyright © 2006 Wanda B. Campbell
Published by W.B. Campbell Publications/Micah 6:8 Books

First Printing 2020

ISBN 10: 0-9897968-1-7
ISBN 13: 978-0-9897968-1-1

Library of Congress Control Number: 2014915840

Cover Design: Tywebbin Creations

Printed in the United States

NOTE FROM THE AUTHOR

For those who have read *First Sunday in October*, *Liberation* and *Unresolved Issues*, and thought, *Hey, did I miss something?* Well, here it is. *Games* is the second book of the Simone Family Series.

You'll remember how young Brian and Shay connected from the beginning, but the paths they choose may surprise you. Not as wise as their parents, Reggie and Julia, the young pair make immature mistakes and play games that could cost them their future together.

I sincerely hope you enjoy Brian and Shay's journey. Perhaps their story will bring back memories of your younger game-playing days.

As always, I love hearing from readers. Feel free to join my Facebook group, Wanda B. Campbell Readers & Supporters. Or email me at wbcampbell@prodigy.net.

Thank you for your continued support. Without you, this journey would be very lonely and meaningless.

Many blessings,
Wanda B. Campbell

THE FALL

PROLOGUE

Shay looked out over the city from the bay window. From where she stood, the streets of Oakland were a place of peace and tranquility, unlike her mind. Her thoughts and her desires raged a battle so fierce common sense and immorality collided—the pressure giving her a slight headache. Her mind told her run as fast as her size-nine feet would take her and don't look back, but the fire fueled with longing racing through her veins conveyed a different story. One time wouldn't alter her life one bit. One taste of ecstasy wouldn't bring damnation. Or would it?

Shay didn't know what to do. She had never wanted anything so badly in her life. The mere fact that she was still standing in his living room after the many warnings and red flags her conscience sent, confirmed that this was a battle she was about to lose. Shay closed her eyes. "God, please help me," she prayed in a whisper and went back into the den instead of out the front door.

* * *

Brian stared out of the kitchen window. He'd finished the dishes ten minutes ago, but couldn't move. He had a decision to make and didn't trust himself to make the right choice. He'd avoided making a decision for two years, now it was unavoidable. She was different now and so was he.

All evening he told himself this was not right, that God wouldn't be pleased, but his flesh promised him complete satisfaction. Tonight his one-year-old commitment to God was being tested to the max. No matter how hard he prayed

3

the fact remained: He wanted LaShay Hampton in the worst way.

He considered calling his father. Just hearing his voice would bring him back to Earth, but truth be told, Brian wasn't sure he wanted to come back, not yet anyway.

Brian walked into the den, just as Shay turned around. The little strength he had quickly vanished with each step she took toward him. In his eyes, Brian saw that Shay was fighting the same battle as he. Brian placed his arms around her, causing her breathing to accelerate. She returned his embrace and parted her lips. Brian's darkened eyes seemed to look right through her outer shell and directly into her desires. As if she couldn't stand the torture, Shay pulled Brian to her and kissed his lips. After a short feast, he pulled back nearly breathless.

"Shay, this is going to change everything. If you're not ready for that, help both of us and leave now," he warned.

Shay didn't move.

He surrendered then. "Tell me what you want, Shay," his voice deep and loaded with passion.

She didn't say a word, just slowly lifted her tank top over her head.

Brian's heart pounded as he watched her remove the straps to her undergarment. He picked her up and carried her to his bedroom.

Later

"Oh, my God, what have we done?" Shay murmured while covering herself with what little sheet remained on the bed.

"We had sex," Brian answered regretfully.

"This was a big mistake. I shouldn't have allowed this to happen."

Shay's words added injury to his emotional wounds. He'd sinned against God and in the process he hadn't physically pleased Shay. Brian sat on the side of the bed with his back to her. "Sorry, I was that bad."

Shay leaned over and stroked his back. "Brian, that's not

what I meant. What we shared was beautiful. Something I'll always remember. Thank you for giving me the gift of womanhood. But what we did was wrong. We committed sin."

"I know." He sighed. "I should have stayed sexually pure. I should have been more responsible."

"Where do we go from here?" she finally asked.

"I don't know, but we can't do this anymore."

She agreed. "I know. I can't handle this emptiness, this guilt."

He finally turned to face her. "Shay, we cannot go back to the way we were. We-I need to put some space between us. I'll always remember this night, it was wonderful, but I don't know if I'll ever overcome this guilt either."

Shay quietly retrieved her clothing and dressed without saying a word. Just before she left his bedroom she kissed him on the cheek and softly told him good-bye. He stayed in the same spot, long after he heard the front door close.

CHAPTER 1

Shay cried all the way home. Her first sexual experience was supposed to bring her joy. It did, for a moment. Then the guilt of committing fornication overwhelmed her, sending ecstasy out the window. She no longer felt like a secure twenty-three-year-old woman. Willfully committing sin brought an instant feeling of shame and vulnerability that she'd never known before. And exposure. She felt as if the driver of every passing vehicle on I-680 knew she wasn't a virgin anymore. Everyone knew she'd just spent two hours in the bed of a man that wasn't her husband and for the most part, enjoyed it. She didn't feel worthy of any favors from God, but she was thankful her mother and stepfather were already in bed when she arrived home. Shay didn't have the strength to face anyone; right now she could barely face herself. Inside her bathroom she soaked in a hot bubble bath and tried to understand why and how she ended up in bed with Brian Pennington.

They were introduced to each other over three years ago, shortly before her mother married his father. With only an eleven-month difference in their ages, they had a lot of things in common. From the beginning they were inseparable and instantly became best buddies. Back then, Brian was someone for her to hang out and debate with, nothing more. At least that's what she tried to make herself believe. In truth, she became possessive of Brian from day one.

Shay would never admit it to him, but she had always

admired Brian for being so focused at a young age. He always knew exactly what he wanted to do with his life. From day one, all he talked about was being a criminal defense attorney. Shay, on the other hand, wasn't so sure what she wanted to do with her life, but being around him made her want to figure it out. Brian unknowingly brought direction into her life along with companionship.

When her mother gave birth to her little brother two years ago, their relationship took a turn. That was the first time their attraction for each other surfaced and since then they had an unspoken commitment to each other. It was impossible for either of them to date other people, because they spent all of their free time with each other. They talked on the phone often and shared the important events of each other's lives. She was the first to call him on his twenty-first birthday and Brian was the first to congratulate her upon graduating from Stanford University. Brian escorted her to school and social functions. Shay accompanied him nearly wherever he went. The two even traveled together. Their parents were not blind to their closeness, but they never discussed it with them.

Now, at age twenty-three Brian was no longer a young boy with no rhythm; he was a man. And he looked like a man. The once-oversized goofy kid had transformed into a fine six-foot-four-inch two-hundred-forty-pound smooth dark-chocolate specimen. Brian was her type of man: tall, dark and thick all around. Shaving his head bald only made him that much more appealing to her. That alone, should have been enough for her to stay away from him, but it wasn't.

She'd heard the warning signals loud and clear, but told herself she could handle it. She told herself she could tolerate the constant hugs and affectionate kissing that escalated to petting.

At first they started with friendly little pecks on the cheeks; then graduated to soft kisses on the lips. From there, deep-seeded passionate kisses with plenty of tongue. The other day when they'd enjoyed a swim, something they'd done hundreds of times before, Shay nearly hyperventilated when he stepped from the pool in black briefs. She became instantly stimulated and had to drape a towel around her chest when he rubbed lotion onto her shoulders. That day she vowed never to go swimming with him again. Even as she made that vow, she knew she wouldn't be able to keep it. Fact was, she liked being with him and constantly fantasized about being intimate with him.

Today they'd gone ice-skating. She hadn't planned on coming back to the house with him, but at the last minute changed her mind. They had made tacos for dinner and went into the den to watch a movie. Halfway through *The Bodyguard*, she ended up straddling his lap, nearly intoxicated from kissing him. A soft moan escaped when she felt the tenderness of his fingers underneath her tank top. But then he suddenly lifted her from him and went into the kitchen.

"Why didn't I just leave?" she groaned as she squeezed the water from her sponge. Shay knew the answer: She really didn't want to.

Shay's heart warmed as she reminisced about how good Brian made her feel. After the initial penetration, Brian was so gentle and caring, fumbling his way. She appreciated him for taking his time to try and please her. When she reached the pinnacle of womanhood, she cried softly. If she didn't know any better, she'd think she was in love with him.

She bolted upright, splashing water on the floor. "Oh, God!" Panic filled her, now realizing how irresponsible she'd behaved. She and Brian had had intercourse twice without any protection!

"Oh, God, please don't make me pay for my sin with an unwanted pregnancy," she prayed. She would have to wait at least a week for the answer to that prayer.

Before climbing into bed, she kneeled down and prayed. "God, please forgive me for yielding to my flesh and committing fornication. Forgive me for enjoying it. And,

God, please take away this guilt and please take this desire from me."

CHAPTER 2

After a long hot shower, Brian lay in bed unable to sleep. He looked at the now-empty space next to him. Changing the sheets hadn't changed the facts at all. Brian had given his virginity to LaShay Hampton. "How did I get here?" he asked himself for what seemed like the thousandth time. He already knew the answer; Brian wanted to be with Shay, had wanted to for a long time.

For the last two years, she'd been the woman in his life. It didn't start out like that. In the beginning, Shay was just his buddy, someone to hang out with when he visited his dad. That first year, she rarely called him by his name, opting to identify him as "fat head". They had a lot in common, but he thought she was bossy and controlling. Shay always had to have the last word on everything. They couldn't get through the day without at least one argument. Then after his little brother, Josiah, was born things changed. She changed.

She no longer bossed him around, but treated him with respect. Like he was equal to her and she no longer threw the fact that she was eleven months older than him in his face. When he needed someone to talk to, Shay was his best listener and his chief supporter for every idea. She was always there for him.

For two years, he tried to ignore his feelings for her. Brian was successful as long as he didn't see her, which wasn't too often. After he committed his life to God, he thought his feelings for her would go away, at least the physical ones, but they didn't. Shay didn't give him any reason to think she felt the same, so he never voiced his feelings to her.

Brian knew spending so much time with her was lethal to his salvation, but he couldn't help it. He just had to see her, had to hear her voice and rationalized his need for her as friendship. Brian was handling his physical feelings for her well until a few days ago when they went swimming.

Brian was glad that he was already in the pool when she removed her robe, revealing the little red two-piece swimsuit. Somehow when he wasn't looking, Shay had transformed into a woman. The kind of woman he liked. Her five-foot-seven-inch frame owned all the right curves in the right places for him. Her cappuccino skin matched perfectly with her hazel eyes and light-brown hair. Brian wondered what she would have done if she knew what was running through his mind as he rubbed lotion onto her. Shay's skin felt so good, he told himself that was the last time he would touch her until the time was right. Brian knew that day he would eventually have her; he just didn't know it would come this soon and under these circumstances. He'd figured once he finished law school, they would try a relationship.

Today, Brian knew it was risky inviting her inside, but he wasn't ready for her to leave. He didn't have to sit so close to her either. Before he knew it, Shay was straddling him and he was held captive by the sweetness of her mouth. Brian broke his promise not to touch her when he slipped his hands beneath her top and caressed her. He didn't mean to, but her soft skin was too inviting. The deep moan that escaped her lips brought him back to reality and he quickly got away from her.

Brian never asked Shay to leave; he hoped by the time he returned from the kitchen she'd be gone, but she wasn't. When they made eye contact, he knew he had lost the battle for his sexual purity.

There was no doubt in his mind, what happened between them was wrong, but it was also beautiful. Brian gave her part of himself he could never get back and truth be told, he didn't want it back. Being inside the woman he cherished had in a sense stripped him of himself and at the same time ushered in unimaginable guilt and shame. His body was a temple and he defiled it by being one with Shay. Although it was wrong, he was happy they'd shared their first experience with each other.

Before Brian dozed off, he prayed for forgiveness and for God to remove the desire he still held for Shay.

CHAPTER 3

Shay's mother, Julia Simone-Pennington, sat on the floor of the den playing with two-year-old Josiah. He was her miracle baby. After rearing Shay, she'd thought her days of parenthood were over. They were until she fell in love and married Reverend Reginald Pennington. At times, she wished they were younger, because she loved him so much that she wanted to give him a whole tribe of babies. After three years of marriage, she could still count on him to keep every promise he made to her.

"Hey, sweetheart," Reggie said as he slipped his arms around her and kissed her neck.

"I see you've finally gotten enough strength to crawl out of bed," she teased.

"You shouldn't do me like that first thing in the morning. It takes me until noon to recuperate," he said this time kissing her on the lips.

"I'll keep that in mind."

Reggie picked up Josiah. "Brian called and asked me to stop by. He wants to talk to me about something."

"Is everything all right?" she asked

"I don't know, he just said he needed to talk."

Julia was quiet for a moment. "Honey, you should eat before you go." She went into the kitchen to heat his food.

"Some things never change," Julia said when Shay entered the kitchen.

"Good morning, Mom."

"Baby, it's after noon, but that's morning to you," Julia teased her daughter.

"I got in late last night."

"I know. We turned in after eleven o'clock and you weren't here yet." She gave her daughter a stern look.

"Sorry, Mama, I should've called."

"Yes, you should have. I know you're twenty-three, but that doesn't keep me from worrying about you. Next time just call, so I can go to bed without worrying, alright?"

"Alright, Mom." Shay smiled, thinking if she'd called last night she wouldn't be a fornicator this morning.

Reggie placed Josiah's highchair between him and Shay at the kitchen table.

"Good afternoon, sleeping beauty."

"Hey, Dad," Shay affectionately addressed her stepfather.

Julia and Reggie exchanged glances with each other. Normally, Shay didn't address her stepfather by the endearing term.

Shay cleared up the confusion. "I know what I said, Reggie. I called you 'Dad'. Outside of Uncle Jonathan, you're the closest thing to a father I'll ever have, so get used to it," she said flatly.

"It's not that I don't like you addressing me in that manner, you just surprised me," Reggie clarified.

"Life's full of surprises." Shay's mind went back to the previous night. She wanted to smile, but her shame wouldn't allow her. "You never know I might just surprise you and marry your son." When Reggie nearly choked on his cranberry juice, she added, "I'm only playing."

Reggie and Julia exchanged glances again, even more confused about Shay's gleeful demeanor.

"Can I ask you guys something?" Shay didn't wait for an answer. "Is it wrong to feel good about committing sin?"

"Explain what you mean," Reggie said.

"Say you made a mistake and did something you knew was wrong, but what you did felt good and you liked it. I mean, you're sorry for doing it and you feel guilty about it, but that doesn't erase the fact that you enjoyed it and wouldn't mind doing it again."

Reggie responded first. "That doesn't mean you felt good about committing the sin, what that means is that your flesh enjoyed it."

Julia jumped in. "That's normal, because sin feels good to the flesh."

"How long does God make you pay for willfully doing something wrong?" Shay had to know the length of her punishment.

"Shay, there's a penalty to every sin, but God forgives us the moment we ask for forgiveness because He sees us as righteous through the blood of Jesus," Reggie answered.

"But what if you ask for forgiveness, but you're not sure you won't do it again? Then what?"

It was Julia's turn. "Until you gain control over your flesh it will happen again. That's why we have to be watchful and die daily by renewing our minds. We have to make sure our desires are for the things of God and not for the things of this world or the flesh."

"Sometimes what we desire is not wrong, it's just not the right time for us to have it," Reggie added.

Shay thought for a moment then asked, "Can you forfeit what God has for you by moving outside of His will? Let's say you did the right thing with the right person, but at the wrong time?"

"Shay, you have to remember God is forgiving and merciful. Sometimes He'll delay what he has for you, but he won't deny it."

Shay ate the rest of her food without saying a word. Inwardly, she wondered if Brian and she were meant to be together. Deep down she believed they were. True they had a special connection and she really did care about him, for a second last night, she thought she loved him. She wasn't sure, but she thought she heard him say those three words to her right before he released himself. She blinked back tears and wondered if they'd ruined their future.

CHAPTER 4

On the forty-five-minute drive from his Blackhawk home to see Brian in Oakland, Reggie couldn't get his earlier conversation with Shay out of his mind. He thought it was more than a coincidence that both Shay and Brian had something on their minds at the same time. Reggie didn't believe they knew what was really going on between the two of them. Almost from the beginning the two had shared a special connection. The connection they shared was so strong, they even felt each other's pain.

Last year when Shay sprained her ankle rollerblading with her cousins, Brian walked with a limp until she recovered. The funny thing was, Brian didn't even go rollerblading that day. He was tutoring at the True Worship Community Center when the accident occurred. Yet from the moment Shay called him, Brian instantly acquired a limp. Every time Brian caught a cold, Shay would walk around breathing through her nose and sucking constantly on Hall's lemon-flavored cough drops.

Reggie and Julia realized a long time ago, their children were destined to be together, but vowed not to interfere with their lives. Neither Reggie nor Julia ever indicated approval or disapproval of their "non-existent" relationship. It didn't take long for Alysse, Brian's biological mother, to see the connection as well.

"Julia, what's going on with our kids?" Alysse asked one night after Shay accompanied Brian to Arizona to visit her.

"Nothing, if you ask them," Julia answered after placing the call on speaker so Reggie could hear.

"I was not born yesterday. Girl, you should have seen them, they were feeding each other ice cream. I could see if they had different flavors, but they were eating the same kind." Alysse laughed.

"They're quite interesting, I know." Julia laughed with her.

"What are you and Reggie going to do about it?"

"Absolutely nothing," Reggie interjected. "If anything evolves between them, it will be their choice, not ours."

"I wasn't talking to you." Alysse cleared her throat. "As I was saying, *Julia*, would you be happy if it did?"

Julia chose her words carefully. She didn't want to appear bias one-way or the other. "Alysse, as long as my daughter marries the man she loves and he loves her in return, I'll be happy."

"Well, I'm not as conservative as you are. I like Shay and I want to see them together. And if Brian asks for my opinion, or if I just feel like giving it to him, I will let him know that she's the one." Alysse was certain.

Thinking back now on the conversation, Reggie couldn't help but wonder if Alysse's prediction was correct.

Reggie parked his Mercedes in front of what used to be his parents' home. Brian now lived here with his roommate, Todd. Reggie used his key to let himself in.

"Brian," he called.

"I'm in the kitchen, Dad."

Reggie found his son sitting at the kitchen table with his Bible open. As always whenever he saw his son, Reggie walked over to Brian and gave him a tight hug. After missing seventeen years of his son's life, Reggie treasured every moment with him.

"What's going on?" Reggie took a seat opposite Brian and helped himself to some red seedless grapes from the fruit bowl on the table.

Brian lowered his head. "I want your advice on something."

"I'm listening."

"I want to confess something I did wrong and I need help figuring out a way to keep it from happening again."

"Son, what did you do?"

Brian kept his head lowered. "I had sex," he whispered.

So that's it, Reggie thought inwardly. With his thumb and forefinger, he lifted Brian's head. "There's nothing to be ashamed of; we all have sinned and fallen short at one time or another."

"But, Dad, I knew better and I really enjoyed it?"

Reggie's earlier conversation with Shay replayed over in his head. "That's normal, fornication is a sin of the flesh and sin feels good to the flesh." Reggie knew the answer, but he had to ask anyway. "Brian, with whom did you have sex?" Brian's silence confirmed his suspicion. "It was Shay, wasn't it?"

Brian was surprised. "Did she tell you?"

"No, but it's not hard to figure out, since you guys are always together. I'm surprised something like this hadn't happened sooner."

"What do you mean?"

"I mean the two of you aren't teenagers, you're twenty-three-year-old young adults with adult feelings and desires," Reggie clarified. "The two of you have been in a "non-existent" relationship since the summer you met."

"I know, but I thought I could control myself." Brian sounded defeated. "But the more I tried the harder it got."

"Son, never play games with your flesh. If you know you're weak to something, stay away from it until you're strong enough to overcome it."

"I know. I did see the warning signs and I wanted to stop, but I just kept going. I mean, Shay is a beautiful woman." Brian tried unsuccessfully to hide the smile that always creased his face at the thought of Shay's physical attributes.

Reggie studied his son. "Why do you think you didn't

stop? Was it all physical for you or do you have feelings for her?"

"No, it wasn't *all* physical," Brian answered.

Reggie knew his son was stalling. "Son, how do feel about her?"

"I feel good about her?" Brian answered evasively then looked away.

"Brian, do you love her?" Reggie asked plainly.

Brian looked his father in the eye and answered, "Yes, I do."

"Does she know that?"

"I think so."

"You think so?"

"I told her, but I don't think she heard me. Even if she does know, it wouldn't make a difference, because I told her our relationship was over and I was going to put some space between us."

"So, you had sex with her and then told her you needed space?" Reggie paused. "I don't want to steer you into doing something you're not ready to do, but what do you see in the future for the two of you?"

"Whatever plans I may have had were ruined last night."

"You made a mistake, but with some work and discipline, you can move past this."

"I don't know if I'll ever stop feeling guilty and ashamed of what we did," Brian admitted. "At least not enough to be with Shay again."

Guilt and shame were two things Reggie knew a lot about. He almost lost his precious Julia behind it. "Have you asked God for forgiveness?"

"Yes."

"Do you believe He's forgiven you?"

"I think so. I'm not really sure. It seems too easy."

"Brian, if you're going to live by that Bible you're reading, then you're going to have to believe what it says. The Bible tells us that if we confess our sins, God is faithful and just to forgive us of our sins and He will cleanse us from all unrighteousness." Brian listened attentively.

"That same Bible tells us that if we walk after the things of the spirit and not after the flesh, there is no need for us to feel condemned about our past sins and mistakes. We are made righteous by the blood of Jesus. I know what it's like to live like a prisoner after you've been set free. I almost lost Julia behind it and if you don't dismiss the guilt by forgiving yourself, you and Shay don't have a chance."

"How do I do that? How do I forgive myself?" Brian earnestly asked. "I mean, I knew what I was doing and I knew it was wrong. But to be totally honest, I wanted to do it."

"Brian, first take responsibility for your actions. Accept that you handed control of your life over to your flesh. Then leave the sin in the past. Do what it takes to build up your spiritual man and not your flesh and be watchful."

"For instance, you and Shay have been intimate. Don't tempt yourself by being alone with her. Meet in public places or come out to the house, but don't hang out here alone. Don't play little kissing and touching games, because you will find yourself right back in bed. And, son, you need to talk to her, to get a clear understanding of where your relationship is headed. That's part of the problem. You and Shay have never defined your relationship. You won't even admit that you have one. Invisible boundaries are easy to cross, but if you draw the boundaries together, you're less likely to cross them because you'll know what's expected of you."

Reggie spent the rest of the afternoon with his son. Before he left, he prayed for him. Only time would tell, if he got through to him or not.

* * *

Shay's head had barely touched the pillow when her phone rang.

"Hello," she said, without checking the caller ID.

"Did I wake you?" Brian asked.

Has his voice always been this sexy? "No, what's on your mind?"

"Us."

"There's no us remember; you need space," she said sarcastically.

"You're right. I just wanted to make sure we have an understanding."

"And the correct understanding would be—"

Brian breathed deeply into the phone. "That you and I will always be friends."

Shay felt like she'd been punched in the stomach. Part of her had hoped they could build a relationship. All afternoon, last night replayed in her mind and she was almost certain he'd told her he loved her. Maybe that's what people say when they're at the zenith of satisfaction, she guessed.

"Brian, how do you feel about me?" She had to know.

"After all this time, you don't know?"

"I'm not sure."

In the dead silence that covered the line, Shay's breathing accelerated and the pulse in her neck throbbed. "Brian?"

He cleared his throat. "LaShay Hampton, you're a beautiful woman and my best friend and after last night, you'll always have a special place in my heart."

Shay didn't bother saying good night. She hung up the phone and cried herself to sleep.

CHAPTER 5

Shay tossed and turned in her bed. For the third night in a row she couldn't fall asleep without thinking about the pleasure she'd found in Brian's bed. She hadn't seen him in two weeks and every inch of her seemed to be crying out for his touch. Her ears longed to hear his voice. Since he announced his need for space, her eyes were opened to see how much he really meant to her. No matter what she told herself, the truth was she wanted him so badly, she could smell him. It wasn't all physical; she could have sex with anyone, if that were the case. She missed Brian. She missed his company and conversation. Shay hated to admit it, but she wanted to make love to him again. To release the tension, she increased her exercise routine by an hour and practiced meditation. Nothing worked. In fact, each workout left her more aroused.

Nighttime was the hardest for her. Last night, she had to jump in the shower in order to cool down enough to sleep. When she did fall asleep, her dreams were filled with images of him. She awakened drenched with perspiration.

"God, I can't take this anymore. Why did he have to feel so good?" she cried and held onto her pillow to muffle the noise. "God, I am so sorry for opening this door, please forgive me. Please deliver me from this torture. I promise I'll never do it again. I won't have sex with anyone but my husband," Shay vowed then rocked and cried until she fell asleep.

* * *

Reggie and Julia sat at the kitchen table watching Shay frantically move around, looking like a wild woman with her shoulder-length hair going every direction on the compass. She looked tired, like she hadn't slept in days. It was two o'clock in the afternoon and she still wore pajamas. The white film in the corners of her mouth was indication she hadn't brushed her teeth either. After pulling out every drawer and opening the cabinets, she moved to the den. She never said a word, so they had no idea what she was looking for.

Julia looked at her husband for an answer, but he didn't have one, just shrugged his shoulders. Reggie had noticed Shay's erratic behavior and had a pretty good idea as to what was bothering her. Brian was having similar issues. The other day at Starbucks, Brian went off because the young man gave him a grande instead of a tall caramel apple cider. It didn't matter that they charged him for the smaller size. "That's not what I want!" he yelled until they made him the right size.

Shay stormed back into the kitchen. "Have you guys seen my gold charm bracelet?"

Julia ignored her daughter's rudeness. "Good afternoon, Shay."

"I said have you seen my gold charm bracelet?"

Julia stood and pulled the piece of jewelry Brian had given Shay for her last birthday from her pocket. "Here," Julia said softly. "I found it on the floor in the den."

"Mama, why didn't you tell me you had it? You saw me running around here searching for it!" Shay yelled at her mother.

"This is not going to end well," Reggie mumbled.

Julia swallowed hard. "Next time try opening that big mouth of yours and saying something." Julia's voice sounded too sweet, almost sugary.

Reggie stood.

Shay rolled her neck and screamed at her mother. "I don't have to tell you everything, I'm a grown—"

26

The avalanche came so fast, Shay didn't get the chance to complete her sentence. Julia literally slammed the words out of her mouth. With ease, Julia grabbed her, flung her across the table and slammed her onto the kitchen floor. Shay thought she was about to die. Reggie grabbed Julia from behind and carried her out of the kitchen to keep her from doing any more damage. Shay took the opportunity to run for cover inside of her room.

It took Reggie thirty minutes to calm Julia down and make her promise she wouldn't kill her daughter, before he allowed her to go upstairs.

"Mama, I'm sorry," Shay said when Julia stepped into her room without knocking.

"What is going on with you, Shay? "I'm going to give you a chance to tell the truth, before I read your mail."

"I got upset when I couldn't find my bracelet, that's all." Shay turned away from her mother.

"I'm not talking about just today. You've haven't been yourself for over two weeks. What's bothering you and don't say nothing."

Shay didn't respond, she couldn't without telling her mother the whole story and she was too embarrassed to do that.

"Shay," Julia persisted.

"I can't say," she finally answered between sniffles.

Julia sighed deeply. "I'm turning into my mother." Ana Simone could see through every smoke screen, like she had some kind of truth magnet chip embedded in her.

"Then I'll say it for you. You had sex and now you feel guilty about it because you want to do it again," Julia stated plainly.

Shay looked at her mother in disbelief. "How did you know?"

"The questions you asked about the flesh and sin were a dead giveaway."

"Oh." Shay's voice was just above a whisper. "Do you know with whom?"

Julia twisted her face. "Let me take a wild guess. He's twenty-three, six foot four, dark-complexioned with a left dimple and looks a lot like my husband." Julia folded her arms, effectively daring her daughter to deny it. "Am I close?"

Shay was embarrassed, but also relieved, at least now she didn't have to hide it. "Did he tell you?"

"No he didn't, but the way he's been avoiding you and this house was a good clue."

Shay sat with her shoulders slumped.

"You miss him, don't you?"

Shay exhaled. "Yes."

"Why aren't you seeing each other anymore?"

"Because, we're not going to pursue a relationship, we're going to remain friends only—very distant friends."

Julia looked at her daughter as if she were a stranger. "Girl, what are you talking about? You and Brian have been in a relationship practically since the day you met!"

Shay wiped her face. "But when we slept together, it messed things up."

"How?"

"We willfully sinned, Mama, and we enjoyed it. We have to pay for that."

"And you think you have to pay for your mistake by never having contact with each other again?" Julia questioned.

"Exactly."

Julia felt sorry for her baby. "So you're prepared to be miserable for the rest of your life, because of one mistake? That's going to be kind of hard to do since his father and brother live in this house and I love him like a son." Shay didn't respond. "Do you love Brian?"

"Yes." Shay realized that now that he wasn't around. Actually, she realized it a year ago, but wasn't ready until today to admit it.

"Does he love you?"

Shay thought about their last conversation. "I don't know."

28

"What if he is in love with you? Don't you think God can forgive you of your indiscretion and show you how to build a proper relationship? Shay, you and Brian have something special. Don't allow one mistake to destroy everything."

"I don't think I can have a godly relationship with him, Mama. Maybe if I didn't enjoy having sex with him so much, it might be possible," Shay answered. "All the relating I want to do involves a horizontal position."

Julia narrowed her eyebrows. "Just how many times have you had sex?"

"Just that one time, but we did it twice."

"Just twice, and you've lost your mind?" Julia teased.

"Mama, you don't understand." Shay fanned her face and laid back on her bed.

"Oh, I have a good idea." Julia grinned. "But seriously, honey, don't feel guilty because you enjoyed it. Sex was designed to feel good. Sex feels good whether you're married or not. But the *only* sex that God honors is within the confines of marriage. Repent for committing the act of fornication, and don't do it again."

"You need to be honest with him about your feelings and stop hiding behind being *just friends*. You and Brian are *just friends* about as much as Reggie and I are." Julia smirked. "I guess that's how your little brother was conceived, by spreading all that friendship around."

"Mama," Shay whined.

"Mama, nothing. You need to set some boundaries for yourself. When Reggie and I were dating, I knew if I kissed him on the lips, I'd end up in bed with him. So we didn't kiss until after Pastor Jackson pronounced us husband and wife. You have to find out what you are weak to and protect yourself. The only way the devil can get the upper hand, is if we're ignorant to his devices."

Julia left Shay's room an hour later. "God, please let her take heed to what I've said," she prayed on her way down the hall to check on Josiah.

CHAPTER 6

"Todd, where's the orange juice?" Brian yelled at his roommate.

"We ran out yesterday," Todd yelled back.

"And you couldn't pick up some more?"

Brian slammed the refrigerator door shut.

"Man, it's your week to buy groceries. And while you're there get some toothpaste."

Brian slammed his fist on the table; he had forgotten to buy groceries. He had been forgetting a lot of things lately and he really didn't know why. He had a lot of free time since he'd stopped hanging out with Shay. So there was no reason why he couldn't take care of his shopping or any of his other responsibilities. Then he remembered shopping was something he usually did with Shay. Come to think of it, he did most things with her. Now that Shay wasn't around, he didn't want to do much of anything. He didn't want to clean the house or even make his bed.

"Man, you sure are grouchy lately. What's going on?" Todd asked, folding his arms and leaning against the arched doorway.

"Things, just things." Brian didn't feel like talking.

"These things wouldn't have anything to do with Shay, would they?"

Brian attempted to act nonchalant. "Why would you ask that?"

"Because I haven't seen her around and your cell phone has been quiet."

31

Todd was right. His funky mood had everything to do with LaShay Hampton. Brian missed her so much, but he had to stay away from her. That was the punishment he imposed on himself for committing fornication.

The nights were especially hard for him. Lately he'd been up until one o'clock in the morning lifting weights in the garage. Brian needed to be exhausted before he climbed into the bed he had shared with her or else he would lay there daydreaming about the night they shared. He had to fall asleep with his headphones on to drown out her voice in his head. However, he still kept a picture of her on his nightstand.

Brian turned his attention back to Todd. "What else do we need?"

Todd, realizing Brian was not going to divulge anything, called off a few more items and left.

* * *

Sunday morning service at True Worship was something Brian really enjoyed. Not because his father was the pastor, but he always left revived and ready to tackle the next week. He'd missed the last two Sundays. The excuse he fed himself was he had finals to study for, which was true. But he really felt too guilty to walk into the house of God. Brian was afraid the prayer warriors would zero in on him the second he entered the sanctuary, particularly Mother Elsie, the church mother. She only had a sixth-grade education, but read most people's spirits with one-hundred-percent accuracy.

Pastor Reggie's preference was for his family to sit in the front center section of the 1500-seat sanctuary, but today, Brian thought he would hide in the back. His plan didn't work.

"Hey, Brian, I saved you a seat," Angie said, approaching him on her way to the front.

Angie was Julia's oldest sister. She and her husband Mike had joined the church right before Reggie and Julia got married.

"Thanks," was all Brian could say as he made his way to the front. He knew better than to argue with his aunt. Of course the vacant seat was right next to Shay, who was holding Josiah.

Brian was about to turn and leave, but his little brother stopped him.

"Bi-an, Bi-an," little Josiah called and held out his arms.

Brian took his brother and sat down and played with him for a while, but didn't speak to Shay.

CHAPTER 7

Shay's feelings were hurt. How could the man she'd been crying herself to sleep over, the man she loved. The man she'd given her virginity to. How could he sit right next to her and not say one word? Not talking to her over the phone was one thing, but in person he couldn't even say "hi" or "hello". He didn't acknowledge her presence at all. Brian wouldn't even look at her. Shay folded her arms and glared at him.

The congregation stood as the Praise and Worship ministry took their places on the platform. Hitting Brian's head in the process, Shay yanked her purse and walked out.

She was pulling out of the parking lot when Brian caught up with her.

"Shay, where are you going?"

She rolled her eyes. "I'm giving you some space, fat head!"

He leaned into her car. "Shay, I'm sorry. I wasn't prepared to see you today."

"Shut up, Brian. You knew I would be at church today! I'm here every Sunday."

"But I didn't know I'd be sitting next to you." Brian looked around; they were not alone. A steady stream of people flowed through the parking lot en route to the sanctuary. "Shay, we need to talk. Let's go somewhere where we can talk in private. I want to clear the air between us."

Shay didn't want to go anywhere with him. She also didn't want their business to be headline news for the TWM gossip column. "Meet me at the condo in Emery Bay," Shay barked and drove off.

The minute she let Brian into her mother's corporate condo, Shay got a bad feeling in the pit of her stomach. It was then that she realized that they were alone for the first time since that night. Her conversation with her mother replayed in her head. The part about being alone with Brian was jumbled and undecipherable. *This won't take long. We'll just talk and then leave.*

Shay grabbed a Henry Wienhard's root beer from the refrigerator and sat down on the couch. "You wanted to talk, so talk," she said before taking a swig.

Brian stood in front of her. "You're not going to offer me anything?" he asked trailing his eyes along the shaft of her long legs.

"You don't need anything; you're not going to be here that long," she answered and sat the bottle on the table without a coaster.

He didn't say anything, so she made her announcement. "Brian, I'm leaving California for a while. I'm going to Harvard for my Master's and teaching credential. I'll be gone for a year."

His eyes bulged the precise second his jaw fell. "When do you leave?"

"Right after you graduate."

"But that's only a few weeks from now."

"I know." He remained quiet so she continued. "I would leave sooner, but I don't want to miss your graduation." Shay admitted it was important to her. "The move should give you, excuse me, us enough space. Don't you think?"

Shay's eyes begged him to ask her not to leave, but he didn't. If he wasn't going to ask her to stay, she wasn't going to tell him how she really felt about him. When she reached for her root beer, he took her hand and lifted her to her feet and hungrily kissed her. As he explored the inside of her mouth, his hands roamed her body and every word her mother had spoken went right out the window along with the guilt and the shame of their first encounter. Every promise Shay made to God about not touching him again was placed on hold. The only thing of importance was desire.

Brian felt and smelled so good to her, Shay had to have him. "God, please forgive me, again, for what I'm about to do, again," Shay whispered when his kisses traveled down to her neck. She lifted his head so she could look into his eyes. "Brian, make love to me one last time, then I promise we can go back to being just friends." Without hesitation, Brian lifted her into his arms and carried her to the bedroom.

The orange rays of sunset sprayed the bedroom as they made their way up the third summit. This time it was Shay who couldn't hold back anymore. "I love you, Brian. I love you so much," she said repeatedly, then cried quietly when the reality of this being their last time together in this way came crashing down.

Later in the parking garage, Shay unlocked her car then turned and kissed him on the cheek. "See you later, friend." Shay locked herself in the confines of her PT Cruiser before Brian returned the valediction and before she gave into her emotions.

When Shay went to bed that night, she slept peacefully. She didn't have everything figured out. She didn't know if God would ever forgive her and be merciful enough to give her another chance at love with Brian. Shay wasn't sure if she wanted to love someone other than Brian. One thing was for sure, the love she felt today would help her get through whatever punishment God had waiting for her.

* * *

Brian slept well also. True, he felt bad about yielding to his flesh again, but he didn't feel bad about being in love with Shay. He didn't want Shay to leave and he really didn't want any more space, but she'd made up her mind. If she was willing to leave that confirmed that their relationship didn't mean that much to her. Brian wished he'd listened to his father and been upfront about his feelings with her, but it was too late for that now.

The sound of her telling him she loved him was like music to his ears and that rhythm would help him get through the rough days ahead. If God ever decides to give him another chance at love, he didn't know if he would take it, because he left his heart with Shay.

CHAPTER 8

Brian finished his laps in his father's pool. From the patio window, Shay watched him take laps wondering if she should tell him or just wait it out on her own. He looked so relaxed, now threading and enjoying warm water in the 80-degree clear weather. What she had to tell him would without a doubt disrupt his peace, but what choice did she have. Shay couldn't believe the mess she'd gotten herself into. Behaving as a responsible adult had never been an issue, but that was before she discovered the power of passion mingled with lust. "Please, God, I know I was wrong, but how about some longsuffering and mercy here?" she begged, once more looking toward heaven, before stepping onto the marble tile that led to the pool.

Brian saw her approaching and floated to the side of the pool. Water splashed her feet as he poached his massive body on the tile. They hadn't seen or spoken to each other since the day they shared at Emery Bay.

"You look pretty." Brian took in the soft-pink tank dress and white sandals. Shay grabbed his towel from the lounge chair and handed it to him. "Thank you," Brian said, accepting the towel. "How have you been?"

His casual tone was too impersonal for her. Considering she was the woman he'd given his virginity to and whose he had taken. "Brian, we need to talk," Shay answered, without responding to his question. She then turned her back to him, trying not to remember what it felt like to lay against his now-bare chest.

"What do you want to talk about, Shay?"

Shay folded her arms and nervously looked back toward the house. Reggie and Julia weren't visible through the sliding glass doors, which meant they were probably upstairs in their bedroom. She'd throw herself in the pool and sink to the bottom if they heard her next words. She looked down at her arms in amazement at the goose bumps that had suddenly appeared in the 80-degree weather. "I'm late," she whispered.

"Where are you going?" Brian asked innocently. Too innocently to be the same man who turned her world upside down.

Shay let out a long sigh. "Brian, my period is late."

* * *

At first Brian just sat there staring at her as if trying to process what her words meant. Then he lowered his head and massaged his temples as the impact of Shay's words slammed his frontal lobe. "Oh, God," he finally said, before stepping completely from the pool and wrapping his robe around him. There was only one thing on his mind, what was he going to do if Shay was pregnant with his child?

He was not ready to become a father and he didn't believe in abortion. What was he supposed to do? What about school? He didn't have a job. How was he going to feed and clothe a child? What would his father say? How would his mother feel? "How late are you?" he finally asked to stop the questions from bombarding his brain.

"Two weeks." Shay's voice sounded so low he barely heard her. She still didn't make eye contact with him.

"Have you taken a test?"

"No."

"How long are you going to wait before you find out if you are preg—" Brian couldn't say the word. "You know..."

With fear and anxiety etched on her face, Shay turned away from him. Brian sensed that she harbored the same fear as him. He walked over to her and turned her to face him. Her head slumped, hiding the tears that rolled down her cheek, but Brian knew her too well. He instinctively wiped her cheeks with his fingertips and cupped her face. "I wish I could tell you that everything is going to work out, but I can't. If you're pregnant, I don't know what I am going to do. But I promise you, you won't have to deal with this by yourself. If you have our child, you won't raise it alone."

Brian's sincerity leaped out and seared her heart. She knew he would put his life on hold to take care of his child. But she didn't want it to come to that, didn't want Brian to abort his dreams because of uncontrolled lust. Shay wasn't rich, but by all accounts she was well off. With trust funds from both sets of grandparents and being the daughter of a wealthy developer didn't hurt. Shay would be able to adjust to the cost of raising a child, but not Brian. He didn't have the cushion or support system she had. Because of that it was Brian's desire not to have children until he became a lawyer, wanting to make sure his own children never suffered the things he had endured as a child. Now that might change.

"I know," Shay said softly, and then ran into the house before a flood of tears erupted.

CHAPTER 9

He wanted to follow her, but didn't. Brian stayed outside praying that Shay wasn't pregnant. She couldn't be. Sure they had unprotected sex, but Brian wasn't ready to be a parent. He couldn't take care of himself without his father's assistance, how was he supposed to provide for a child. And what about school? He would have to postpone law school and find a job. Brian loved Shay, but being an unwed father was not on his agenda and he was not ready for marriage. No, Shay couldn't be pregnant, he decided. Not now. "God, please don't let this be," he mumbled, walking back to the house.

Inside the confines of the guest room, he mechanically showered then slid into a pair of khaki shorts and a white T-shirt. The possibility of his child growing inside of Shay robbed him of his rational thinking ability. He paced rapidly in circles until he became dizzy and fell onto the queen-sized bed. He lay there until the ceiling returned to its still-state. The pounding in his chest, which surfaced with Shay's revelation, remained. He counted on that being a permanent fixture until he found out the results of the pregnancy test. Somberly, he made his way to the den to join his father.

Minus the usual passion and intensity, Brian stared at the mounted plasma screen. The San Francisco Giants and the Oakland A's were engaged in the Bay Bridge Series. Instead of professional athletes, the men on the screen were orange, black, white and green dots. His team was winning, but he didn't know that. The numbers danced over the screen like his thoughts. *Shay can't be pregnant. I still have law school. How could I have been so irresponsible? I didn't even think about using a condom.*

"I can't believe that ump! That ball missed the strike zone by a mile." Reggie's protest snapped Brian from his internal rambling.

Brian turned to find his father staring at him, waiting for a response. Quickly, he decided the best way to keep his father from asking questions about his inattentiveness was to play along. He threw his hands in the air. "I can't believe that," he yelled at the television, then stood. "I'm going to get something to drink. I'll bring you back some apple juice." Brian left before Reggie could tell him he already had a glass of cranberry juice.

By the seventh-inning stretch anxiety took over and Brian left without eating dinner and without saying good-bye to Shay. He did manage enough courage to call her as he lay unable to sleep in bed later that night.

"When are you going to the doctor?" he asked.

"Tomorrow at eleven o'clock."

"Where?"

Shay gave him the address. "You don't have to come. I can handle it on my own."

Even as the words left her mouth, he knew she didn't mean them. "Shay, it's me you're talking to. You want me there and I want to be there. We're in this together."

"Thank you," she whispered and after a pause added, "fat head."

He half-heartedly chuckled. "I'll meet you there, Ms. Know It All."

CHAPTER 10

Shay distracted her thoughts by attempting to read the latest cooking magazine. Under normal circumstances the recipe for the triple chocolate torte drizzled with caramel would have held her attention. But her eyes kept moving from the pages and surveying the mauve-colored waiting room. She watched the receptionist check new patients in and then heard those same patients called into the examination rooms. Her heart rate accelerated every time the wooden door opened, afraid a nurse in colorful scrubs would come render her fate. She glanced at her watch, just a few minutes more and she'd be home-free.

Brian sat next to Shay watching the video health monitor. He wasn't interested in the latest allergy medication, but found it to be a good distraction. They had been waiting for the results of Shay's blood test for two hours. To their relief, the regular urine test was negative, but to be sure the doctor ordered the more-accurate blood test since Shay's cycle was two weeks behind schedule.

Brian looked over at Shay who had remained quiet for most of the day. She hadn't given him any indication she blamed him, herself or both for their predicament. Brian placed her hand in his. "I'm sorry about all this," Brian said apologetically.

"What are you sorry about? You didn't do anything I didn't want you to do. As I recall, I extended the invitation."

"True, but I should have been more responsible."

"So should I, especially after that first time. But, Brian, I honestly didn't think it would happen again. After the first time I swore it wouldn't happen again."

"Me, too. I made all kinds of promises and bargains with God," Brian admitted.

"Probably the same ones I made."

They shared a light laugh.

For just a second, Brian allowed his mind to drift back to Emery Bay. How wrong they had been, but yet how good it felt, like they were meant to be. "No matter the outcome, Shay, we're still friends, right?"

Shay gave him a slight smile. "Of course, fat head, you're my best friend," Shay answered then turned her attention back to the cooking magazine. The colorful pages appeared blank to her after Brian reminded her they didn't have a future together. Somewhere deep within, she hoped she was pregnant, just so she could have a little part of him forever. A moment later the nurse called Shay back to the examination room.

Brian waited in the waiting room with his head bowed. He was so deep in prayer, he didn't notice when Shay returned wearing a big grin.

"Congratulations, you are NOT going to be a father!"

Brian let out a deep sigh of relief then said audible words of thanks. "Why are you late?" he then asked.

"The doctor doesn't know, but I'm definitely not pregnant. Could be stress and irregular periods do run in my family."

"Thank God," Brian said again. "God sure does know how to save us from ourselves."

"I know that's right," Shay agreed.

Three days later, Shay stood on the football field at UC Berkeley and watched Brian receive his Criminal Justice degree, graduating Summa Cum Laude. She was so proud of him, when the professor called his name tears rolled down her face. Her best friend was on his way to fulfilling his dreams.

After the ceremony he walked over to join the family.

Shay snapped his picture. While he got hugs and congratulations from everyone, Shay quietly slipped away; she had a plane to catch.

CHAPTER 11

"Thanks, Mom," Brian said to his mother when she handed him a tall glass of ice-cold lemonade. He enjoyed spending his short summer break in Goodyear, Arizona with his mother and stepfather, but with Goodyear being located just outside of Phoenix, he was perched right smack in the middle of the desert heat.

Alysse left and returned with a gallon-sized pitcher filled with Brian's favorite beverage. "Four years in the Bay Area has spoiled you. And that big pool your father and Julia have."

"Come on, Ma. I'm not spoiled." Brian pouted.

Alysse folded her arms across her chest and narrowed her eyebrows. His stepfather cleared his throat.

"Well, maybe just a little," Brian conceded. "What can I say? I have a great dad."

Alysse sat down on the enclosed patio and watched Brian and her husband, Mark, spar off in a game of chess. She studied Brian from head to toe and discovered he was not her baby anymore. Somehow when she wasn't looking, her little boy had transformed into quite a handsome, grown man. Who was she kidding? Brian was the spitting image of his father and Reginald Pennington was ten degrees past fine.

Brian's physical characteristics weren't the only thing that had changed. Brian's attitude had transformed in the last month. He was no longer tense and irritable.

He'd just turned twenty-three and Alysse still wasn't

ready to let him go. Four years ago, she fought tooth and nail to keep him from moving to California, but lost the battle when Reggie, Brian and Mark ganged up on her. Now Brian was on his way to law school in a few weeks. And just liked he'd planned; he'd been accepted into the Boalt Hall School of Law at UC Berkeley.

Business at the travel agency she owned with her husband had been slow lately and Alysse worried about meeting Brian's tuition. Her son never asked for much, outside of an education to fulfill his dream of becoming a lawyer. Now Alysse was afraid she wasn't going to be able to grant him that.

"Brian, when is your first tuition payment due?" she asked, tying to sound cheerful.

Brian shrugged his shoulders. "I don't know."

"Well, how much is it?"

"I don't know." He shrugged again.

"Brian, you start classes in a few weeks and you don't know when or how much is due?" Alysse stood with her fists planted at her waist. "I need to know, so I can figure out how I'm going to pay it!"

Mark narrowed his eyes when Alysse raised her voice. Mark being ten years her senior didn't care too much for drama and Alysse had a short fuse.

"Mom, don't worry about it. I gave all the information to my dad and he took care of it."

Alysse's face contorted. "What do you mean he took care of it and *how* did he take care of it?"

"Mom, I don't know how, but he told me not to worry about it."

"Oh, he did?"

"Alysse." At the sound of Mark's firm tone, she relented.

Alysse didn't press Brian any further, but went inside and called Reggie. As she punched his number, she felt a great relief, because she honestly didn't know how she would come up with the money. She also felt like eating crow.

"Hello, Alysse," Reggie answered on the third ring.

"You must have caller ID. Look, I'm calling about Brian's tuition." Alysse was always direct and to the point with everyone.

"What about it?"

"He told me you took care of it?" Alysse responded cautiously, fearing her son had given her the wrong information.

"That's correct. In fact, I just sent the check off yesterday," Reggie answered.

"When's the next payment due?" she asked, hoping it wouldn't be due for at least three months.

"There isn't one; I paid it in full."

Alysse was speechless. It was times like this when she regretted not allowing him to see Brian until he was nearly an adult. It was only because of Reggie that her son was able to pursue any of his dreams.

Alysse took a deep breath. Chewing crow was tougher than she thought. "I didn't expect you to do that, considering you've already paid for undergrad."

"Brian is my son, Alysse. I told you I would take care of his college education. That included law school."

"I didn't know that." Alysse breathed a huge sigh of relief. "Thanks, Reggie. Lord knows I don't have the money." Glad that was out of the way, she changed the subject. Maybe one day she and Reggie would make peace about their broken relationship, but today was not the day. "What's going on with Brian and Shay?" Brian was a little upset with Shay for leaving his graduation without saying good-bye.

"What are you talking about?"

Alysse hated when Reggie pretended not to know what was going on with Brian. To her envy, her son shared everything with his father. Her son once clung to her, but now all Brian wanted was to emulate the great Pastor Reginald Pennington. "Are they dating or not?" she snapped.

"Brian is there with you, why don't you ask him?"

"I already did, but he won't give me an answer," Alysse admitted.

"Then neither will I. Good-bye, Alysse."

The dial tone greeted Alysse before she could form a comeback.

* * *

Brian finished his third lap and sat on the edge of the pool enjoying the warm Arizona night. The eighty-degree night weather was perfect for swimming. Living next door in California for the past four years, he'd forgotten how quiet and peaceful the desert could be. Nights in the desert were pitch-black, but surprisingly the darkness carried a peaceful calm. In the thickness of the night one couldn't help but be still and reflect on one's life. Brian leaned his head back and contemplated his progress. Thus far, what he had accomplished was remarkable, considering his humble beginnings.

As a child, he lived like a vagabond with his mother. They never had enough of anything, including food or money. And to top it off, he suffered physical beatings from Alysse's drunken boyfriends.

Alysse had grown up in the foster care system, which meant Brian didn't have any close relatives that he could turn to. He spent most of his childhood feeling alone and helpless and very depressed. Then right before he graduated high school, Julia Simone appeared out of nowhere and united him with his dad. The father he didn't know existed.

Brian had a special love for his stepmother, whom he affectionately addressed as, Mama J. If it hadn't been for her popping up, he would have never known his father was alive and well. His mother had told him he was dead. From that day on his life changed. The questions about who he was and where he belonged were finally answered. The emptiness he'd felt all his life now overflowed with his father's love. Brian had friends his own age, but considered his dad to be his best friend and his hero.

Brian dove into the pool when his mind wandered to

Shay. He hoped water would clog his ears so he could no longer hear her constant voice in his head. He hadn't spoken to her since she slipped away at his graduation. He missed her, but knew it was better this way. Brian didn't need any distractions right now and just thinking about the day they spent at Emery Bay and his near-brush with fatherhood was sobering enough. Those memories would both haunt and console him forever.

On more than one occasion he found himself replaying the sound of her voice telling him she loved him. Brian knew he would never hear those words from her again, at least not in the same context. That hurt him, but he accepted that as part of his punishment for breaking his commitment to God. Besides, he didn't believe Shay really meant those words in the same context as he'd used them. Brian loved her, the woman, the individual, not just the physical activity alone. He didn't just love her, he was in love with her, but she would never know it.

Since he'd been in Arizona, he'd been working on getting his spiritual life back on track. He prayed every day and read his Bible. He attended bible study with his mother and stepfather and watched the Word Channel whenever he could. When he drove his Rav4 around Phoenix, he blasted his favorite gospel CDs and when he went to sleep. But all of that didn't remove her memory from his mind or his heart.

Brian did notice that he wasn't the least bit interested in other women, like the other day when he walked to Cold Stone Creamery. While he sat on the store's patio eating his ice cream, he didn't notice the young lady eyeing him from the next table. When he didn't respond to her flirtations, she boldly approached him.

"Would you like some company?"

Brian gave her a quick once-over and without any regard said, "No," and continued eating. Looking dejected, the young lady walked slowly back to her table.

Brian wore a pair of shorts and tank top when he accompanied his mother to the grocery store on yesterday.

When Alysse turned down the opposite aisle, a bold woman approached him. "I would love to wrap my legs around you and ride off into the desert night," she said and held out a card with her number on it. Instead of being flattered, Brian was offended. He didn't say a word to the woman, just took the card and tore it up right in her face then handed the pieces back to her. His craving for sex was satisfied. What Brian wanted was love from Shay.

CHAPTER 12

Shay sat Indian-style on her bed reading over lecture notes. Since her arrival at Harvard four weeks ago, her days were consumed with studying and more studying. The accelerated Masters and Teaching Credential program was only a year in length. That left little if no time at all for recreation. She was glad, because it kept her mind off home. She'd taken a year off after completing her undergraduate work at Stanford and it took her a minute to get back into the flow and organization of a full schedule. Added to the stress, was the fact that this was her first time living so far away from her mother and the Simone family. While at Stanford, Shay lived in the dorms, but that distance was only an hour drive from her mother's Blackhawk estate. Her aunt Angie lived near the college. During her first week in Cambridge, Shay called home every day. Now she had so much work to do, she limited her calls to the weekend.

Overall, she liked the New England atmosphere. Surprisingly, Cambridge was a major metropolitan city similar to Oakland and Berkeley. Massachusetts Avenue, or as the locals call it, Mass Avenue, reminded her of Berkeley's Telegraph Avenue with its many multicultural gift shops and street vendors. One could find everything from clothing to exotic art on the street corners. On a real good night, one could even find the kind of candy that would help you stay awake and study all night.

The mixture of cultures impressed Shay. Whereas the Bay Area was mostly populated with minority groups like

Hispanics, Asians and African Americans like herself, New England was filled with West Indians, the Irish, Puerto Ricans and Haitians. Each group had their exclusive area, yet everyone coexisted peaceably together.

On Sundays, she opted out of church services, attempting to dodge God's wrath for sleeping with Brian again after she vowed not to. She didn't pray anymore since she thought God had turned a deaf ear. Her Sundays were spent in her apartment studying or reading in Harvard Square.

Engrossed in her reading material, her cell phone rang three times before the disco ringtone caught her attention. She read the caller ID then smiled.

"Hey, Uncle." It was her closest uncle, Jonathan Simone. He was only fourteen months older than her mother and after Shay's father died, Jonathan made it his responsibility to look after his niece.

"How are you doing, baby girl?" he asked in the voice Shay always thought similar to James Earl Jones.

"I miss you guys, but I'm adjusting."

"I'm proud of you for taking on such a challenging program."

Shay sucked her teeth. "Thanks, but I hope I didn't bite off more than I can chew. It's a little tougher than I expected. I'm not going to give up though."

"You can't give up, you're a Simone and—"

"Simones don't give up," she helped him complete one of the many Simone- family slogans. The Simone family was a very close-knit and loving group. Her French- born grandfather, Carey Simone, Sr., whom everyone affectionately referred to as Papa, and her African-American grandmother, Ana Simone, had been married for fifty-three years. Together, they raised eight children. Her uncle Jonathan was the fourth born and her mother, Julia was number five.

Forty years ago, Papa founded the Simone Company and turned it into one of the most sought-after architectural and construction businesses on the West Coast. The Simone family was just as wealthy in family values and love as they were in money and possessions. Papa and Ana taught their children and grandchildren to always place God and family before anything material. Because of their strong faith in God, all of the Simone children were successful and always gave to others.

"I know, Uncle, there's no way I'm leaving here until I'm finished," Shay declared. She then asked him about his family.

"Your aunt invited Alysse and Mark over to the house on yesterday. They showed us the pictures from Brian's graduation." Jonathan practiced criminal law in Scottsdale, Arizona.

Shay knew what was coming next and she tried to steer her uncle into a different direction. "Brian wants to be a criminal defense attorney, maybe you can mentor him?"

Jonathan understood his niece well. "That might be possible if he moves to Arizona. Shay, I didn't see you in any of the pictures, what's going on?"

"That's the day I left for Cambridge. I left early so I could get to the airport in enough time to make it through the security checkpoint." She hoped he bought her excuse. He didn't.

Jonathan, along with the rest of the family, recognized from day one, Shay and Brian were stuck on each other. If she left early, it certainly wasn't because of an airplane schedule. The family's private plane would have taken her anywhere she wanted to go. A pregnant pause followed. Jonathan didn't press further. "I'll be speaking at a conference in Boston next month. We'll get together then. In the meantime, if you need anything, all you have to do is call."

Shay pumped her fist in the air in celebration of the reprieve. "I know, Uncle, thanks." She talked to him for a few more minutes then asked to speak to his daughter, Taylor. She and Shay were the same age and had grown up more like sisters than cousins.

"What's up, cuz? How's New England treating you?"

"Everything's fine. You should come up during winter break?" Shay suggested.

"I just might do that, if you promise to hook me up with a couple of them fine Harvard men." Taylor laughed.

"Girl, I've been so busy with classes, I haven't had time to notice if the men are fine or not."

"If you weren't busy, you still wouldn't have noticed," Taylor asserted.

Shay twisted her face. "What do you mean by that?"

"Everybody knows you only have eyes for Brian."

Shay knew her cousin spoke the truth, but since she was already a sinner, she lied. "That's not true; Brian and I are only friends."

"Yeah, and I was born yesterday. It's nothing to be ashamed of, Shay; Brian does look good, especially since he shaved his head. Lucky for you, you're my cousin. If you weren't I might have to fight you for him," Taylor teased.

Shay needed to end this conversation. Just thinking about how good Brian looked made her instantly think of how good he made her feel. Shay didn't want to think about that anymore. "Hey, cuz, I have some things I need to take care of. I'll call you later," Shay said then quickly ended the call.

CHAPTER 13

"Hey, folks," Brian called when he entered the Blackhawk estate. He found his father and stepmother in the eat-in kitchen with Josiah. Brian greeted them by hugging his father and kissing Julia on the cheek.

"We didn't expect to see you today," Julia said. "Are you hungry?"

Before he could answer Julia reached into the cabinet and began making him a plate. Brian didn't object. He, like his father, loved Julia's cooking. Her candied yams, cabbage and fried chicken were among his favorites. Today she topped the meal off with pineapple-coconut cake.

"Bi-an, Bi-an," little Josiah called to him from his highchair.

"Hey, little man." Brian lifted his younger brother from his chair and tickled him. Little Josiah's giggles echoed throughout the kitchen.

Brian eyed his father watching their play and wondered if Reggie's current thoughts were the same ones he'd voiced on numerous other occasions. Reggie wore his pride in his sons in the broad smile that showed nearly all of his pearly whites. Brian and Josiah were nineteen years apart with different mothers, but they looked so much alike. Josiah was a shade lighter than he and Brian, but everything else was the same, right down to the left dimpled cheek.

Julia set a heaping plate of food and a glass of lemonade on the table and Brian dug right in without saying grace.

"So what's going on?" Reggie asked when Brian took a swig of lemonade.

"Nothing much."

"Are you nervous about law school?"

"Not really. I'm looking forward to the distraction," Brian answered his father without thinking. He didn't want his parents to know how much he really missed Shay. Brian kept eating, hoping they'd missed his comment.

They hadn't. Julia gave Reggie a sideways glance. Reggie shook his head, which was an indication to leave the subject of Brian and Shay alone.

"So, have you talked to your mother lately?" Julia asked. "Jonathan told me she and Mark came for a visit in Scottsdale."

"Yeah, my mom told me about it. She'd take a trip across country to show off my graduation pictures."

"She's proud of you and so are we," Reggie said proudly.

"I understand, but it's still embarrassing," Brian said before biting into a fried chicken leg.

"If you think she's doing a lot now, wait until you finish law school."

Except for an occasional comment, Brian focused on the decreasing mound on his plate. When he helped himself to a second serving Reggie and Julia watched with amazement. The plate Julia had made for him was loaded. They were used to him eating a lot, but this was excessive even for him. "Brian, when was the last time you ate?" his father asked.

Brian thought for a moment. "Two days ago."

"Why haven't you eaten in two days? Are you sick?" Julia asked and at the same time placed the back of her hand against his forehead.

"No, I just haven't had much of an appetite lately," Brian answered without realizing the implication.

This time Julia didn't look in Reggie's direction. "Brian, have you spoken to Shay lately?"

"No," Brian said and quickly filled his mouth with cabbage.

Julia started, "Maybe if you'd call her—" but abruptly stopped at the sound of Reggie's fork clanging against his plate. She ate the rest of her meal in silence.

CHAPTER 14

Shay stretched and let out a long yawn. She'd been studying three hours straight. Her neck was stiff and her shoulders tired. Her lower back ached and she was hungry. The clock beside her queen-sized bed read 10:00 P.M. She still had time to make her weekly check-in call to her mother.

"Good evening, Pennington residence."

At the sound of Brian's voice, Shay nearly dropped the phone. She didn't expect to hear his voice, and certainly didn't expect for it to be so soothing.

"Hello," Brian greeted the caller again.

Shay took a deep breath. "Hello, Brian," she said. "I didn't expect to hear your voice."

"I dropped by for dinner. I'm watching *Barney* with Josiah while the folks are out taking a swim. Is everything all right, you sound tired?"

She smiled slightly at his concern. He hadn't heard her voice in weeks, but he immediately knew she was exhausted. "I am, but that's to be expected with this program."

Brian listened as she gave him the highlights of her short time in Massachusetts.

"I missed you at my graduation, Shay," Brian finally said when she was finished.

"What are you talking about? I was there. I have your picture to prove it on my dresser."

"Shay, you know what I mean."

She did know. "Brian, I couldn't say good-bye to you again," Shay answered honestly. Shay wanted to tell him that she wanted to start over with him. She wanted to say that no matter how much she studied, she couldn't get him out of her mind or her heart. She missed his smile and his laugh. Shay wanted to say how incomplete her life was without him. She wanted to say how her heart ached whenever she thought of how much she loved him. Instead of saying what was in her heart, she asked, "Are you seeing someone?"

The question enraged Brian. "How could you ask me that after what we shared at Emery Bay? That was only eight weeks ago. A month ago, you feared you were carrying my child and now you want to know if I'm seeing someone? Why would you ask me something like that?"

Shay didn't know why she'd said that considering she really didn't want to see him with anyone but her.

"Shay, answer me. Is that what you really want? Are you seeing someone?"

Shay held her breath in an attempt to keep from crying. "No, I'm not seeing anyone, but it might be a good idea if we did."

Brian took a deep breath. "Shay, did you mean what you said to me at Emery Bay?"

Shay knew what he was talking about, but she stalled. "What did I say?"

"I should just drop it, but I need to know. Did you mean it when you said you loved me?"

Shay wanted to scream YES! What came out of her mouth was, "You know as well as I do that in the heat of the moment, one will say anything. You can't hold a person responsible for words screamed out in a wave of passion." She gave a manufactured laugh to camouflage her nerves.

Brian didn't see the humor. "I'm glad you enjoyed the moment," he said and slammed the phone down.

"That's the end of that." Shay stared into the receiver and cried. She started to call him back, but didn't. "It's better this way," she told herself an hour later when she was still crying.

* * *

Brian left the house right after he hung up on Shay. He despised himself for thinking she loved him. Brian had given his heart to her and all she considered him to be was a good time. Brian wanted to tell her that he didn't want her to say good-bye, not that day or any other day. Brian wanted to tell her how much he missed her and that he wanted to start a real relationship with her. He wanted to tell her that he meant it when he'd told her he loved her. Brian wanted to say so many things, but didn't.

Shay's words made him feel empty and used, something he never wanted her to feel. It was obvious to him that she'd moved on and now it was time for him to do the same. Brian made a decision: Tomorrow he would start living his life completely without LaShay Hampton. No sooner had the angry words left his mouth, he knew it was impossible to do. Yet he would try.

THE
REPLACEMENT

CHAPTER 15

S hay sat in the café sipping hot chocolate and working frantically on her laptop. She'd been at it for over an hour and decided now was a good time to stretch and take a quick break. Looking out of the store's front window she took in the New England scenery. It was quite different from the sunny Bay Area. The beautiful trees that lined the streets of Harvard Square were now filled with brown and orange leaves. Most of the branches were bare as the leaves littered the pavement, creating a unique collage. In her opinion, the orange leaves were a good match for the ivy-covered, red-brick buildings.

Shay sipped her hot chocolate and wondered how she would handle her first Thanksgiving away from her family. Maybe she'd cook a traditional dinner or better yet order one of those prepackaged holiday meals from the supermarket. She hadn't told her mother yet, but she planned on skipping the holiday at the end of next month, using her heavy workload as an excuse. Of course the real reason she didn't want to go home was Brian. She hadn't spoken to him since he hung up on her two months ago. It was hard, but every day she fought to not think about him. She was successful less than half the time. No matter how much she studied and read, there was no replacing him in her heart.

Shay still wasn't attending church which was really hard for her, because she grew up in the church. Even before her mother got saved, the two of them attended church regularly. Now, she didn't feel worthy enough to walk into a church and sit on the back pew. When walking past a church she hung her head. The other night she tried to pray, but stopped after a couple of sentences. To her, the prayer sounded hollow and insincere. Shay had heard all of her life that God was a forgiving God, but how could He keep forgiving her after she piled sin on top of sin? First, it was committing fornication twice. Then she broke her promise to God to never to do it again, by having intercourse three more times at Emery Bay. She didn't outright lie to Brian, but she led him to believe a lie. She lied numerous times to her mother and Reggie about why she had to leave California. That made her a fornicator and a liar and completely unworthy of God's mercy.

She was sure her mother knew the real reason for her sudden decision to apply to Harvard had something to do with Brian. Reggie knew too, he told her as much the night before Brian's graduation. "Nothing has happened that can't be worked out, Shay. You and Brian are young, you have time," he'd told her. Reggie was probably right, but Shay didn't believe God would give her another chance. Shay wasn't sure if she were God, she'd forgive own self.

Shay massaged her forehead after another sip of smooth chocolate then started typing again. Ten minutes later her flow was interrupted.

"Hi, LaShay, I have my half of the research completed," Rhonda said and dropped a binder on the table. Rhonda was her classmate. They'd befriended one another the first week of class and were now working together on a project depicting the different learning styles in children.

"Great," Shay said, but didn't stop to look at the work.

"I also got us some help," Rhonda added.

Shay released the keyboard and gave Rhonda her undivided attention. "That's great. Who?"

"Jason. He should be here any minute."

Shay frowned. She had no idea who Jason was, but if he was going to help her complete this project, she would welcome him with open arms.

Shay and Rhonda exchanged binders and laptops to study each other's notes. They were still reviewing when Jason arrived.

"Sorry I'm late. I had to stop by the library," he said while pulling a chair from an empty table next to them.

"No problem, let's see what you've found," Rhonda said and held out her hand expectantly.

Shay looked up from Rhonda's work long enough to greet the newest team member. "We haven't met, my name is LaShay Hampton," she politely said and extended her hand to him.

Shaking her hand and smiling Jason responded, "Hello, LaShay. I'm Jason Alexander and actually we have met on several occasions. I usually sit behind you in our morning class."

Shay's caramel cheeks burned with embarrassment. She really couldn't recall having ever laid eyes on him before. She studied Jason's appearance and understood why she'd overlooked him for nearly three months. He did not have the physical characteristics that would make her take notice. For starters, he was fair-complexioned. His five-foot-ten-inch height made him only three inches taller than her. He was slim all around. She guessed his waist was no bigger than size thirty-two. She surveyed his upper body. Not much to brag about there either. No, he was definitely not someone she would have given a second glance or would have left a lasting impression. The biggest turn off was his dreads. Shay preferred the tall dark-chocolate bulkier clean-cut type. Someone like Brian.

"Sorry, I'm so engrossed in class that the only person I notice on the regular is the professor."

"She's right," Rhonda added, "I had to introduce myself three times before she remembered my name."

"No problem, we can get to know each other now."

Jason's grin was too casual for Shay's taste. "What we can do is work on this assignment. Let's see what you're bringing to the table."

Jason must have picked up on Shay's no-nonsense tone. His smile faded and he turned the focus of the conversation to schoolwork.

After an hour of working on the project, Shay packed up her laptop and prepared to leave. As she zipped up her parka Jason asked, "What time are we meeting on Wednesday?"

"This time is perfect for me." She turned to Rhonda. "What about you?"

"I don't get off work until six on Wednesdays, but I can come right after," Rhonda answered.

"I don't finish at the bookstore until five-thirty," Jason stated. "Shay, do you have to work late on Wednesday nights?"

Once again Shay was reminded of how blessed she was to be at Harvard. Thanks to her mother's success as a real estate developer, she was able to attend one of the most prestigious schools in the country and not have to worry about tuition or living expenses. It was her family's connections that got her into the program at the ninth hour. Both her uncle and aunt were Harvard alumni and the Simone Company contributed heavily to the school on an annual basis.

"No, Jason. I don't work, so I'm flexible," she finally answered.

"Let's meet at six-thirty, that way we can get at least two hours in," Rhonda suggested.

"Six-thirty it is." Shay picked up her laptop and braced herself for the cold air.

* * *

From the doorway Jason watched her walk down the sidewalk and get into the new small white SUV and drive off. He had approached Rhonda about working with them as a way to get to know LaShay, since he wasn't having any luck with her in class. From day one, he'd noticed her, but she proved today that the attraction wasn't mutual.

"Is she always so stiff?" he asked Rhonda when she made her exit.

"Yes. LaShay's all about business."

"I'll have to do something about that. No one should be that serious."

Rhonda adjusted the shoulder strap on her book bag. "I wouldn't focus on LaShay Hampton if I were you. You have better odds at passing the program than you do with getting close to her."

Jason stuffed his free hand into his front jacket pocket. Maybe Rhonda was right. Pursing the beautiful LaShay could prove useless. There was only one way to find out.

CHAPTER 16

Done with his study session, Brian looked at his watch. He still had two hours left before Bible Study. He was proud of himself. His spiritual life was back on track and he felt good about his life again. At the beginning of the semester, he'd ended his weekly counseling sessions with his father and no longer felt dirty and unforgiven for committing fornication. In his heart, he knew he still loved Shay, but accepted that they would never be anything more than friends. However, he still kept a framed picture of her on his nightstand and every day he fought the urge to call her.

Law school was challenging, but fun because it was what he always wanted to do. He still shared the house with Todd, who was now in medical school at UCSF, but most of the time he was alone. On Sundays, he went to church. Whenever he had a light Saturday, he volunteered as a tutor at True Worship's Community Center or he'd spend time with the Simone family.

Today's agenda included hanging out with brothers, Marcus and Craig, and Justin. The Simone first cousins met him at Reggie and Julia's house. They'd agreed to meet in Blackhawk in hopes of talking Julia into letting them borrow her new Jaguar.

"Come on, Auntie. Let us take her on the highway," Justin pleaded.

"Why don't you ask your father for his car?" Julia asked with her fist planted at her waist. Justin was Julia's older brother, Stephan's son. She then turned to her oldest brother Carey's sons, Marcus and Craig. "And your father has a brand new Bentley in his garage."

"Auntie, you know my dad won't even let us look at that car without leaving a vital body organ for collateral," Marcus answered.

"Mama J, I promise I'll drive and I'll be extra careful." Brian flashed the smile he knew would work. "We're only going to Dave and Buster's. I promise we'll come straight back after we're done."

Reggie handed Brian the keys. It was common knowledge Julia could not say no to Brian, especially when he smiled displaying that deep left dimple. Reggie had used that same smile on her in the past and it worked every time.

"Don't think you're getting over on me," Julia said sternly and narrowed her eyes at Brian. "If I find one scratch on my car, I'm going to beat all four of your behinds."

Brian and her nephews kissed Julia on the cheek and made a dash for the door.

Later inside Dave and Buster's the young men were enjoying a friendly game of pool, when a young lady approached Brian. He had just called his shot in the corner pocket when the woman leaned over the table and in a sultry voice asked, "Mind if I join you?"

The Simones laughed as Brian lost his concentration. The low-cut top the young lady wore gave him more than an eyeful.

Brian cleared his throat and regrouped. "Excuse me, Miss, but we are in the middle of a game. When we're finished, you can find someone who wants to look at your breasts then you can play with them."

"Ouch!" Marcus and Justin shrieked.

"Man, that was nasty!" Craig added.

The young lady's smile disappeared and she slowly retreated back. They resumed play. Brian didn't give her a second look the whole time he was playing; he actually forgot she was there. As soon as his game ended, she approached him again. This time she adjusted her top so her breasts were covered.

"Hello, my name is Shannon. I'm sorry if I offended you earlier."

"Hello, Shannon, my name is Brian. I accept your apology." Brian turned away to talk to the boys, but Shannon wasn't finished.

"I only interrupted your game because you're so handsome and I would like to get to know you," the young lady flirted.

Brian gave her a good once-over. Shannon wasn't unattractive; she just wasn't his type. His preference was lighter-complexioned taller women and she was too skinny. He estimated her to be a size six, but he liked women with a little more substance to them. Shay's size-ten was perfect. He did like her long hair, but he could tell it wasn't naturally grown, at least not on her head. The green eye color wasn't natural either and she wore far too much makeup.

"Like I said, my name is Brian, besides that there isn't much to know."

She stepped closer to him. "I think there's a whole lot more to you." She licked her lips as the words flowed.

Although Brian had little experience with women outside of Shay, he detested overly aggressive females. He preferred to do the chasing. Brian looked to Marcus for help.

"Sorry, Shannon, he's already taken," Marcus offered.

"I don't see a ring on his finger." She rolled her eyes at Marcus then frowned. "Unless you mean the two of you are an item? That would be such a waste."

Justin and Craig snickered, but Brian and Marcus glared at Shannon.

"What I mean is if my cousin Shay catches you in his face, you won't be able to see anything by the time she finishes with you," Marcus clarified in a tone that conveyed his dislike for the annoying woman.

"Trust us, we're trying to keep you from danger," Justin added.

77

Shannon looked back at Brian who smiled and shrugged his shoulders, but remained quiet. Finally, she said, "Here's my number, just in case you find yourself available." She slipped her number into his pocket and slowly walked away.

After she was out of earshot, the men laughed and made fun of Brian. For someone who wasn't available, he certainly received his share of attention from women. Brian took the jesting in the spirit it was given. He didn't think it was a good time to tell them that he and Shay were nothing more than friends. It didn't matter because he wasn't interested in Shannon and would never see her again. What Brian didn't know was that Shannon had spotted him in the parking lot getting out of Julia's Jaguar and she was going to make it her business to find out more about him.

Two weeks later, Brian had the privilege of being interrupted by Shannon once again as he studied on campus.

"Brian, is that you?" She was wearing dress slacks and a V-neck sweater.

"Hello," he paused, "do I know you?"

"It's me, Shannon. We met at Dave and Buster's."

It took a moment for Brian to recall the long hair and colored contacts. "I'm surprised to see you here," he said referring to UC Berkeley's law library. "Are you a student?"

"I work on campus in the admissions office. What about yourself?" Shannon took the liberty of sitting next to him.

"First year at Boalt."

"So you're going to be a big-time lawyer." Shannon smiled.

"I hope so."

She placed her hand on his shoulder. "Brian, I know you're going to be successful," she said a little too sweet for Brian's taste.

"Thank you."

"I knew there was more to you than playing pool," she said and leaned forward without revealing any cleavage.

"Maybe you're right," he said trying not to focus on her

long brightly painted nails. He closed the law book and turned to her. "Shannon, tell me about you since it seems our paths keep crossing."

"Are you sure your girlfriend won't mind us having a conversation?" Shannon mused.

"I don't have a girlfriend and right now I'm not looking for one," Brian answered firmly.

"But your boys said—"

"I know what they said," he cut her off, "but the person they were referring to is just a good friend." Brian looked away after he made that statement. It was the first time he'd said it out loud and it didn't sound right to him. If Shannon noticed the change in his demeanor, she didn't address it.

"So when we met at Dave and Buster's, you just didn't like me? Is that why you were so rude?" she asked, incredulously.

Brian closed his notebook. "To be perfectly honest, yes. You're not my type."

His blatant dislike of her physical appearance didn't seem to bother Shannon at all. "Exactly what is your type?" she asked.

"It doesn't matter, because I'm not interested in a relationship, remember?"

"Well, can I at least know your last name and a little more about you?" she asked still holding a smile. "I don't see why we can't be friends."

Brian hesitated before answering. Perhaps a friendship with a female would take his mind off Shay. "My last name is Pennington. I moved here almost five years ago from Arizona."

Shannon twisted her face. "Pennington," she mumbled to herself repeatedly. "Are you related to that Pastor Pennington in East Oakland? I think the church is True Witness or something?"

"He's my father," Brian answered, "and it's True Worship."

"How does it feel to be the son of a wealthy pastor?"

Brian smirked as sheer fascination veiled Shannon's face. "I wouldn't exactly call my father wealthy."

"I've seen True Worship. It's probably the fastest-growing church in the Bay Area with state-of-the-art facilities."

"Since the community center opened two years ago, membership has surged. My father is considering having three services on Sunday to accommodate everyone," Brian announced proudly.

"Maybe I can visit one Sunday," Shannon suggested, the key word being maybe.

"Are you a Christian?" Brian wondered out loud. Considering her provocative mannerisms he would have thought not.

Instead of looking him in the face, Shannon looked over his shoulder at a stack of periodicals. "I believe in God, but I don't attend church regularly."

"Hearing my father or Mama J preach one time would change that," Brian said with confidence.

"Your mother preaches too?" Shannon questioned.

"No, but Mama J does. That's what I call my stepmother. My mother lives in Arizona," he clarified.

He thought he read disappointment on her face. "So, Julia Simone is your stepmother? I read somewhere that Reverend Pennington is married to the wealthy real estate developer."

"That's correct, but I'm very close to my stepmother," he continued. "There's nothing I wouldn't do for her. Now, tell me about you," he said, leaning back in his seat.

"What would you like to know, Brian?" Shannon placed her hand on his and Brian casually moved his hand away.

"How old are you? Where are you from? What's your story?"

"For starters, I'm twenty-five. I was born and raised in Oakland. I don't have any baby daddies and I'm available." She added a wink to the last part of her answer.

"That's good to know, the baby daddy part, I mean."

She rubbed his forearm and spoke softly. "Brian, who is Shay?"

80

Brian moved his hand away, again. "Shay is a special friend," he said almost sadly. "Very special."

"How long have you known her?" Shannon probed.

"Why?" Brian asked sharply.

She shifted in her seat. Like she knew she'd just worn out her welcome. "How old are you, Brian?"

"Twenty-three."

"So was Shay your college sweetheart?" Shannon wouldn't let it go.

Brian shifted in his seat, mainly because he hadn't come to terms with the answer. Shay wasn't his college sweetheart. She was much more than that. "No, but LaShay Hampton is my friend and she will always be special to me. Now, if you want to continue this conversation, don't ask me anything else about her."

Shannon leaned back in her seat. "I'm sorry I didn't mean to hit a sore spot."

"Well, now you know. My relationship with Shay is private." Brian looked at his watch; suddenly he was ready to leave. "I'd better get going if I'm going to make it to Bible Study on time." He turned back to Shannon. "Would you like to join me?"

"Maybe next time; or maybe I'll come with you on Sunday. Why don't you give me your number and I'll call you and let you know if I can make it," Shannon innocently suggested.

Brian scribbled his cell phone number and handed it to her. "For the most part, it was nice talking to you. I hope you make it to church one Sunday." With that he gathered his books and laptop and was gone.

* * *

Watching Brian walk away, a million thoughts raced through Shannon's mind. She'd have to play it very careful, if she were going to win Brian. It was evident he had strong feelings for this Shay person. He was probably in love with her, but she didn't care. A man didn't have to be in love with her, for her to spend his money. Brian was definitely her meal ticket, even if Julia Simone wasn't his biological mother. His father received more than enough money from that church and like Brian said, Julia Simone treated him like a son. To add to the windfall, Brian was going to be a lawyer. If she was careful, she'd be Mrs. Pennington before Brian took the bar exam.

The sound of a ringing cash register and floating dollar signs filled Shannon's head. She'd finally hit the jackpot. Shannon had to blink her eyes to stay focused. From working in the admissions office, she knew the financial status of most of the students' families. She clearly remembered processing a cashier's check from Reginald and Julia Pennington for full payment of law school. She was so curious about the writer of the check, that she'd Googled their names on the Internet and learned that Reginald Pennington was the pastor of True Worship Ministries and his wife Julia Simone-Pennington was the founder and CEO of Pinnacle Developments, the driving force behind the revitalization of Emery Bay.

Shannon could barely contain herself. Her main goal in life was to find someone who could take care of her and give her a life of luxury. She viewed working on campus as a means to accomplish this. She would find a man with a bright future and lure him in. Brian was the perfect candidate, especially now since he didn't have a girlfriend.

CHAPTER 17

Shay sat in a booth at Olive Garden with Rhonda and Jason celebrating the completion of their project. When Jason sat down next to her, Shay second-guessed her decision to enjoy an evening outside of her apartment. She wasn't interested in Jason outside of class assignments, but she sure could tell he was interested in her. The entire two weeks they'd worked together Jason tried without success to get her telephone number. At first he used the project as an excuse. When that didn't work, he plainly told her he would like to spend time with her.

"I don't have time for dating," is what she told him.

"Neither do I, but I think you're worth making time for."

Instead of blushing, Shay fought to keep her displeasure from showing in her facial expression. She was certain she'd frowned. "Look, Jason, I'm not ready to date and if I were, I wouldn't date you. So let's just focus on finishing this project, please." She thought she'd said enough to hurt his feelings and make him back off, but she was mistaken.

"That's because you don't know me," Jason persisted. "You only know me as a college student, outside of school, I'm really quite fun."

"It wouldn't make a difference, trust me," she said, without blinking.

Jason backed off and didn't press her again until tonight.

He started by sitting next to her although there was more room on Rhonda's side of the booth. Shay rolled her eyes at him when he "accidentally" placed his arm around her shoulder. He promptly removed it when she picked up her knife and waved it in his direction.

Jason grinned. "At least you didn't cut me."

Shay pursed her lips and replaced the knife on the cloth napkin, but before they placed their drink orders Rhonda's cell phone rang.

"Sorry, guys, that was my job. I have to go in," Rhonda announced after a brief phone conversation.

Shay's eyes bulged as she mentally searched for a solution. Being left alone with Jason Alexander was not an option. "I thought you were off tonight?"

"I was, but one of the other waitresses called in sick and I can really use the money."

Shay was about to offer to pay her a night's salary, or even a week's salary to keep her from leaving her alone with Jason. She just couldn't figure out how to do so without coming across as a snobbish rich girl. In the time it took for her to figure it out, Rhonda had grabbed her coat and left the building.

Jason interrupted her thoughts. "Looks like it's just you and I this evening."

"Maybe we should do this another time, when Rhonda can join us. She worked just as hard as we did and she deserves a chance to celebrate," she said just as the waitress asked for their drink orders. Having decided her plan made sense, Shay grabbed her jacket.

Jason made eye-contact with her. "LaShay, it's only dinner. If it'll make you feel better, I'll move to the other side of the booth, but don't leave."

The waitress waited patiently as Shay weighed her options. She was hungry and it did feel good to be out on a Friday evening. Maybe having dinner with Jason would cure his infatuation and he'd leave her alone. "I'll have an iced tea," she finally said then removed her jacket.

Jason smiled. "I'll have the same."

As soon as the waitress left Shay reminded him of his promise to move to the opposite side of the booth. He didn't protest, but now instead of being alongside her, he was staring her in the face. Smiling like he had just won the lottery.

"LaShay Hampton, I've been working with you for two weeks and I still don't know anything about you. Tell me about yourself, or shall I go first?"

"You can go first, second and third for all I care," she retorted.

Jason ignored the sarcasm and gave her his story. She learned he was born and raised in Chicago and had attended Howard University on a full scholarship. He planned to move back to Chicago and teach high-school English. He was from a two-parent family and had an older brother and a younger sister. He was the first in his family to attend college.

"What about you?" he asked after the waitress delivered the drinks. "What's your story?"

Shay took a sip of her drink and in an attempt at nicety, she offered him a smile. "What do want to know, Jason?"

"For starters, why do you always act so cold?"

She could tell by his tone that he'd grown tired of her attitude and fake smile. However, his assessment surprised her. "So you think I'm a cold person because I won't go out with you?"

"That, and every time I try to have a simple conversation with you, like now, you put up this wall of ice. I can't even ask you a simple question, like where are you from, without getting sarcasm. It's fine if you don't want to date me, but at least you can be polite."

Shay twisted her mouth; maybe she was being a little too hard on Jason. He really hadn't done anything wrong other than show interest in her. Getting to know him didn't mean she had to date him. "Alright, Jason. I was born and raised in the San Francisco Bay Area. I graduated Magna Cum Laude from Stanford and now I'm here. I want to teach elementary education, preferably kindergarten. Is that enough information?" Shay smirked slightly.

"It's a start. It's also quite impressive. What about your family?"

"I was raised by my mother. My father died in an automobile accident before I was born."

"I bet your mother was happy when you received the scholarship to Stanford, with her being a single parent and all," Jason clarified.

Shay pushed her glass away. She hated when people assumed she was on a scholarship simply because she was an African-American. It especially bothered her when it came from other African Americans, like they didn't believe there were successful people of color with enough money to pay college tuition.

She interlocked her fingers before responding to him. "Jason, I didn't receive a scholarship for Stanford, nor did I receive one for Harvard. My mother wrote a check. You do know African-Americans are allowed to have savings accounts with more than a fifty-dollar balance?"

After the waitress took their dinner order, Jason continued. "That explains it."

"Explains what?"

"I was wondering how you can afford a new SUV and an apartment without a job. You're from a wealthy family."

"Does that bother you?" Shay hoped it did. "True, my family is well-off, but I worked hard for my degree," Shay defended. "And I'm working hard for this Master's and Teaching Credential."

"I've seen you in action. I know you work hard. And no it doesn't bother me at all that you're well-off." He reached for her hand. "What does bother me is why you don't like me."

"It's not that I don't like you, Jason, I really don't know you," she answered, trying not to bruise his ego again.

"Are you seeing someone?"

Shay immediately thought of Brian. Although they weren't on speaking terms, they still shared an unspoken commitment to one another, especially after sharing their bodies. "No, I'm not seeing anyone."

"Let me guess, you like the tall and dark type."

She smiled. Tall and dark; definitely Brian. "Something like that."

"Nice"

Confusion masked her face. "What's nice?"

"Your smile," Jason explained. "This is the first time I've seen you smile. You should try it more often."

Shay was glad the food arrived because she couldn't get Brian out of her head. He liked her smile and her hazel eyes among other things.

They talked more over dinner and she learned a lot about him. Jason was actually quite likeable and had a wonderful sense of humor. Like her, he was an avid reader and dabbled in poetry. She still wasn't attracted to him, but decided he would be a good person to hang out with, a way to chase the loneliness away. When he walked Shay to her car, she accepted his invitation to the movies the following Friday and finally gave him her cell phone number.

CHAPTER 18

The *Mission Impossible* ringtone on his cell phone sounded just as Brian's hand touched the doorknob. He pulled the Smartphone from his waist clip to answer the call and immediately recognized Shannon's number. She had called him every day since he had given her his number four days ago. Talking to Shannon helped Brian realize just how much he really missed Shay. Up until the night he took Shay into his bed, a day rarely went by that he didn't hear her soft feminine voice. But for now Shannon Yates would be his replacement for female conversation.

Each day he talked to her for at least an hour and yesterday morning Brian joined her for a jog around Lake Merritt. Walking toward her in Lakeside Park, Brian couldn't help but wonder why Shannon jogged in the first place. It certainly wasn't to watch her weight. Shannon didn't look like she had an ounce of fat on her; she barely had meat on her bones. He kept his curiosity to himself and enjoyed the fresh winter morning, not wanting Shannon to get the wrong idea that he harbored an attraction to her body.

Outside of a few clouds, the Oakland morning was beautiful. The mid-sixty- degree weather attracted a large amount of seagulls equal to the number of runners. On the four-mile trail, Brian had to admit that he enjoyed both the jog and the conversation. Not one time did Shannon mention Shay or flirt with him. Instead, she centered the majority of the conversation on Brian and his father.

WANDA B. CAMPBELL

"My father is my best friend," was what he told her when she asked about his relationship with his father.

"Have the two of you always been close?" she asked slowing her slow jog to a brisk walk.

"Since we met five years ago." Brian went on to explain the events to Shannon.

"That's amazing; no wonder you're so close to your stepmother. Does your father pressure you into becoming a minister like him?"

Brian slowed his pace. "My dad doesn't pressure me to become anything that I don't want to become. He encourages me to be me, not walk in his shadows. If I do pursue the ministry, it'll be because I hear a call from God in my heart; not pressure from my father."

"I'm going to block that call," Shannon teased. They made more small talk about him, but she didn't talk about herself. Brian noticed, but didn't press the issue.

Drawing his attention back to the ringing in his hand, Brian pressed the green answer key button. "Good morning, Shannon," he answered while locking his front door.

"Good morning, Brian. I hope you slept well. I didn't. I was lonely," Shannon whined.

"I'm on my way to church. Is there something you want?"

She cleared her throat. "I was wondering if you could pick me up for church this morning."

Her request surprised Brian. During their previous conversations Shannon hadn't mentioned a desire to attend today's worship service. "I'm glad you want to come to church, Shannon, but it's a little late for me to pick you up. Why don't you just meet me there?"

"That's too bad, Brian, I really wanted to see you today." She pouted.

"Sorry, but I don't like being late for service. If you're sure you're coming, I'll have the usher save you a seat," Brian offered as he started his RAV4.

Shannon wasn't happy and said as much. "It's too early for

90

me to throw a temper tantrum, so I'll drop it for now. Will I be sitting next to you?" She sounded like a wounded puppy.

"No, but you'll have a good seat." Brian didn't tell her that as his father's personal adjutant, he sat on the dais with the ministers.

"I guess this is the only way I'll get to see you today?" she conceded.

"It sure is. I'll see you later." He ended the call and turned his attention to the road.

As always, Brian knocked on Reggie's office door before turning the knob and entering. "Do you need anything, Dad?" he asked, leaning his head inside.

Reggie sat in his chair holding Josiah. Brian stepped inside and immediately Josiah threw his hands up and called out, "Brian!" He took his little brother from his father and tickled him.

"Julia is preaching this at morning's service," Reggie answered with an expression that conveyed how much he cherished the opportunity to watch his children play.

Reggie studied his eldest son's face. Brian worked very hard to keep up in law school, but Reggie suspected there was more on his son's mind than just school. "What's going on with you and Shay? I'm not one to pry into your personal business with Shay, but I don't want you to make a huge mistake either."

Brian turned so he couldn't face his father and focused on Josiah. "Nothing."

"Nothing?" Reggie asked incredulously

"We're just friends, like always."

Before he asked, Reggie guessed the answer to his next question by Brian's mannerisms. "You haven't told her how you really feel about her and that you want to build a relationship with her? She doesn't know that you're in love with her?"

"Kind of, but the feeling isn't mutual. We're just friends."

Reggie rested his elbows on his desk and lowered his head. What Brian said didn't make sense. Reggie knew for a fact that Shay was in love with Brian; she'd told him so before leaving for Cambridge, but that was something Brian should hear directly from Shay.

"Is that what she told you? Did she actually say she didn't love you?" Reggie wanted clarification.

"No she didn't actually say that, but she implied it."

"I see. I remember how hard it was for me to communicate my true feelings to Julia at age forty-one. Brian, I really feel, no, I know, you and Shay need to sit down and have an honest heart-to-heart talk, before one of you takes a wrong turn."

Brian listened to his father's words, his dad was probably right. "Maybe next week at Thanksgiving, I'll try talking to her again."

"I'm sorry, Brian. I guess I forgot to tell you. Shay's not coming home for Thanksgiving. She said she needed to spend that time studying."

"Oh." Brian tried to conceal his hurt, but wasn't too successful. He felt like his heart had been pulled from his chest and stomped on. He knew without a doubt the only reason Shay wasn't coming home for her favorite holiday, was to keep from seeing him. He moaned and asked himself, *Does she hate me that much?*

"You don't have to wait until she returns home, you can give her a call or better yet, you can go to Massachusetts," Reggie suggested.

"Yeah, right." Brian sat Josiah down and left the office.

Halfway through Praise & Worship, Brian spotted Shannon walking down the far right aisle. He couldn't believe what she'd worn to church. He never understood why some women liked to wear skimpy clothing in the wintertime and then try to keep warm with an oversized winter coat.

Shannon looked like she was headed to a nightclub instead of Sunday church service. The black V-neck tank dress barely came halfway to her thighs. Even from where he sat, Brian could tell she wasn't wearing a bra by the deep cut down the front of her dress. The black straps from her shoes wrapped around her bare ankles added to the nightlife look. She must have gotten a new weave, because instead of black, her hair was golden which Brian considered too light for her dark-brown complexion. Brian watched, embarrassed, as Shannon argued with an usher about finding her a seat up close. When Brian finally made eye contact with her, Shannon folded her arms and glared at him. With Shay's latest rejection of him still fresh, Brian didn't have the energy to worry about Shannon's attitude. He ignored her for the rest of the service.

* * *

"I'm a guest of Brian Pennington and I'm supposed to be seated up front," Shannon barked at the usher.

"Miss, I would seat you closer, but you are inappropriately dressed. If you would like to wear your overcoat for the duration of service, I'd be happy to seat you up front," the female usher responded firmly.

"Why would I wear my overcoat while I'm inside?" Shannon fumed. When she realized that she wasn't going to get anywhere with the usher, she rolled her eyes and sat down on the fifth row.

After the choir's second selection, the congregation stood as Pastor Julia Pennington stepped to the podium. She began by praying. Shannon was impressed with how "religious" Julia looked in her ministry attire. Shannon perceived that Julia took preaching seriously and she prayed like she really knew God. She didn't look or sound at all like the millionaire she was and that bothered Shannon. Besides her five-carat wedding ring, she didn't even have on any flashy jewelry. "When I become a millionaire everyone's going to know it, from my hair all the way down to my feet," Shannon mumbled as Julia began her sermon titled, "Overcoming Evil Desires."

Shannon didn't pay attention to the sermon Pastor Julia preached. She hadn't come to church to hear anything about evil desires. She came for one purpose only and that was to draw Brian into her and secure herself a meal ticket. In the few days she'd spent talking with him, she had learned just about everything there was to know about him. She knew all of his favorite foods, colors, places to go and even his favorite movies. She knew his ambitions, likes and dislikes. There were only two walls she hadn't managed to penetrate yet. One was his commitment to God and the church. No matter how hard she tried, Shannon couldn't get him to talk about this Shay person. That bothered her, because Shannon liked to know as much as possible about the competition.

As soon as service ended, Shannon sashayed to the front of the sanctuary and stood directly next to the church mother, Mother Elsie, in search of her prey.

"Baby, did you forget its wintertime?" Mother Elsie asked as she took in Shannon's attire.

"Excuse me, but you don't know me well enough to make comments about my clothing." Shannon rolled her eyes and neck at the elderly mother.

Mother Elsie stood her ground. "I'm not commenting about your clothing, I'm commenting about your lack of clothing. You're right I don't know you well, because if I did, you would have never walked in here looking like you're on your way to a street corner. Have more respect for yourself and put some clothes on next time." With that Mother Elsie walked away and greeted two ministers.

Shannon dismissed the old woman's words. "She just mad, because she can't wear this dress," she grumbled and rolled her eyes in Mother Elsie's direction. She then quickly directed her attention back to searching for Brian. She spotted him walking toward the back with the pastor and first lady.

"Brian, honey," she yelled.

She not only got Brian's attention, but Reggie and Julia's as well. When Brian didn't respond fast enough, she yelled again. "Brian, honey!" This time she got the attention of everyone within fifty feet of her.

Embarrassed, Brian looked as if he wanted her to shut up. He left his father and stepmother and walked over to Shannon.

"Who is that? Why is she referring to Brian as honey?" Brian heard his father ask.

Julia had an answer for him. "That's the devil."

"Shannon, I'm busy right now. I'll call you later." Brian's attempt at brushing her off failed.

She whined, "But, honey, I thought we could spend the afternoon together since you're done with the church thing."

Brian narrowed his eyes. "Shannon, I never told you that. I'm spending the afternoon with my family and friends."

Shannon smiled then decided to use the back door instead of the front. "Can you at least introduce me to the pastor and first lady before you go?"

Brian rubbed his forehead in frustration. "Come on. Since you've caused a scene, I'll have to explain your presence. This will be quick and then you can go."

Shannon slithered over to Reggie and Julia. Brian tried to stay a step ahead of her, but Shannon interlocked her arm with his.

"Dad, Mama J, this is Shannon. Shannon, this is Reverend Pennington and First Lady Pennington," Brian said dryly and looked away.

Reggie and Julia looked back and forth between the two before they said, "Hello, Shannon."

"It's so nice to finally meet you," Shannon said with an overabundance of cheerfulness. "I've heard so much about you, I feel like we're family."

Julia raised an eyebrow. "Is that right? We haven't heard anything about you." Julia looked at Brian who was having a hard time making eye contact.

"Yes, Brian talks about you guys all the time. I mean there's not a day that goes by that he doesn't mention you." Shannon thought she was making a good impression, so she continued, "Since Brian and I are so close, can I call you Mom?"

Brian stepped back and gave Shannon an I-don't-believe-you-just-said-that look, but she didn't care

"No you cannot!" Julia answered quickly and sternly.

Her harsh response took Shannon by surprise. "I'm sorry," Shannon whimpered. "I just thought that since you and Brian are so close, it would be a good idea if you and I could be close also." Shannon gave her best impression of her feelings being hurt and then cried fake tears. But Julia wasn't buying it, especially after Shannon fell onto Reggie for support. Other than hand Shannon his handkerchief, Reggie seemed confused as to what to do

Standing directly in front of Shannon, so she could say exactly what she wanted to without being heard by others, Julia let her have it. "Let's get a few things straight. First of all, I don't care how close you claim you and Brian are, you will never call me 'Mom', 'Mother', or any other derivative of the word. Second, you can stop with all the drama and the crocodile tears, because I'm not buying it. And lastly, the next time you decide you want to meet a young man's parents put some clothes on! If you want to make a good impression, don't walk into his father's church looking like a whore!" With that Julia turned and left. Reggie followed.

Shannon was insulted, but she wasn't angry. If anything she'd gained respect for Julia Simone-Pennington. Here she was a self-made millionaire who wasn't afraid to speak her mind. She knew how to and wasn't afraid to protect what was hers. I want to be just like her, Shannon thought to herself.

Brian, on the other hand, appeared utterly humiliated. "Shannon, I think you should leave. Now."

"Brian, I'm sorry."

"Whatever! Like I said before, I have dinner plans with my family." Brian turned to leave, but Shannon grabbed his arm.

"Brian, give me another chance, let me join you for dinner.

I promise I won't dress like this again. I'll even go home and change," she pleaded.

"It's not just your clothing, Shannon. You lied to my parents. You made my parents think that you and I are in a relationship."

Shannon thought this would be a good time to condescend. "You're right, Brian, I was wrong. I won't let that happen again. Just give me another chance to redeem myself. I promise at dinner, that I'll clear up any misunderstandings I may have caused," Shannon promised. When he didn't answer she knew she had won him over. "Why don't you follow me to my apartment and I'll change into something more appropriate. It'll only take me a few minutes; you don't even have to turn the engine off."

Brian didn't look at her when he said, "Hurry up."

In the parking lot, Brian unlocked the door to his RAV4. "Why aren't you driving the Jag?" Shannon asked, pointing to the new gold luxury vehicle.

"Because this is my car," he said abruptly and climbed into the RAV4.

Shannon was speechless as she walked to her Ford Focus.

CHAPTER 19

Brian waited in his RAV4 while Shannon changed her clothing. He was still upset with her for giving his parents the impression that he was in a relationship with her, but he wasn't sure if he was overreacting because of the earlier news about Shay. All he knew was that he didn't want to be involved with Shannon outside of being causal acquaintances and that he needed to see Shay as much as he needed air.

Shannon finally appeared from her apartment wearing a long black skirt with a cashmere sweater and three-inch heel black boots. "Is this better?" she asked climbing into the SUV.

"Much better." Without taking a breath he added, "Shannon, I have not changed my mind, I do not want a relationship with you. Do you understand that?"

"I do understand, Brian, and I promise I will never make that mistake again." Shannon almost sounded sincere. She sat back and fastened her seatbelt. "So where are we going for dinner?"

"To my parents' house. Mama J made Sunday dinner."

"Where do your parents live?"

"Blackhawk," he answered nonchalantly.

Shannon nearly screamed. Blackhawk was home to some of the wealthiest people in the Bay Area. She had always wanted to visit the exclusive and inclusive private community. Shannon sat in her seat smiling uncontrollably. Brian didn't acknowledge her excitement, he was thinking about Shay and how lonely his Thanksgiving would be without her.

When Brian pulled into the circular driveway, Shannon nearly jumped out of the vehicle, awestruck by the ten-thousand-square-foot Mediterranean-style home. She walked around the perimeter, admiring the manicured lawn and the granite fountain in the center of the lawn.

***

Inside the kitchen Julia, Angie and Nikki were busy preparing the feast. Reggie and the rest of the males were in the den watching a football game.

"Girl, have you calmed down yet? I thought you were going to beat the devil out of that girl or at least snatch her bad weave out." Nikki laughed. Nikki Thompson-Davis was Julia's oldest and best friend.

"Nikki, I'm fine. I just didn't like the way she was clawing all over Brian," Julia answered as she placed the macaroni and cheese into the double oven.

"The mother in you rose up, huh?" Julia's oldest sister, Angie, asked.

"I'm not a mother and I wanted to knock her out under the power." Nikki balled her fist to emphasize her point.

"Now if Alysse were here, Ms. Shannon would have gotten slayed, and it wouldn't have been in the spirit," Julia added.

"I know that's right," Angie and Nikki agreed.

Angie turned from stirring the collard greens. "What's going on with Brian and Shay?"

"Nothing, that's the problem," Julia answered her sister.

Nikki set the knife she was using to slice the ham on the cutting board. "What are you talking about?"

"Everyone knows that they are in love with each other. They know it too, but neither of them wants to admit it to the other. So instead of talking to each other, they avoid one another," Julia said plainly.

"Girlfriend, you remember how crazy we were at that age. We didn't know what or who we wanted and then when we figured it out, we were too scared to say something," Nikki said then resumed cutting.

"You remember the, you-tell-me-first-then-I'll-tell-you games we used to play?" Angie added. "Brian and Shay are meant to be together, just like you and Reggie were. They might linger in limbo for a minute, but eventually they will come together."

"I know you're right. I just wish Shay hadn't run off like she did. You know that left the door wide open for Ms. Shannon and everyone else." Julia finished just as Brian and Shannon entered the kitchen.

"Hi, Aunties." Brian kissed Angie and Nikki on the cheek. Nikki had been around the Simones for so long, she was considered part of the family.

"Hello, Brian." They waited for him to introduce Shannon. When he didn't, Angie asked, "Aren't you going to introduce your guest to us?"

"I'm sorry, Aunties. This is Shannon. I met her last week at Dave and Buster's."

Julia almost dropped the rolls in her hand. "I was under the impression that you've known her a lot longer than a week." Julia gave Shannon a sideward glance and Shannon turned away.

"Hello, Shannon. It's nice to meet you," Nikki offered.

"Really?" Shannon asked excitedly.

"Of course. We like to know all the females chasing after our young men," Angie said without smiling.

Shannon didn't know if she should smile or feel insulted.

Nikki handed Brian a Henry Wienhard's root beer before he headed to the den to watch the football game, leaving Shannon standing alone in the corner of the kitchen.

"Hey, Aunties," brothers Marcus and Craig Simone walked into the kitchen and kissed the women. Shannon watched from her spot in the corner. She clearly remembered Marcus and Craig from last week, but she didn't speak.

While exiting the kitchen, Marcus made eye contact with

Shannon. "What are you doing here?" he asked with a look of disdain.

"I'm here with Brian," Shannon answered proudly.

Marcus twisted his face and left the room without saying another word.

"Remember the message you preached this morning," Angie told Julia as she and Nikki left to set the dining room table.

Once she was alone with Julia, Shannon tried to mend fences. "Mrs. Pennington, you have a lovely home."

"Thank you, Shannon." Julia tried to smile, but her smile vanished with Shannon's next statement.

"After dinner, I'll have my honey give me a tour of the estate."

Julia didn't respond, just gave Shannon a blank stare.

"Mrs. Pennington, I'm sorry if I offended you earlier."

Julia was not in the mood for games and said as much. "Shannon, don't play with words. Just say you're sorry for lying about giving the impression that you are in a relationship with Brian."

Shannon suddenly realized she was not going to pull the wool over Julia's eyes with her innocent act. She thought she'd try the straightforward approach. "You're right. I'm not in a relationship with Brian, but I would like to be. I think Brian is a very loving and sensitive person."

"That's very insightful, considering you've only known him a week." Julia's sarcasm was lost on Shannon.

"I know a good man when I see one. I—"

Julia cut her off. "Or do you know a meal ticket when you see one?"

Before Shannon could respond, Reggie walked into the kitchen. "Is everything all right in here?" he asked nervously.

"Everything is just fine. Shannon and I have just reached an understanding on where we stand with each other." Julia gave Shannon a half-smile and left the kitchen.

"Wow!" Shannon gasped twenty minutes later when she walked into the formal dining room. While Reggie said grace, she scanned the room and admired the elegant setting. By her estimation, the mahogany dinner table that seated twenty people easily and the matching buffet server and cabinet must have cost at least one-hundred-thousand dollars. The beautiful tiered crystal chandelier hanging from the vaulted ceiling was the focal point of the room. It hung perfectly over the center of the table. At her family gatherings, she ate on paper plates, but she didn't see a piece of paper anywhere. The dinner plates and flatware that rested on the ivory scalloped-edged lace tablecloth were lined with fourteen-carat-gold trim. So was the stemware. On the floor was the plushest carpet her feet ever felt. The ivory color gave the mahogany set a more regal look. "I would love to live here," she almost said out loud.

Shannon observed how the people around her interacted with each other, especially the married couples. Mike and Angie were very affectionate with each other. So were Tyrone and Nikki, holding hands while Reggie said grace. Even at the dinner table Reggie held his wife's hand and kissed her on her face. *I want that*, Shannon thought. Shannon looked at Brian with renewed determination, but he was busy playing with Josiah. Just as Shannon was about to sit down next to Brian, he put Josiah's highchair next to him. Marcus and Craig were unsuccessful with holding in their laughter when Shannon's face fell. With her head held high, she sat in the seat next to Josiah.

Halfway through dinner, Shannon decided to take a fishing expedition. Since Brian refused to tell her anything about Shay, she opted to see what she could learn from the family.

"Mrs. Pennington, where did you learn to cook like this? This food is delicious." Truthfully, Shannon really did enjoy Julia's food.

"My mother taught all of her daughters how to cook," Julia answered with forced politeness.

"That's wonderful. I bet you can't wait for a

granddaughter, so you can pass your skills on to her." Shannon smiled at Brian.

Julia didn't respond to her last statement, instead hurriedly stuffed collard greens into her mouth.

Shannon continued, "Is this the first time Brian has brought one of his special friends home to meet the family?"

Brian dropped his fork. "Shannon, mind your own business."

The rest of the family all exchanged looks.

"Shannon, you're the first female Brian has *brought* here," Julia finally answered.

Shannon smirked at Brian. "I must be more special than that Shay girl."

Shannon, too caught up in the moment, didn't notice the adults had stopped eating and were now staring at her.

"Shannon, what do you know about Shay?" Angie asked calmly, almost friendly.

"I told you my relationship with Shay is none of your business," Brian reminded Shannon through clenched teeth.

"No, let her talk. I want to hear what she has to say," Julia responded setting her fork down and placing her elbows on the table.

Shannon gave Brian what she thought was a triumphant smile, and then proceeded to sink to the bottom of the ocean. "I don't know anything for sure because Brian won't tell me much. He keeps her a secret like she's some goddess or something. But my guess is that she wasn't good enough for Brian. She certainly wasn't on the same level as Brian and the rest of the family, that's why you never met her. She didn't have the ability to appreciate his intellect, like I do. That's why he's with me." Shannon smiled proudly.

"Shannon, you've just committed suicide," Marcus said, shaking his head. The other men hurriedly stuffed their mouths, like they were pretending not to hear or see anything.

"So," Nikki began, "you don't think this Shay person, as you call her, is good enough for Brian?"

"And you are?" Angie jumped in.

Shannon couldn't respond to their questions, because when Marcus made his comment, she remembered that he'd referred to Shay as his cousin at Dave and Buster's. *Uh-oh,* she thought.

"Let me handle this," Julia said to her sister and best friend. Reggie bowed his head in prayer.

"Shannon, you give yourself way too much credit. You're not special at all and you're not too bright either. LaShay Hampton is a very intelligent young woman, who graduated Magna Cum Laude from Stanford and is now working on her Master's at Harvard, so you see she and Brian are very much on the same level. The reason Brian has never brought Shay home to meet us is because this is her home and we are her family. You, on the other hand, are an unwanted guest and I would appreciate it if you would leave."

The dining room was completely quiet. Even Josiah was still.

Shannon held her head down as Brian stood and waited for her to get up. Before she could leave the room, Julia stopped her. "Let me give you some free advice. Don't ever talk bad about someone to his or her mother; you'll lose every time." Shannon's confusion must have showed on her face, because Julia explained. "LaShay Hampton is my daughter."

The entire ride back to her apartment, Brian didn't say one word to Shannon.

"I'm sorry. I didn't know that Julia is her mother," Shannon pleaded.

"Get out of my car, Shannon. I told you Shay was none of your business."

"What about us?"

"Shannon, there is no us. Good-bye."

She knew she wasn't going to get anywhere with Brian at that moment, but tomorrow was another day. She had all night to figure out how to get back into Brian's good graces. "Good night, Brian," she whispered and closed the door.

He drove off before she made it to the door of her apartment building, not caring if she was safe or not.

CHAPTER 20

Shay gave herself one last look-over before she answered the door. She took her time admiring her toned body in the full-length mirror, knowing the visitor wasn't anyone but Jason and he would wait for her all night. Since they'd shared dinner three weeks ago, they'd begun studying together and had gone to the movies a couple of times. Jason was easy to talk to and when she wanted company he was always available. An attraction to Jason was still missing, which made him a safe replacement for Brian. She could enjoy his company without an emotional attachment.

Shay missed Brian so much at times she would cry herself to sleep, aching to be near him. It wasn't the sex that she craved. She missed the friendship they'd shared since the day they met. Whenever something good happened in her life, Brian was always the first person she would call after her mother. He was always excited for her and encouraged her in everything. If she were down about something, he would do little things like cook her favorite meal or take her on a drive up the California coastline just so she could take her mind off her problems. On a few occasions, she'd dialed his number to tell him about her progress in the program, but changed her mind on the first ring. It was better this way. If she were going to recover and move on with her life without Brian as the center, it was best to go cold turkey.

"I wished I'd realized how much I love you, before I messed everything up," she mumbled to his graduation picture she kept on her nightstand while outlining his face with her fingertips. Jason buzzed again. Shay set the picture of the man she loved down and went to open the door for his substitute.

"Hey, you. You look nice tonight," Jason referred to her black pantsuit.

"Thank you. Let me get my coat." Shay turned away from him.

She grabbed her coat and reached for the doorknob, but Jason restrained her. "The movie doesn't begin for ninety minutes. Can you and I talk for a moment?"

She shrugged her shoulders and walked back to the couch. "Sure," she said as she sat down and crossed her legs.

Jason rubbed his hands together and unsteadily looked around the room, like he was afraid to say what was on his mind.

"What's on your mind, Jason?"

Jason took a deep breath and exhaled into his cupped hands, like he was trying to warm them. "LaShay, we have been going out for three weeks now and I really enjoy your company. I would like to start a relationship with you."

Shay mentally slapped herself for being foolish enough to encourage Jason's interest in her. Sure she enjoyed his company, but in no way was she ready to have a relationship with him or anyone else. "Jason, I have to admit that I enjoy spending time with you, but I'm not ready for a serious relationship." She hoped to sound empathetic, consoling even.

"Why not? Is it because I'm not the tall and dark type? I mean, we enjoy each other's company."

Brutal honesty spilled from her lips. "Emotionally, I'm not ready to handle a relationship right now. And besides, Jason we are on two different paths. You're going back to Chicago in less than a year and I'm going back to California. I don't do well with close relationships, so long distance is completely out of the question."

"So you're worried about us separating after we graduate?"

Jason hadn't understood what she'd said, so she tried a different approach. "Jason, if you and I were to have a relationship it wouldn't be what you expect."

Jason's facial expression turned upward. "What do you mean?"

"For starters, I will not have sex until I'm married. Nor will there be any sexual "favors" or feeling me up." He would back off now. Jason wasn't ready for this type of commitment, so she thought.

Jason sat there as in thought for a moment. "I figured you were a virgin, by the way you interact with me and other males."

Shay's head snapped up. "What?"

"Never mind," Jason waved his hands, "I'm up for the challenge, if you'll give me a chance."

I don't believe this! Shay wanted to scream. Why did Jason Alexander have to be the one noble man left in Massachusetts?

"Look, Jason, I don't think this is a good idea. I have old scars and I don't want you paying for my past mistakes." Thoughts of Brian returned. "It may turn out bad for you and I don't want to hurt you."

Jason held her hand. "I'm a twenty-seven-year-old man; I can take care of myself."

Shay's hot gaze bore into Jason long and hard. Maybe it won't be too bad. He'll probably lose interest in a couple of months anyway, Shay reasoned, tuning out the voice from deep within warning her of the big mistake she was about to make.

"Alright, Jason, we'll give it a try and see what happens," she finally answered.

The wide jubilant grin on Jason's face said she'd just made him the happiest man in the world. Even still, his quick lift and embrace caught her off guard. An attempt to relax in his arms proved futile. Jason didn't feel like Brian. He didn't smell like Brian. He didn't hold her the way Brian had. She didn't feel the security Brian's arms had always given her. To put it plainly, Jason wasn't Brian.

When he released her and softly brushed her lips with his, Shay had tears in her eyes. Jason must have assumed she was crying because of how much she cared for him. She did in a casual-friend kind of way, but those tears washed her cheeks because for the first time she realized that Brian was the only man she would ever want to touch her. She did more than give Brian her body; she had given him her heart. Crossing this bridge would be much harder than she had anticipated.

CHAPTER 21

"Happy Thanksgiving!" Brian was half-asleep, but when he heard Shay's voice on the phone, he sat straight up.

"Shay, is that you?" he wanted to make sure he wasn't dreaming about her like he'd been doing lately.

"Who else would it be?" Her soft voice sent feather-like touches down his muscular biceps.

Due to Brian's wandering childhood, the holidays were very special to him. A time he cherished with the enthusiasm of a child on Christmas Eve. Shay knew this and made every effort to make sure he enjoyed every holiday. Her voice was the first sound he heard every holiday, birthday and special event.

Brian felt a tug at his heart. "My Shay, always looking out for me."

"Brian, I'll always look out for you. You're special to me."

"I thought you forgot about me. You know, threw me away like old clothes."

"Why, because I didn't come home for Thanksgiving?" she asked, "Is it because I'm talking to you through telephone wire and not there with you?"

"That and because of our last conversation. You know I'd rather hold you in my arms instead of this cold telephone."

"I'd like that too," she admitted. "Brian, I'll never throw you away."

Brian closed his eyes and took a deep breath. "Why, Shay? Why won't you throw me away?"

Her quivering voice was just above a whisper. "Because I gave you my heart. Don't you know that?"

The declaration overwhelmed Brian to the point it took him a minute to align his thoughts and gain control of his voice. Shay took his silence for rejection. By the time he'd steadied his voice enough to speak, she had hung up. He attempted to call her back, but was greeted by her voicemail.

CHAPTER 22

Brian stopped mid-stride when he recognized Shannon standing next to his RAV4. He had been avoiding her persistent telephone calls since she pulled that stunt at his parents' house. Now there was no way he could avoid her.

"What do you want, Shannon?"

"I need to talk to you," she whined.

Brian unlocked the car and sat his laptop in the back passenger seat. "You and I have nothing to talk about."

"Brian, I don't think you're being fair to me."

Brian twisted his face incredulously. "Shannon, you disrespected me and my

parents and not to mention Shay. Whom you don't even know, and I'm not being fair?" Brian reached around her to open the driver's side door. "Playing the victim won't help your case."

She folded her arms across her chest. "Think about it, Brian, if you'd been forthright with me about Shay, I wouldn't have had to draw my own conclusions."

"I told you, what happens between Shay and me is none of your business." Brian jumped into the car, closed the door and to his surprise, Shannon started crying.

"Brian, I'm sorry, I just wanted to know everything I could about you. I want to be a good friend to you."

"You want to be a good friend to me? Shannon, you don't even know me." He started the engine.

Between sobs she answered, "I know I have only known

you for a short period of time, but I know you're special and if you give me a chance, you'll see that we can be good together."

"Shannon, listen to me very closely. You and I will never be anything but friends—if that."

"How do you know if you won't give me a chance?" she sniffled.

His visual head-to-toe inspection confirmed his thoughts. While the skin-tight leggings and low cleavage would have been a turn-on to some, for Brian the outfit was distasteful. "Shannon, I just know."

High-pitched sobbing erupted. "You don't think I'm good enough for you! Why?"

He handed her a tissue from his glove box. "Shannon, that's not what I said."

She blew her nose loudly. "Then why won't you give me a chance?"

Brian wasn't used to women crying in front of him and wanted her to stop.

Neither did he want her to get the wrong impression of him. He knew firsthand what it felt like to have people look down on you, because of economic status and living environment.

"Shannon, I can't have a serious relationship with you, because you're not a Christian," then added hesitatingly, "and because I'm in love with someone else."

Shannon wrapped up the crying routine. She had all the information she needed.

"I see, so you are in love with Shay. Well, maybe you can help me become a Christian. I can start going to service with you on Sundays. I promise I'll dress like a respectable lady," she stated hopefully.

"Shannon, you can become as devout as Mother Theresa, but you still won't win my heart."

Shannon was fast on her feet, like rejection was nothing new to her. "No, I won't, but at least I'll have your friendship and respect."

Brian shifted the gear into reverse. "Whatever, Shannon."

Before he completely pulled out of his parking stall, she called after him. "What time shall I be ready on Sunday?"

"Ten o'clock," he yelled back.

Shannon had a wide smile on her face on her way back to the admissions office. Everything was going to be just fine. She could fake the church thing long enough to get Brian into her. By her calculations she had until the summer to help him get over his infatuation with Shay. All spring she'd break him down until his sweet Shay was nothing but a distant memory.

CHAPTER 23

With just two weeks left before Christmas, Alysse flew in from Arizona to visit Brian. Alysse hadn't planned the trip, but her last few conversations with Brian had left her with a bad feeling. Brian sounded lonely to her. She figured his disposition was due to Shay's living in Massachusetts. After she arrived and observed that he'd lost more than a few pounds, Alysse knew the problem had to be deeper than mere loneliness. Her baby boy was in love and he missed his woman.

Alysse worked in the kitchen while Brian took a shower. She'd gotten up early Saturday morning and went to the supermarket. She was on a mission: If she had to cook nonstop, Brian was going to gain his weight back.

"Mrs. Green, you've got it smelling real good in here," Todd said as he entered the kitchen.

"You look like you could use some home cooking too." She looked up and down at his tall thin frame. "Don't they teach you to eat in medical school?"

"Yes. It's just hard sometimes to find regular solid meals," Todd answered.

"It must be hard in law school too, because Brian has dropped at least one waist size."

Todd smirked. "Mrs. Green, I think Brian's weight loss is due more to matters of the heart than his food intake." Todd gave Alysse a knowing look. "He hasn't been the same since Shay left."

"That's what I figured. I can't wait for her to come back."

"Me neither," Todd agreed. "His mood swings are becoming unbearable."

"Smells good, Mom." Brian kissed his mother and joined Todd at the table. "My mood swings aren't that bad," he said to his roommate.

"It's about time you came out of hibernation," Alysse scolded.

"It's only ten o'clock, Mom."

"Brian, I know you miss Shay, but if you don't eat, there won't be anything for her to hold on to when she comes back," Alysse teased.

Brian's chocolate cheeks burned. "Mom, I don't know what you are talking about."

"I'm your mother so don't play with me. You know Shay loves holding onto your tall, dark, used-to-be thick self. I've seen the two of you together, feeding each other and holding hands like you're scared you're going to lose one another."

Todd laughed, but Brian remained silent.

Alysse continued. "And you know you like them hips and those long legs she has."

"Alright, Mom, you win. You can stop now." Brian conceded because hearing his mother describe Shay's physical attributes made his mind go places it shouldn't. Brian had made up his mind; he was not going to have sex again. Not until after he married. In his heart he prayed it would be with Shay, but this morning he couldn't think about that.

Alysse—never the type of mother to allow her child to tell her what to do—continued to talk and pile food onto the platter at the same time. "I like Shay. She's everything I want for you. She's smart, clean and pretty. She can cook, but most importantly, she respects your mother. You don't find that too often these days. Julia has done a good job with raising her." She placed the huge platter of pancakes, sausage, bacon and scrambled eggs on the table next to the pitcher of orange juice. "I hope to take care of myself when I'm older, but just in case I need some help, it's good to know that Shay has been raised to respect and care for her elders." Alysse set a plate in front of Todd and Brian. "I've been watching the Simone family. All of them grandchildren treat the adults with the utmost respect, even the adult grandchildren. And they all address Mark and I as Mr. or Ms."

Brian piled his plate. "I'm glad you like her. I like her too."

Alysse smacked her lips. "Boy, there you go playing again. You're in love with her, that's why you can't eat. You miss her."

The doorbell chime spared Brian a response.

"Are you expecting company this morning?" Alysse asked, removing her apron.

"No, it's probably someone trying to sell magazines or something."

"You stay here and eat; I'll take care of it."

The persistent unexpected guest pressed the doorbell again before Alysse managed to open the door. "Can I help you?" she asked, holding the door open.

"I'm here to see Mr. Pennington."

"I'm sorry, but he's eating breakfast. Is there a message I can give him?"

"No, there isn't a message you can give him, but you could run along and tell him Shannon is here to see him."

Alysse gripped both hands on the heavy oak door and squeezed. As a rule she didn't tolerate disrespect.

"Did I speak too fast for you? Let me try it again." Shannon spoke to Alysse like she was a two-year-old child, "GO TELL MR. PENNINGTON THAT SHANNON IS HERE TO SEE HIM. Now!"

Alysse slapped her hands on her hip. "Little girl, I will hang you from that light pole by that bad hair weave of yours, if you don't get out of my face!"

"Who do you think you're talking to like that?" Shannon rolled her neck.

"The question is, who do you think you're talking to?"

"The maid, the hired help," Shannon yelled.

Alysse stepped back. "Come back on Tuesday, that's the day Brian puts the trash out." With that she slammed the door in Shannon's face.

Alysse stormed into the kitchen. "Brian, who is Shannon and why is she here to see you?"

Brian washed down the pancakes with a gulp of orange juice. "What are you talking about, Mama?"

"Some little skinny girl with a bad hair weave just mistook me for a maid."

The doorbell chimed once again. Brian abruptly left the kitchen and went to the front door.

"Shannon, what are you doing here? How did you know where I live?" She moved her mouth to answer, but he tossed another question. "What did you say to my mother?"

Shannon's mouth fell open. "Your mother? Oh...Um."

Alysse stepped in front of Brian and pointed her finger in Shannon's face. "Let me tell you something. I am not a close friend with Jesus, like Brian's father is. Me and Jesus are just getting acquainted and I haven't learned to turn the other cheek yet. If you ever disrespect me again, I promise you, Jesus will have to save your life."

Shannon didn't say a word, just lowered her head.

"Do you understand?" Alysse yelled.

"Yes, I'm sorry." Shannon's voice was so low, Brian couldn't tell if she'd responded or not.

"Did you hear what my mother said?"

This time Shannon nodded her answer.

"And why are you here?" Alysse demanded.

Brian didn't say a word; he knew not to interrupt Alysse when she was angry.

"I'm here to see Brian," Shannon's voice quivered.

Alysse looked her up and down. "What do you need to see my son about? I can look at you and tell you're not a classmate."

"Brian and I are friends."

Alysse stepped closer and pointed her finger at Shannon. "You listen to me. I wasn't born yesterday. I've lived on the

120

streets longer than you are old. I've seen and played every type of game there is. You can take your little manipulative seductive game back down the hill away from my son." Alysse stormed away.

Shannon's head hung low. "Brian, I'm sorry, I didn't know she was your mother. I just assumed you would have a maid with you living in this exclusive neighborhood."

He ignored her explanation. "Shannon, I didn't give you my address. How did you find out where I live?"

"I got your address from work and I shouldn't have come over here without calling first."

"You're right, you shouldn't have come here uninvited nor should you have used your job to gain my personal information."

"I'll see you tomorrow at church," she said and walked back to her car with her shoulders slumped.

* * *

Wrapping his arms around Julia, Reggie kissed her neck. "Good morning, beautiful."

"Is it still morning?" Julia rolled over and snuggled against him.

"It's after ten."

Julia stretched. "I better get up before Josiah destroys the house." She tried to sit up, but Reggie held her down.

"He's fine. Did you forget that Marcus and Justin are here?"

She relaxed. "I sure did."

He pressed her closer to him. "Let me see what else I can make you forget."

The intercom sounded, it was her nephew Justin. "Do you guys want some breakfast? We have waffles, eggs and bacon."

"Maybe later," Reggie answered then turned the speaker off and directed his attention back to Julia just as the telephone rang.

Reggie sighed. "Don't move." He kissed her again before answering the phone.

121

Good morning, Pennington residence"

"What's so good about it?" Alysse snapped.

"I should have let the call go to voicemail," he mumbled, but said out loud, "Is something wrong, Alysse?"

"Something is very wrong. Reggie, did you know there's a gold digger chasing after Brian?"

Reggie rubbed his head. "Are you referring to Shannon?"

At the mention of Shannon's name, Julia sat straight up.

"Yes I am and I don't like her. Do you know that little trifling wanna-be had the nerve to talk to me like I was a child and then called me a maid?"

Reggie covered his mouth so Alysse couldn't hear him laugh. "Alysse, I hope you're not calling me from jail. Please don't tell me you've been arrested for assault and battery?"

"What happened?" Julia asked.

"Reginald Pennington, stop laughing. I am not in the mood for your tired jokes," she yelled. "Anyway, I didn't beat her down this time."

Reggie breathed a sigh of relief. "Thank God."

"But I promise to the next time she gets out of line," Alysse added.

"What happened?" Julia asked again.

"Alysse, where did you see Shannon?" Reggie asked.

"She showed up on Brian's doorstep this morning, looking like both Delilah and Jezebel."

It was Reggie's turn to sit straight up. "What? Shannon was at the house?"

"What?" Julia started to get out of bed.

"Reggie, let me talk to Julia. We're not about to have this foolishness. If I have to move back to Oakland, I will. I've invested too much into my son for this mess!"

Reggie shook his head and handed the phone to Julia.

"Shannon was at the house?" Julia went straight to the point.

"Girl, yes, and let me tell you what she did." Alysse gave Julia the highlights from her unexpected visitor. "How long have y'all known about this?"

"Brian introduced her to us at church a few weeks ago and lately she's been coming to Bible Study." Julia didn't mention the disastrous Sunday dinner.

"What is she doing at church? That devil ain't trying to find Jesus?"

"I think you're right about that." Julia laughed. "Alysse, I don't think we have anything to worry about. Brian's not interested in her."

Alysse would not be pacified. "I know he's not interested in her, because I raised him better than that. I know he's in love with Shay, but that won't stop ms. thang from trying something. I can see the dollar signs all in her eyes. She sees Brian living in this house on this hill and she knows he's going to be a lawyer. That girl is going to try to trap my baby."

"I bet she's rolling her neck and wagging her finger," Julia whispered to Reggie. "Now you know, Julia, I am not about to have that!"

"I know, Alysse, neither are we," Julia stated calmly.

Alysse continued to rant. "You know that boy is not too old or too big for me to beat some sense into him."

"I know, Alysse."

Julia watched Reggie leave their bed and walk into the bathroom. A moment later she heard the shower. "Alysse, I'll call you later and we can talk about this some more, but I need to take care of something first." Julia hung up the phone and headed to the shower.

CHAPTER 24

During Sunday service Shannon performed a good show by participating in Praise & Worship and by taking notes during Reggie's sermon. To her surprise, she actually found what he was saying interesting. Today's topic was "Unconditional Love", taken from First Corinthians Chapter 13.

"Love is patient, love is kind. Love bears all things and endures all things. Love never fails," Pastor Pennington read.

Shannon's mind drifted back to her childhood and the horrific trauma she'd endured. "Love isn't for everybody," she said snidely.

From the dais Julia watched Shannon the entire service. She didn't want to admit it, but she felt that God was leading her to Shannon. "I really could do without the drama," was what Julia told the Lord in her early-morning prayer time, but like always the Lord didn't change His mind.

Shannon started in Brian's direction after service, but Alysse gave her a warning glare causing Shannon to quietly retreat. She was about to turn and leave when Julia called after her.

"Shannon, can I speak to you for a moment?"

Reggie's sermon had left Shannon feeling a little vulnerable and she wasn't in the mood for another argument. "What is it?" she asked defensively.

"I know something is bothering you, but I'm not going to ask what, or who it is. Shannon, it's no secret that you and

I got off on the wrong foot. But if you'll allow me, I'd like to help you."

Shannon smacked her lips. "You want to help me?"

"Yes, Shannon. I want to save you from experiencing more embarrassing moments like the one you had yesterday morning and when you were at my house for dinner."

Shannon rolled her neck. "And just how do you plan to do that?"

Julia ignored the attitude. "By giving you a few simple rules on life."

Shannon rolled her eyes again and smacked her lips. "What rules?"

"For starters, don't try to make yourself look good at the expense of making someone else look bad. It will only backfire."

Shannon remained quiet, and Julia continued. "Don't ever prejudge someone based on where they live or the job they hold. If Alysse were in fact a maid, that wouldn't have given you the right to be rude to her. Shannon, never think you're better than another person. And Shannon, if you want to land a good man—other than Brian of course—never show up at his house uninvited. It shows desperation. Don't force your way in; wait until you're invited. You'll get to stay longer."

Shannon's face twisted. Julia had given her more instructions on life in two minutes, than her own mother had done her entire childhood. Shannon flung her blonde curls over her shoulder and smirked. "Anything else, Mrs. Pennington?"

Julia saw right through Shannon's hard shell, the young woman really didn't know as much as she portrayed. "No, I think I've give you enough to think about. If there's anything I can help you with Shannon, don't hesitate to ask."

Shannon turned and walked out of the sanctuary. Outside in her car she pulled out her notepad and wrote down everything Julia had said to her. By Shannon's standards, Julia had everything Shannon wanted: money, a big house, her choice of luxury cars and not to mention that five-carat rock on her left ring finger. Shannon thought she'd learn all she could from her before she broke her daughter's heart by marrying Brian.

CHAPTER 25

On Christmas Eve Shay found herself sitting anxiously on her bed, staring at the small parcel box. Several presents already surrounded her small optic Christmas tree, but this white box with black lettering was special. The return address and handwriting belonged to Brian. They hadn't talked since Thanksgiving day and her feelings for him had not changed. With trembling fingers she finally opened the little cardboard box and read the short enclosed note.

You gave me your heart, now I'm giving you mine.

Inside of the white velvet box was a flat silver heart on a silver chain-linked bracelet. Rhythmically, her hand covered the cavity that enclosed her own heart as she read the endearing inscription.

B&S

4Ever

Tears flooded her eyes as she ran her finger over the letters. Her nerves instantly settled and involuntarily she picked up the phone to call the man she loved, when the man she dated knocked on her front door. Reluctantly, Shay ran into the living room and answered the door. As she did so, she slipped the new chain around her wrist.

"Jason, have a seat, I'll be right back." She let Jason in then returned to her bedroom and closed the door. She dialed the number and paced the length of her queen-sized bed. He answered on the second ring.

"Hey, you."

She could tell he was smiling from the jovialness of his voice. "Hello, Brian, I got your present today."

"I hope you like it. Although I know you do from the sound of your joyous voice."

"It's perfect," she paused, "I'm wearing it now."

Silence remained until Brian cleared his throat. "Shay, I was thinking about coming to see you next week."

"Really?" She'd yearned to see him since their brief conversation when she'd recklessly admitted her feelings.

Shay's ecstatic response pleased him. "Good. I thought I'd fly in on Tuesday and stay until Friday."

"That's great," was what she was about to say when the sound of Jason turning on the television quickly brought her back to reality. Brian couldn't come to Cambridge. Not because of Jason, she'd dismiss him in a second for Brian. Truth was, Shay didn't trust herself alone with Brian for three days. She hadn't worked on her spiritual relationship with God and she knew if Brian were in Cambridge, there was nothing to prevent her from sleeping with him again. If that happens, she may never find her way back to God. She had to think of a reason to keep Brian in California without telling him the real motive. She walked over to the window and looked out at the white powdery streets and found the answer.

"Brian, on second thought, that might not be a good idea. We're experiencing a very heavy snow season and I would feel better if you didn't fly in bad weather." That was the truth.

"I didn't think about that," he said with disappointment that touched her. "I just wanted to see you."

Shay blushed. "I want to see you too."

"I miss you. I miss our conversations. I miss your company. I just miss us."

"I miss being with you, too, but I will come home during spring break for Marcus's CD recording."

"But that's four months away," he whined.

"That's the best I can do. Maybe in the meantime we

could—you know—communicate more often." It amazed Shay how easily her heart controlled her mind where Brian was concerned.

"I'd like that. I'm not the same without you," Brian admitted to her. "Shay," he broke the silence that followed.

"Yes, Brian."

"You now hold my heart in your hands as well. Take care of it."

"Take care of mine, she whispered back." If only their relationship wasn't so complicated.

"Always, Shay, always."

Long after Shay hung up the phone a big smile creased her face. She wasn't quite sure what he meant by asking her to take care of his heart, but she was elated he hadn't taken what she'd told him about giving her heart to him, for naught.

She returned to the living room to find Jason watching a basketball game. In her elation, she'd nearly forgotten about him.

"Is everything all right?" Jason asked.

"Everything is just fine." Shay sat on the couch next to him, still smiling.

Jason's eyes moved from her face to the silver on her wrist. "Is that a new bracelet?"

"Huh?" Shay wasn't prepared for his question.

"The bracelet on your wrist, is it new?"

Shay's eyes looked away from him and focused on the television. "What made you ask that question?"

"I don't recall seeing you wear it before, that's all."

Shay took the defensive approach. "And I'm sure I have seen all of your personal items, right?"

"Well, no," he admitted.

Shay knew she'd wiggled out of this one. "Then don't assume something is new, just because you haven't seen it before."

Jason held up his hand and shrugged in defeat. "It's nice, where did you get it from?"

Instead of answering his question, she got up and went into the kitchen to make hot chocolate. When she returned with two steaming mugs Jason didn't question her again about that, but did go on an expedition into her past.

"Have you dated before?" he asked after sipping the hot warm liquid.

"Why are you always digging into my past?"

Jason sighed. "LaShay, if you would open up to me, I wouldn't have to dig."

He was right. Every time Jason asked her a question, she'd clam up or answer his question with one of her own.

"I'm sorry; I have been unfair to you," Shay acknowledged. "I dated in college, but it was nothing serious."

"So, I'm not competing with the memory of an old love for your affections?" he asked then slowly sipped the chocolate.

Shay often wondered if Jason was psychic. He always seemed to hit the nail on the head when it came to her past. She looked deep into his eyes, debating if she should tell him about Brian. She decided against it.

"The guys I dated at school didn't hold my interest. Our relationships were more like that of old buddies." That was true. She and Brian did not attend the same college.

Jason set his mug on the coaster and leaned closer to Shay. "LaShay, have you ever been passionately kissed before?"

Her mind immediately went back to the first and last kiss she and Brian shared. Both times and every time in between were remarkable. Remembering the warmth of Brian's touch, a soft moan attempted to escape from her lips. "Why?"

Again, Jason assumed she was being evasive to hide her inexperience and said as much. "I want to show you what passion feels like."

It surprised her how much the thought of someone other than Brian kissing her upset her. Shay's defensiveness snatched any hope Jason had of getting a kiss underneath the mistletoe.

"Look, Jason," she snapped, pushing him away. "If you want to keep dating me, you'd do well to remember that my passion is reserved for my future husband." An image of Brian flashed before her. "If you keep pressuring me, I guarantee you that man won't be you."

Jason quickly moved out of her space. "LaShay, I'm not trying to pressure you. I just really like you a lot. I like to express my feelings and when you're ready, you'll return them."

Shay started to tell him she couldn't imagine ever being affectionate with him, but the sincerity in his eyes wouldn't allow her to break his heart, at least not on Christmas Eve.

"Maybe one day," was Shay's response before going into the kitchen for more hot chocolate.

CHAPTER 26

Shay walked through Harvard Square enjoying the colorful blossoms of spring. Of the four seasons, spring was her favorite. For her, blossoming flowers and trees always promised something new and exciting, a new beginning. That was exactly what she was hoping for: something new. She could hardly wait until September, when she'd complete the fast-paced teaching program. The program was tedious, but she'd managed to maintain a 3.8 GPA since arriving at Harvard and was very proud of herself for rising to the challenge. Today, excitement over her trip home next weekend and the anticipation of spending much-needed time with Brian caused her to step with the rhythm of her humming.

They'd been talking on a weekly basis since Christmas. She still hadn't shared the depths of her heart, but at least she got to hear his voice every week and that helped fill the void. It was almost like old times; they talked about everything, except what really needed to be discussed: their non-existent relationship. And of course, she never mentioned Jason. In her mind, she didn't need to, because she'd decided to break things off with Jason when she returned from California. Jason was a nice guy, but he wasn't what she wanted. Jason had proven to be a man of great determination and honor. Someday he'd make someone a good companion, but not her.

The enthralling aroma of hot cinnamon rolls from the corner bakery crammed her mind with more thoughts of

Brian. Suddenly she felt like cooking again. Brian loved to eat her homemade cinnamon rolls right out of the oven. She continued down the brick walk, past the Italian ice shop and remembered sharing ice cream with Brian every day they were in Arizona. "I bet he'd love mango Italian ice," she said audibly. And so it was, every store she passed, she had thoughts of what Brian would like and what she wanted him to try. Forty-five minutes later, frustrated with thinking about him, Shay pulled out her cell phone and punched in his number.

* * *

Brian turned the engine off and looked over at Shannon. "Do you want anything?" he asked.

"Just a tall vanilla cream. Thank you," she answered politely.

Shannon smiled as she watched Brian disappear inside Starbucks. Everything was working according to her plan. She'd kept her word to Brian and had attended church every Sunday for the last four months. She'd gotten used to the songs that the Praise & Worship team and the choir sang to the point sometimes she would stand and sing along with them. She especially enjoyed listening to Julia sing, but she didn't understand why Pastor Pennington always wore an expression of love and respect for Julia, and she likewise for him. Every Sunday before Pastor Pennington took his seat next to her, he always kissed her. And sometimes he would hold her hand while the deacons received the offering or as the choir sang. When one of them administered prayer to the congregation, the other was always present. From where Shannon sat, it looked as though they were protecting each other. Shannon had never seen such an open display of real affection between two people. In the household she'd grown up in that never happened. She still took notes on the sermon every Sunday, but she also took notes on Julia Pennington.

Shannon observed everything about her. How she talked and how she walked. She took note of how she sat with her legs crossed at the ankles and how her skirts were always long enough that she never needed a lap scarf. It amazed her that although Julia never showed cleavage and her clothing never hugged her hips tightly, she possessed a natural sensuality and sexuality that was foreign to Shannon.

Every Sunday Shannon made a point of speaking to Julia, to see what she could glean from her. So far she had gleaned enough to know how to convince Brian to pick her up every Wednesday for Bible Study and Sunday morning for church. Soon she'd have enough to convince him to shop for a ring.

Shannon's thoughts were interrupted by Brian's cell phone that lay on the console. Normally she didn't answer his phone, but she couldn't resist when she saw Shay's name on the caller ID. She pressed the green answer call button after checking to make sure Brian wasn't coming.

"Hello," she said in her most sexy and seductive voice.

"I'm sorry, I have the wrong number." Shay was about to disconnect when Shannon spoke up.

"If you're trying to reach Brian Pennington, this is the right number."

The response seemed to confuse Shay. "Um...is...um... May I speak to Brian please?"

"I'm sorry, but he's um...Let's just say he's busy right now. Is there a message I can give him when we're done?" Shannon breathed heavily between sentences.

Shay's voice escalated. "Who are you?"

A devilish grin spread across Shannon's face; she'd succeeded in ruffling Shay's feathers. "I'm Shannon, Brian's significant other. And you are?"

Shay's earlier adoration for Brian turned into hot anger. "Don't worry about who I am! You're not that significant, if I've never heard of you." Then she ended the call.

***

Shay was still angry when she returned to her apartment. She paced from the living room to the kitchen to the bedroom and back again, talking out loud and yelling at the furniture.

"I can't believe he had the nerve to let some woman answer his phone! And what on earth was he doing that he couldn't take my call? Is that why he calls me on the weekend, because he's with her during the week? So you want to play games, mister? I'll show you how to play."

She stomped over to the nightstand, picked up the cordless telephone and punched the numbers without thinking rationally.

"Hello," the sleepy voice answered.

"Hi, Jason. How would you like to spend a couple days in California with me next weekend, my treat? My cousin is recording his CD at my parents' church on Saturday night."

"Are you asking me to meet your parents?"

She could tell he was smiling, but Shay was not in the mood to stroke his ego. "I'm asking you if you want to go to my cousin's live recording, and yes you'll meet my mother and stepfather and the rest of my family. Do you want to go or not?"

"I'd love to. When do we leave?"

"Friday morning and we'll return Sunday evening."

"LaShay, thank you for inviting me. I really mean that. I've been working hard to impress you and now it's paying off. If you think enough of me to introduce me to your family, your feelings must be growing."

"I'll see you later." Shay replaced the headset back on its holster. She looked at the picture of Brian on her dresser. "Let's see how you like it when you get served."

CHAPTER 27

Brian checked himself one last time in the full-length mirror on his bedroom door. He'd chosen the black silk casual pants with the matching button-down shirt, because Shay liked him in black. Earlier that morning he'd gone to the barbershop and had his head freshly shaved and his newly acquired goatee trimmed. After splashing on both his and Shay's favorite cologne, he checked his watch. If he didn't leave now he'd be late picking Shay up at the airport. He still needed to stop at the florist and pick up red roses.

***

Shay literally shook as the plane made its final decent into Oakland.

"Calm down, the plane is not going to crash land." Jason must have assumed she worried about the landing. That was the furthest thing from her mind. In less than thirty minutes she'd be face-to-face with Brian, her love. Originally Reggie had agreed to pick her up, but called to say he was sending Brian at the last minute. Shay was certain the alteration was planned. She hadn't seen Brian in eight months and after the incident with Shannon, she'd stopped answering his calls. However mad, the closer she got to Oakland, the stronger her desire to see him grew. Her palms sweat. Her mouth went dry and a lump lodged in her throat. "Will someone please tell this pilot to hurry up?" she mumbled.

She wondered if he would like the changes she'd made to her appearance. While in Massachusetts, she'd decided to let her hair grow. Her once-shoulder-length hair was now

139

three-inches down her back. At the hair salon three days ago, she'd made the decision to lighten her brown hair. It was now honey blonde. Jason didn't care for the color change, but she didn't care what he thought. She loved it. Due to her busy schedule, she didn't prepare home-cooked meals too often. That meant she ate out a lot and consumed more calories than normal and it showed in her hips. If she didn't start cutting back soon, her size-ten clothing would be too small by the time summer rolled around.

Ten minutes later the plan landed. Shay went to the restroom while Jason located the baggage claim area.

***

Brian's six-foot-four-inch frame made it easy for him to search through the flood of travelers approaching the baggage claim area. He spotted her the moment she stepped out of the restroom. "Shay!" he called out in a loud voice.

She stopped mid-stride and slowly turned around. The grin on his face nearly showed all thirty-two teeth.

Her mouth hung open and her legs weakened as she watched him take quick long strides toward her. He looked better than she remembered. His upper body was broader and his new goatee made him that much more handsome to her and that baldhead. Oh, how she loved that baldhead!

When Brian reached her, he gathered her into his strong arms and held her tightly. Without hesitation, she received his embrace by wrapping her arms around his neck.

"My Shay, I've missed you," he whispered repeatedly in her ear while holding her against his chest.

She deeply inhaled his scent. He smelled so good. He felt very good. She couldn't resist any longer, she stroked his baldhead and moaned. "I've missed you so much."

They finally separated after what Shay thought was too soon. Brian stepped back and studied her. His voice full of adoration and his eyes full of appreciation. "Shay, I love the new look. I love your hair, that color highlights your skin tone and eyes perfectly." He gently stroked her cheek. "You're more beautiful than I remember."

140

"I didn't think you could get any finer, but you've proven me wrong," Shay said outlining his goatee with her fingertips.

She blushed as he stroked her hair and then took her right hand in his. Shay nearly lost her balance when he brought her hand to his lips and kissed her wrist where the silver heart he'd sent her lay. He then stroked his cheek with her wrist. His strong arms caught her just as her knees buckled.

"Let's get your luggage," Brian said, reveling in the affect he had on her.

Shay's world quickly came tumbling down as she remembered she was not alone. At that very moment she hated herself for dragging Jason along with her. The anger that motivated her to invite Jason had dissipated and all she wanted to do was have Brian hold her like he'd just done. She lowered her head. "Brian, there's something I need to tell you." Her smile was gone, replaced with what Brian interpreted as sheer fear.

"What's the matter, baby?"

Hearing him address her by the endearing term, made her want to run back to Massachusetts, but she couldn't. She had to face the music. "Brian...um...I didn't come alone."

"What are you talking about?"

Shay couldn't look him in the face any longer. Focusing on the floor, she uttered, "I...um...I"

"Hey, babe, I have our bags," Jason announced when he joined them and placed his arm around Shay.

Shay would never forget the look on Brian's face. The handsome face that was moments before joyful and full of contentment was now etched with pain and confusion as he gazed from her to Jason. She couldn't look at Brian for longer than a second. She lowered her head again and this time folded her arms. She suddenly found the multi-colored carpet fascinating.

In a subdued voice, Brian spoke first. "Shay, aren't you going to introduce me to your guest?" He was not going to make it easy for her. He wanted to hear it from her. He wanted her to tell him she was seeing someone, that she'd moved on with her life.

Shay cleared her throat, but didn't make eye contact. "Brian, this is Jason Alexander. Jason, this is Brian Pennington."

"Welcome to California," Brian said, casually, but not friendly and shook Jason's hand.

"Are you one of LaShay's cousins?" Jason asked.

"No. My father is married to Shay's mother. And your relationship to Shay would be?"

"I'm LaShay's boyfriend," Jason answered proudly.

"Oh really?" Brian said and gave Shay a smile completely void of sincerity.

Shay closed her eyes and rubbed her forehead. A major migraine was headed her way.

"We had better get going if we don't want to get stuck in traffic," Brian announced still holding the stale smile. Before Jason or Shay could respond, Brian turned and headed toward the exit.

Except for the Fred Hammond CD, the ride to Blackhawk was quiet. Scared that Brian would strangle her, Shay chose to sit in the backseat with Jason. From time to time she'd look up and see Brian staring at her in the rearview mirror. Shay leaned her head against the window and cried quietly, devoid of tears. *What am I doing?*

CHAPTER 28

When Brian stormed through the door, Reggie and Julia were preparing lunch. Before he headed upstairs, he dumped the roses he'd bought for Shay into the trash.

"Where's Shay?" Julia called after him.

Brian stopped on the third step and took a deep breath. "She's outside—with her boyfriend," he said and continued climbing the stairs.

Julia looked at Reggie with confusion written on her face. "Did he just say Shay's outside with her boyfriend?"

Before Reggie could answer, Shay and Jason entered the kitchen.

"My baby!" Julia hugged and kissed her daughter then held her back and studied her. "I love your new hair color."

"It looks good on you," Reggie concurred.

"Hi, Reggie." Shay stepped into Reggie's embrace.

Three-year-old Josiah ran in from the den. "Shay! Shay!" She squatted and welcomed her little brother into her arms.

Reggie motioned toward Jason. "Aren't you going to introduce us to your guest?" he asked Shay.

Shay released Josiah and stood up. "Mom, Reggie this is Jason Alexander, we're in the same teaching program. These are my parents, Reginald and Julia Pennington."

"Welcome to California, Jason," Reggie said politely although Jason's presence confused him.

Shay's uneasiness was not lost on Julia either. Her attempt to make eye contact with her daughter proved futile. She turned to the visitor. "Jason, so you and Shay are classmates?"

"Yes, and we've been dating for six months," he answered proudly.

"It's good to meet you, Jason." Julia directed her attention to Shay, who couldn't stop rubbing the back of her neck. "Come help me with lunch." Julia smiled, but Shay knew her mother was about to lay into her.

"I need to show Jason where the guest room is," Shay stated.

"Don't worry about that, I'll take care of Jason," Reggie offered.

As soon as Jason was out of earshot, Julia scolded Shay. "Have you lost your mind? What do you think you're doing?"

Shay knew playing innocent wasn't the answer, but that was the only response she had. "What do you mean?"

"You know good and well what I mean! Why have you been dating someone you don't even like for six months and why did you bring him here, when you knew Brian would be here?"

"Mama, how do you know I don't like Jason? He's a very nice person."

"I don't doubt that he's a nice person, Shay, but he's also more than a little naïve if he thinks he has a real chance with you."

Shay hated when her mother was right. "What makes you say that?"

"Maybe it's the way you hid him from us for six months. Or maybe it's the fact that he's the total opposite of the kind of man you're attracted to. Or, Shay, maybe it's because he's not Brian!"

"Mama, I know you think Brian and I should be together, but that will never happen."

"Shay, cut the crap! I've never pushed you toward Brian; you did that all on your own. You falling in love with Brian had nothing to do with me. Now, I sent you to Harvard to gain knowledge, not lose all of your common sense. Shay, it's just plain foolish to be involved with Jason when you know your heart is with Brian. And to parade Jason around, girl, are you crazy? Brian has been counting down the days until your return. He was hoping to spend some quality time with you." Julia rubbed her temples and shook her head. "Did you ever tell Brian how you really feel?"

Shay's silence conveyed the answer Julia needed. Julia took a deep breath and tried to speak calmly. "Shay, you need to tell Brian how you really feel about him. If you're not careful, the heart you break may be your own."

Shay rubbed her forehead. She felt a major migraine coming again. "Mama, I'm sorry, I didn't mean to cause confusion. I—"

"You have a beautiful home, Mrs. Pennington." Jason and Reggie were back.

"Thank you, Jason. Have a seat in the den, lunch will be ready soon."

When Jason stepped out of the kitchen, Julia whispered to Shay, "You had better clean up this mess!"

CHAPTER 29

Brian stayed in the room he called his when he stayed at Blackhawk until he was composed enough to join his family downstairs for lunch. Food was the last thing on his mind, but he didn't want Shay to know that she'd cut him as deeply as she had.

When he first saw Shay at the airport, the world around him came to a standstill and the only person that mattered to him was LaShay Hampton. The sun rose and shone on her. When he held her, his world was complete and then she dropped the sledgehammer that cut him to the core of his being. Despite the fact that they didn't have a real commitment to each other, he never thought he would see her with another man, especially someone so opposite of him.

What happened? he kept asking himself. *Was she just toying with me the past four months? Is he the real reason she didn't want me in Cambridge?*

Before Brian returned downstairs, he prayed for understanding and for better control of his anger. At the airport, he wanted to break Jason's arm when he put it around Shay. She belonged to him alone. Since then, he realized his fight wasn't with Jason, it was with Shay and before the night was over, he would have words with her and wouldn't spare her feelings.

For the rest of the day and evening, Brian intensively observed the interaction between Shay and Jason. Jason appeared to be infatuated with her, but there wasn't any chemistry flowing from Shay. It was challenging, but Brian did manage to engage in conversation with his father and Jason. After watching and talking to Jason, he concluded that Jason was intelligent and knowledgeable and a nice guy, but he was not the man for Shay. He was.

No sooner had Jason turned into the downstairs guest room for the night, Brian knocked on Shay's bedroom door. He stepped inside and closed the door without waiting for her to invite him in.

"What are you doing with Jason?" he demanded.

"The same thing you're doing with your girlfriend, Shannon," she shot back, rolling her neck.

Brian twisted his face. "Shannon is not my girlfriend. And how do you know about her? What does she have to do with anything?"

"She answered your phone last week. She said that you were too busy with her to come to the phone." She pushed his chest and he grabbed her arms.

"What?"

"That's right, Brian, she introduced herself as your special friend." The emphasis Shay put on the word special nearly made Brian sick. Didn't Shay know she was the only one worthy enough to wear that title?

He released her arms. "So that's what this is about? You thought I had a girlfriend, so you brought Jason here to get back at me?"

Shay didn't answer, but rolled her eyes instead.

"Why didn't you just ask me about Shannon instead of ignoring my calls over the weekend?"

Shay rolled her neck again. "Because I didn't want to be your weekend girl anymore."

Brian pointed at her. "I can't believe you. You know the reason I only call you on weekends. I'm busy with law school during the week."

"You weren't too busy for Shannon on Wednesday!" Shay retorted.

He raised his voice to match hers. "I picked her up for

Bible Study. If you would've bothered to ask, I would've told you so."

Shay's perplexed expression indicated she didn't know what to say to his explanation. She stood there staring at him.

Brian's voice was calm. "I'll ask you again. What are you doing with Jason?"

"Wouldn't you like to know?" She gave him a defiant smile then turned away from him.

This time Brian raised his voice and pounded his fist into his palm. "Shay, grow up! You're almost twenty-five years old; stop acting like you're a sixteen-year-old school girl!"

She turned back around and matched his voice. "How do you know that Jason and I aren't serious?"

Brian brought his voice down and spoke flatly. "Shay, for once be honest with yourself. Jason is just a replacement, a substitute. You're only spending time with him because I'm not there."

It was a true statement, but she wasn't going to let him know it. "Who do you think you are, Brian?"

Brian stepped closer to her, in her space. "I'm the one you gave your heart to among other things. Remember?"

His arrogance and possessiveness appalled her. He acted like she belonged to him. Shay quickly stopped the smile that tried to creep onto her face and placed her hands on her hips "Look, Brian, just because I had sex with you twice, doesn't mean you own me."

"Five times." Brian raised his opened hand for emphasis. "We had sex five times, Shay. And I know you haven't forgotten one minute of it. I don't own you, Shay, but I have a part of you no one else will ever have and I plan to keep it."

She had to say something to fracture his ego. "How do you know I haven't given anything to Jason?" She folded her arms and smirked.

He stepped as close as he could and lifted her head and stroked her chin with his thumb and forefinger. His voice, just above a whisper. "That's the easy part. The way you surrendered into my arms this afternoon told me you missed me just as much as I missed you."

Her arms fell to her sides as he ran his fingertips down her cheek and outlined her lips. Involuntarily she moistened her lips with her tongue.

"The way your breathing accelerates every time I'm this close to you, let's me know that I excite you."

She held her head back and a moan escaped from her lips when he traced her neck with his fingertips. He reached for her hand.

"And as long as you wear my heart on your wrist, you'll never give yourself to another man."

This time instead of kissing her wrist near the silver heart, he joined their torsos and kissed her lips. The soft kiss was so powerful Shay's knees buckled and this time he didn't catch her. He let her fall backward unto her bed. Brian let her lay there with her mouth hanging open.

"Serves you right. Don't ever parade another man in front of me." With that he left the room.

CHAPTER 30

Shay lay on her bed bewildered. She thought she was going to serve him and instead, she got served.

Ten minutes later, she was still sitting on her bed trying to figure out when had Brian become so possessive of her. Brian had never verbally committed himself to her, but the look in his eyes and the tone in his voice, told her she belonged to him whether she liked it or not. What bothered her most was that every word Brian had spoken was the truth; he would always own a part of her, if not all.

Joyous singing flowed from Shay's lips and filled the kitchen the following morning. Although her mother claimed she couldn't carry a musical note in a bucket, Shay thought her rendition of Mary Mary's "God in Me" was comparable to the gospel duo's version. The early Saturday morning sun sprayed its rays through the tempered glass windows and brightened the gourmet kitchen. The second she felt the dough oozing between her fingers, Shay remembered how much she enjoyed baking. Kneading dough always relaxed her and homemade cinnamon rolls were her specialty. This morning the caramel and pecans she'd added mingled with the cinnamon aroma and promised her palate a heavenly treat.

"You're in a good mood this morning. I hope you slept well," Brian greeted her, but she didn't respond to him. She placed her hand in the potholder and removed the pan from the oven.

Brian sat down at the table and watched Shay add icing to the hot rolls. "It smells good in here."

Without speaking or making eye contact with him, Shay set a plate with two cinnamon rolls loaded with extra icing, just the way Brian liked them, in front of him.

"Thank you."

Shay continued to ignore him while she poured him a tall glass of milk. After she placed the glass on the table, she stood at the sink with her back to him.

"Shay, if you choose to act like a juvenile, that's fine with me. You don't have to speak to me. At least I know you took what I said last night seriously."

Finally, she turned to face him. "What makes you so sure about that?"

He licked the icing from his fingers. "You got up early and made my favorite rolls, just the way I like them."

"That doesn't mean anything." Shay refused to give him the satisfaction of knowing her so well. "You're not the only person in this house. And why are you here anyway? Don't you have a home to go to? Why don't you go there? I don't want you here."

"That's what your mouth says, but the moan you let out last night when I kissed you tells a different story." Brian grinned sheepishly, like he had the advantage and knew it.

Just as Shay was about to give Brian a piece of her mind, Jason walked in. "Good morning, gorgeous," Jason said to Shay.

As Jason hugged her she took the opportunity to roll her eyes at Brian. "Have a seat, I hope you like fresh baked cinnamon rolls." Shay gave Jason a warm smile, but it was more to irritate Brian than to make Jason feel welcome.

"I love them." Jason took the seat opposite Brian, so that his back faced the counter where Shay stood.

Shay took note of Brian's pulsating temporal vein as she served Jason a heaping plate of cinnamon rolls. His chewing slowed when Shay placed her hands on Jason's shoulders and slowly massaged him.

"These are delicious, who made them?" Jason asked, relishing in the affection he was finally receiving from his girlfriend.

Brian jumped in before Shay could answer. "Everyone knows that Shay makes the best cinnamon rolls." Shay glared at Brian.

Jason leaned his head up and sideways, so he could see Shay's face. "Really, I didn't know you like to bake."

"I hadn't had the desire since I've been in Massachusetts," she answered. When Jason's head turned down again, she gave Brian the hardest stare she could muster.

Brian continued. "The two of you have been dating for what—six months? I'm surprised Shay hasn't found the time to give you a sample of something."

Shay folded her hands to keep from reaching across the table and slapping Brian.

Naïve, Jason continued, "School takes up most of our time; we only see each other socially once a week."

"I know what you mean; law school takes up all of my time," Brian answered with a victorious smile. Brian's satisfaction of knowing there wasn't really anything special between the couple irked Shay. "Jason, do you swim?" Brian asked when Shay acted childish and stuck her tongue out at him.

"I love to swim," Jason answered.

"There's a pool out back. We can take a few laps in a couple of hours," Brian suggested.

"That sounds like fun."

Shay stopped massaging Jason's shoulders and dropped her hands at Brian's next question.

"Shay, would you like to join us?" Brian asked with a devilish grin.

Shay wanted to scream. Brian was toying with her and knew he'd come out victorious. After the previous night's show of possession and aggression, Brian would, without a doubt, drown her with his bare hands, if she pranced around in front of Jason in a swimming suit. Besides that, Brian knew she wouldn't be able to hide her attraction to him, once he was wearing nothing but trunks. But she wasn't going to let Brian see her sweat.

"I think I will." Shay ran her tongue slowly across her lips. Brian's smile vanished. She continued looking Brian straight in the eyes, "I still have that cute little red two-piece from last summer." She stepped from behind Jason and looked down at her body. "I think I can still fit it, don't you, Brian?" She didn't give Brian a chance to respond before she left the kitchen and went upstairs to her room.

Shay didn't have any intentions of going swimming, but Brian didn't know that. "Serves you right." She smirked at the picture of them on her twenty-third birthday that sat on her bureau. Shay wasn't the least bit surprised two hours later when Brian came up with an excuse not to go swimming.

CHAPTER 31

At four o'clock in the afternoon everyone except Shay was dressed and ready to leave for the church. Upstairs in her room, Shay's nerves felt like stickpins up her arms and her stomach moved to its own rhythm. Tonight would be the first time she'd be inside of a church since that Sunday she walked out and spent all day at Emery Bay in bed with Brian. In the chambers of her heart, she still felt the shame of what she'd done and was afraid once her foot crossed the sanctuary's threshold, the sin spotlight would cause her to stand out.

She applied the last bit of makeup and focused on how good it would be to see her grandparents and the rest of her family. That helped her to relax and brought a smile to her face. She took one final look in her full-length mirror. She smiled with pleasure at the way the gold silk and chiffon dress fit. The capped sleeves and fitted waist made the dress hang perfectly. The asymmetric skirt fell just below her knees. The four-inch gold ankle-strapped heels with rhinestones completed the ensemble.

"Shay, the limo's here," Reggie called up.

Shay checked her hair one last time. She hadn't worn her hair up since Brian's graduation. "Perfect," she said to her reflection and grabbed the gold purse from her dresser.

"Shay," Reggie called again just as she made her way down the stairs. Both Brian and Jason waited at the bottom of the winding staircase.

"WOW!" Jason exclaimed. "This is the first time I've seen you in a dress and heels. You're stunning."

Shay acknowledged Jason with a slight head nod, although her eyes quickly traveled to Brian. The black tuxedo looked as if it were cut out to fit his big muscular body. Brian didn't say a word to her, but his eyes conveyed his satisfaction with her appearance.

When she finally made it to the bottom of the staircase, Jason stepped forward and held out his arm for her. Brian turned his attention to Josiah while Jason leveled lavished compliments on Shay.

"You clean up REAL nice." Jason had the biggest grin on his face. "I couldn't have dreamed of a more beautiful woman."

"You're not too bad yourself," she said referring to his black double-breasted suit.

Julia must have sensed Brian's uneasiness. "For the second time in as many days I feel like wringing Shay's neck," she mumbled in Reggie's ear, but Shay heard her. Then voiced a loud, "We had better get going; I have sound check at five o'clock."

Shay and Jason followed Reggie and Julia out to the waiting limo. Brian and Josiah slowly trailed behind. Once Brian sat Josiah inside of the limo, he changed his plans. "I'm going to drive my car, I'll meet you there," he said to no one in particular.

Julia understood. "Alright, we'll see you there." She then scowled at her daughter.

As the limo pulled away, Shay looked out the window. She didn't want to see the disappointment on her mother and Reggie's faces. Shay knew they were angry with her; at the moment she was angry with herself. The image of Brian standing alone pulled at her heart strings. I'm sorry, she mouthed.

As the luxury vehicle passed the golf course, Shay closed her eyes and envisioned the limo stopping with her jumping out and running back into Brian's arms. There, she tells him how much she loves him and can't live without him and he communicates the same. When Shay finally opened her eyes, the limo was turning out of the gated community.

Shay looked over at Jason. He was grinning like he had just won the grand prize at the state fair. *I'm sorry for what I'm doing to you, too.* Jason reached for her hand and she turned her attention to her little brother and adjusted his bow tie.

Little Josiah smiled at his big sister. "Shay, you look pretty."

Shay reached for Josiah and placed him between her and Jason. "Thank you. And you're the most handsome three-year-old I've ever seen." She pinched his cheek.

Outside of Shay and Josiah's playing, the ride to True Worship was quiet.

By five-thirty, the fifteen-hundred-seat sanctuary was nearly filled to capacity. Shay went around greeting the members of True Worship before she joined the Simone clan. Jason trailed behind her, smiling.

"Hey, Auntie and Brother Tyrone." Shay affectionately hugged Nikki and her husband Tyrone.

"Girl, you're looking good. I like that dress and you're working that hair."

Shay blushed modestly. "Thank you."

Nikki directed her attention to Jason. "And who's this?"

"Guys, this is Jason. He attends Harvard with me."

Shay figured as Julia's best friend, Nikki already knew who Jason was. Probably the entire Simone clan was aware of her status with Jason. Of course, no one admitted that to Shay, wanting to see how she was going to weasel her way out of the mess she'd created.

After Jason exchanged pleasantries with Nikki and Tyrone, Shay moved on to Mother Elsie, the church mother.

"Hello, Mother." She hugged the elderly woman.

"Hi, baby. Are you almost done with school? We sure do miss you around here."

"I miss you too, Mother. I still have four months to go before I complete the program, then I'll be back."

Shay introduced Mother Elsie to Jason then said hello to a few other members. "Papa! Grandma!" Shay hugged her grandparents, who were seated on the front row. "I've missed you so much."

"Welcome back, *ma cheri*." Carey Simone kissed his granddaughter's cheek.

"I like the hair change," Ana Simone said when she released her. "You look almost as good as me."

"Thank you, Grandma." This time Shay remembered Jason. "Papa, Grandma, this is Jason Alexander, we're in the same program. Jason, these are my grandparents, the foundation of our family, Carey and Ana Simone."

"It's an honor to meet you both," Jason said, after studying the olive man and the bronze beauty.

Shay noticed Jason's confused expression. "Is something wrong?" she asked.

"Your family name is familiar. Are you related to the Simones of The Simone Company?" Jason asked.

"I started the company forty years ago, now my children run it," Carey answered proudly.

Jason looked at Shay and then back at the elder Simone. "LaShay, you never told me you were part of the renowned Simone Company. Your grandfather's business built nearly half of the northern Chicago suburbs."

Shay was about to respond, but her cousins Taylor, Staci and Leah came and whisked her off to the ladies' room. She did notice Brian watching her from the back of the sanctuary.

CHAPTER 32

Brian stood in the back of the church watching Shay introduce Jason to her grandparents. He was so engulfed, he didn't hear Shannon approach him from behind.

"Good evening, Brian." Shannon didn't waste any time mending fences with last night's angry one-sided conversation still fresh. He'd told her to never answer his phone again then slammed the phone in her ear. "I'm so sorry I forgot to tell you Shay called last week while you were inside Starbucks."

He noted a hint of sincerity in her tone. "How is it that you made it a point of telling her that you're my special friend?"

Shannon pouted. "Brian, we are friends. At least that's what I thought." Her fingertips slowly glided down the black fabric covering his muscular arm. "I have respected your wishes concerning us and have tried to be nothing but a good friend to you."

"Have you, Shannon?"

"Yes, I have. You've made it crystal clear that you don't want me."

Brian didn't feel like debating with Shannon; his heart was still bleeding from Shay's latest stab. He didn't find it fair for Shannon to take the heat intended for Shay. "We'll discuss this later," he finally said.

"How do I look?" Shannon stepped back and modeled for him.

Shannon actually didn't look bad. He didn't tell her, but

he had noticed how her attire had changed for the better over the past couple of months. Her black dress was styled similar to Shay's, but Shannon's skirt wasn't flowing like Shay's. The matching pumps and small purse were accented with rhinestones. In his opinion, the only thing that ruined Shannon's look was the extra coating of makeup. It was almost like she was trying to lighten the color of her skin. He still didn't like the blonde hair on her either.

"Shannon, you look fine," he said, hoping she wouldn't continue with this line of questioning.

"I'm glad you like it," she said then interlocked her arm with his. "So, where are we sitting?"

"I don't know where you're going to sit, but Marcus has reserved the first two rows for family."

"His family can't take up that many seats!" Shannon exclaimed.

Brian laughed. "Oh, yes they can. You can follow me if you want, but I can't guarantee that you'll get a seat."

Shannon smiled and followed Brian to the end of the second row on the far left side.

CHAPTER 33

Inside the restroom Leah checked the stalls to make sure the cousins were alone. After Leah gave the thumbs-up, Taylor let loose.

"Girl, what do you think you're doing, bringing that scrawny little man here?"

"You are not right for doing Brian like that," Staci added.

"If you wanted to make him jealous, why didn't you pick someone you liked?" Leah questioned.

"You and Brian need to stop playing this friendship game and get serious. You know you're in love with him. Why are you playing around with Jason?" Taylor pushed.

Shay finally opened her mouth. "How did you know his name?"

Staci smacked her lips. "Girl, please, you already know how fast news travels through the Simone family, especially, this kind of foolishness."

"So everyone knows that I brought Jason here to get back at Brian?" Shay couldn't believe everyone saw through her little game of get-back.

"We didn't know why you brought him, but we knew it had something to do with Shannon," Leah clarified.

The statement piqued Shay's curiosity. "What do you guys know about Shannon?"

"Nothing, outside of her chasing after Brian for the past several months. But he's not interested in her," Staci answered.

"Justin told me how she pounced on Brian at Dave and

Buster's and how your mother had to set her straight when Brian brought her out to Blackhawk," Leah added.

Shay jumped in. "Oh no, Brian didn't bring her into my house!" Shay threw her small purse onto the counter and slapped her fists against her hips.

"First of all," Taylor waved her index finger in Shay's face, "it's not your house. It's your mother and Reggie's house. If you would take care of your business, you wouldn't have to worry about Shannon. You need to stop playing and tell Brian how you feel."

"Taylor, you sound just like my mother." Shay pouted.

"You need to listen to your mother; she's got a man," Staci said handing Shay her purse. "A fine man at that."

Shay rolled her eyes at her cousins. "I am not about to tell Brian nothing. He already thinks he owns me."

"And why does he think that?" Leah asked. "I mean, besides the obvious."

Shay hadn't meant to say that. "He just does." Shay looked in the mirror and started twisting one of her hanging curls.

Staci gasped. "I knew it! You and Brian had sex!"

This time Shay placed both of her hands on her hips and rolled her neck. "My sex life is none of y'all business!"

"So, you admit that the two of you burned a hole in the sheets?" Leah charged.

"This makes perfect sense now. You had sex with Brian and he blew your mind. That's why you're half-crazy." Taylor threw her hands in the air.

"When did it happen?" Leah pressed.

Shay didn't think it was appropriate to lie in church, even if she was in the bathroom. "Right before he graduated," she answered honestly.

"Then why did you leave?"

"I know why," Staci answered for Shay with a blank look on her face.

Leah turned to Staci. "Will you please explain it to me?"

"We can continue this later, but it's almost show time and

you know my big brother, Marcus, will start on time," Staci said and started for the door.

"She's right. Let's get to our seats before Marcus embarrasses us over the microphone. But we will continue this later, missy." Taylor glared at Shay, following Staci's lead.

"Taylor, you had better be glad I love you, otherwise, I'd beat you down." Shay was serious.

"Whatever." Taylor waved the threat off.

CHAPTER 34

"Who is that?" Shannon inquired.

"Who are you talking about?" Brian asked.

Shannon motioned toward Shay. "The lady wearing that bad gold dress with the golden hair. She looks like a model."

A smile creased Brian's face. "She is beautiful, isn't she?"

"Do you know her?"

"Yes, I do," Brian said softly, still smiling. "She's Marcus's cousin."

Brian watched her for a second longer before gaining Shay's attention and motioning for her to join him. He then turned to Shannon. "I'm sorry, Shannon, but the young lady needs a seat and she is part of the Simone family."

If the news disturbed Shannon, she concealed it. "I understand." She gathered her purse then stood to find the young woman standing next to Brian.

"She's moving, so you can have her seat, that is, if you don't mind sitting next to me?" Brian informed Shay.

Shay looked around. "Where's Jason?"

"He's on the far right front row with my dad and Josiah."

"I wonder if Reggie planned it that way," she mumbled then turned to Shannon. "Thank you so much for yielding your seat."

"No problem. I love that dress and those shoes are to die for." Shannon beamed.

"Thank you," Shay responded modestly. Both women looked at Brian with smiles, as if waiting for him to introduce them.

Brian looked from Shay to Shannon. "This is Shannon. Shannon this is Ms. LaShay Hampton."

Both of their smiles disappeared at such a rapid pace, Brian questioned if he'd actually seen their teeth.

Shay's effort not to twist her face failed. "It's good to finally put a face with a voice."

Shannon stood speechless with her mouth ajar. Brian never mentioned Shay was coming to Marcus's CD recording and no one stated Shay's beauty.

"Shannon, they're about to start, you should run along and find a seat." Shay offered a fake smile then sat down and crossed her long legs at the ankle. Brian shrugged his shoulders and sat down. Having been dismissed, Shannon searched for a seat.

***

Brian placed his arm around Shay's shoulder in a blatant display of possession. "You are so beautiful," he whispered in her ear.

She looked up at him and felt that familiar tug at her heart and she offered him a big smile. His compliment was the only one that mattered to her. "Brian, I'm sorry for overreacting and bringing Jason here. I should have asked you about Shannon instead of jumping to my own conclusions, but honestly, I can't handle the thought of you with another woman any more than you can stand seeing me with another man."

"That's one thought you honestly don't have to dwell on," Brian responded, then squeezed her shoulder. "You're the only woman in my life, Shay; always have been. Although we've never defined our relationship, I think we want the same thing."

Shay released the breath she'd been holding when the lights dimmed and the MC took the stage. One more minute and she would have told Brian everything that was in her heart. No matter how much of a heathen she considered herself to be, she couldn't lie in church.

For the next ninety minutes Shay clapped, swayed and

sang to the music. Marcus had written a good mixture of fast and slow praise and worship songs and Shay loved every one of them. Shay hadn't felt this close to God in a long time and she really missed the peace she felt while in the presence of God. More than once, Brian handed her his handkerchief to wipe the tears that rolled down her cheeks. Shay listened intensely to the song lead by Marcus and her mother on restoration and made up her mind to start working on her estranged spiritual relationship. It was time. She was tired of feeling incomplete and barren. She was tired of the guilt and shame.

Toward the end of his repertoire, Marcus introduced his parents to the audience, and then his aunts and uncles along with their families joined them onstage. The collective group sang a song Marcus had written as a tribute to his grandparents. Since Shay didn't know the words to the song, she remained seated, opting to enjoy her stolen time with Brian.

CHAPTER 35

The actual size of the Simone clan amazed Shannon. She had never seen a family as diverse as the Simones either. Like the United States, they were a big melting pot. They were all different shapes, sizes and colors. Watching them together on stage, reminded Shannon of the old *We Are the World* video. Tall, short, fat, skinny all came together as one and gave honor to the family's pioneers. They all appeared to love and care for one another. "How do they do it?" Shannon asked quietly. Shannon sprinted toward Brian as soon as the final song ended and Marcus took a final bow.

***

Brian remained seated on the second row with Shay. "What an awesome performance."

"I am so proud of Marcus." Shay smiled. "He's really anointed to play and sing.

Who knew that clumsy kid would grow up to be so anointed and powerful?"

"Yeah, and who knew that a bossy Ms. Know-It-All would cocoon into such a beautiful woman?"

Shay opened her mouth to comment about Marcus again until she realized Brian was talking about her. She studied Brian's face and decided to give as good as she got.

"And who would have thought that a naïve high-school baseball player would steal my heart and turn my world upside down?" *Why did I say that? I've got to get out of this church before I propose to him*, Shay scolded herself.

Brian's full grin gave the impression that he couldn't have

been happier with her last statement. Before he could throw a comeback, Jason appeared.

"Where were you?" Jason asked. "I saved you a seat."

Shay was happy to see him. She needed to put some space between her and Brian. Shay stood and stepped away from her seat. Brian stood also. "I didn't see you, so I sat in the first open seat I could find," Shay answered. That was the truth.

"I was with Reggie. Right before the show started he rescued me from your aunts," Jason explained.

Shay gave Brian a knowing glance. "I'll have to thank your father later."

Just then Shannon joined them by interlocking her arm with Brian's. All of a sudden, Shay was ready to leave. "Brian, I'll see you at the Snow Building. Try not to eat the entire buffet before everyone gets there," she teased then turned to leave.

Shay hadn't taken two steps before Shannon's sultry voice reached her ears. "Brian, dear, do you mind if I ride you tonight? I mean, do you mind if I ride with you to the reception?"

Shay wanted to turn around and slap Shannon across the sanctuary, but Taylor's words rang loud and clear in her head. *If you would take care of your business, you wouldn't have to worry about Shannon.* Shay continued walking at an increased pace.

Shay strolled around the lavishly decorated Snow Building on Jason's arm. She felt bad because she'd deserted him earlier and was trying to make up for it by giving him her undivided attention. On the ride to the reception he chatted more with Reggie, than he did with her. She knew something was bothering him. That something was probably Brian.

"So, Jason," she started once they were seated at a reserved family table, "did you enjoy the performance?"

He nodded. "It was good. A little too spiritual for my taste, but good."

Shay frowned. "What do you mean, it was too spiritual? I

did mention to you that Marcus was recording a gospel CD at my parents' church, didn't I?"

"Yes, you did, but I didn't know your family was so deep in religion. I didn't know you attend church until recently."

Jason didn't know it, but he had just insulted her in the worst way; he told the truth. Shay had kept her belief in God a secret, like she was ashamed of it. In actuality, she was ashamed of herself for falling victim to fornication. She sat back in her chair and watched Jason. She tried to recall if Jason had ever shared his faith with her. He hadn't.

"Jason, do you have a relationship with God?" she finally asked.

"Yes, I do, but not the same kind of relationship your mother and Reggie along with the rest of your family believe in."

"What do you mean?"

Jason leaned into her. "Well, for starters, I don't believe it's necessary to attend church regularly in order to be close to God. I'm definitely not into all the dancing and screaming that you Pentecostals do." Jason paused to see if Shay would respond to his last statement. She didn't, so he continued, "I think it's unrealistic to tell people they can live free from sin. God knows we're human and that we will make mistakes. I believe that the good deeds we perform will balance out our shortcomings. And to be absolutely honest with you, I believe there's nothing wrong with two people living together or having sex outside of marriage as long as they are committed to each other."

For the first time, Shay saw just how different she and Jason really were. They were on two different paths, heading in opposite directions. His profession of beliefs, or lack thereof, convinced her beyond a reasonable doubt that she needed to end their so-called relationship soon.

"Jason, I respect your beliefs. I don't agree with them, but I respect them as being yours. Now, I may not shout it from the rooftops, but I do believe the Bible to be the truth and the final authority in all matters."

Jason leaned closer to her. "Can I ask you a question?"

"Sure."

"Do you plan on remaining a virgin until you're married?"

Shay was careful to answer him. He had assumed she was a virgin and she had never told him any different.

"Until my wedding night, sex is not an option," she plainly stated.

Jason looked disappointed, but she wasn't going to pacify him; she meant what she said.

Shay's attention turned to the front door when the room erupted in a thunderous applause for Marcus and his group.

"Come on," she grabbed Jason's hand," let me introduce you to Marcus."

Before Jason could respond, Shay was on her feet. Jason followed along somberly.

"Congratulations, cousin!" Shay and Marcus exchanged hugs and kisses.

"Thanks for making the trip."

"Anything for you, dude. I love your music. I didn't realize how talented and anointed you are," Shay complimented her cousin.

Marcus imitated an old woman's voice. "Baby, you pray my strength in the lawd."

When Marcus finished laughing, he looked at the man with locks, standing next to Shay.

"You must be Jason; I'm Marcus Simone." Like the rest of his family, Marcus shook Jason's hand instead of embracing him.

A slight smile crossed Jason's face. "It's good to meet you, especially since LaShay has already told you about me. I hope it was all good."

Marcus gave Shay a smile, and she knew he was trying to conceal his laughter. He probably didn't know Jason existed before his sister Staci or someone alerted him through the Simone family's public service announcement system, also known as text messaging.

"I didn't hear anything bad."

Shay and Jason chatted with Marcus a few minutes longer before they returned to their table. Shay nearly tripped when she saw Shannon seated next to Brian at the same table.

Taylor walked past Shay on her way to the buffet and mumbled, "Handle your business."

Shay rolled her eyes at her cousin's back and sat down next to Brian. Jason sat down on the left side next to Shay.

"Aren't you guys hungry?" Shay asked Reggie and Brian.

"Your mother is making my plate," Reggie answered.

"I was waiting for you—and Jason," Brian answered.

Shay understood Brian's hidden message and so did his father. Reggie never made his own plate when Julia was around. Neither did Brian when Shay was around. That was a tradition passed down from the family matriarch, Ana Simone. All of the Simone women made sure their men had plenty to eat.

"Well, I'm here now. Let's eat," Shay announced and headed for the buffet.

Jason and Shannon stood.

"I'll get the drinks," Brian said then asked Jason and Shannon what they would like.

By the time Shannon returned to the table with what she thought was a plate for Brian, he was already eating and discussing the show with his father and Julia. Shay gave her an innocent smile and continued eating. She'd seen Shay making a second plate, but she assumed it was for Jason, who had lingered behind.

"You must be very hungry," Brian said when Shannon set the second plate on the table.

"I'm starved," she said then smirked at Shay.

Jason sat down a moment later with his plate. "How did you get your food so fast?" he asked Brian.

"Someone was looking out for me," Brian answered and kept eating.

Shay didn't say a word. Neither did Reggie and Julia, although it was obvious what was going on.

During the meal, Jason and Shannon were too busy eating

173

to notice that Brian and Shay were holding hands underneath the table most of the time. Reggie and Julia noticed.

"If he slips and calls her 'baby', somebody's going to get hurt," Julia mumbled loud enough for Shay to hear.

"I know, that's why I've been praying since the moment they sat down," Reggie responded.

"That's my song!" Shay exclaimed and jumped from her seat when the music started.

Jason looked at her strangely. "I didn't know you knew how to dance."

"It's time to dance," Shay announced and automatically pulled on Brian. "Come on."

He stood without hesitation; they always danced together.

"What is she doing?" Julia sneered underneath her breath.

"Shay, what about Jason?" Reggie called after her.

"He's not into church or gospel music," Shay called over her shoulder then proceeded to get her dance on with the man she loved.

Shannon sat with her arms folded, fuming. Jason was too busy fielding questions from Reggie and Julia about what he had against the church and gospel music.

On the dance floor, Brian and Shay fell in sync like always, doing the Electric Slide to the upbeat praise song.

"I miss dancing with you," Brian said after the first song. "Although I think it's kind of shady how you left Jason."

Shay tilted her head to the side. "Would you rather I dance with him?"

Brian's smile evaporated and he stopped dancing. "Just in case I didn't make myself clear last night, I'll say it again. I won't share you with anyone."

His words threw her off balance and she tripped and fell into him. He caught her and steadied her. Shay stared into his darkened eyes and realized this was the moment she'd been waiting for.

"What exactly are you saying? What do you want from me?" Her heart thumped in her chest waiting for his answer.

Brian's eyes drifted over her head to where his father and Julia were then back at Shay. At that moment, he desired to kiss her and...but this was not the time, nor the place to reveal his heart to the woman he was still holding in a compromising position. After all, her boyfriend was seated a few feet away. He quickly whisked her out the side patio door. Out on the balcony, in one swift motion, Brian pressed her into his body and finally satisfied his desire.

The fervent and passionate kiss ignited an inferno so hot and intense, Shay moaned with pleasure. After a fulfilling feast, Brian broke the kiss and held her securely against his rapidly beating heart until their breathing slowed to a normal rate.

"Does that answer your question? We'll talk later," he said after he drew back.

"Okay," she said, barely audible. Brian released her and followed her back inside, but didn't return to their table.

An hour later, Shay stood outside in the moonlight waiting with her family for their limo. Her eyes were glued on Brian as he engaged in a conversation with Jason a few feet away, about politics. Shay admired his reflection in the moon's glow. Brian was simply beautiful and not just physically. It was his personality. It was his demeanor, his sincerity. It was just him.

"He's a nice specimen, isn't he?" Shannon asked from behind.

"Excuse me?" Shay turned around to face her adversary.

"You were looking at Brian and admiring how attractive he is, weren't you?"

Shay turned her back to Shannon without responding.

"I don't mind, because I know he's mine," Shannon's voice dripped with arrogance.

Shay turned to face her again. "Shannon, I wouldn't count on that. I hear he's given his heart to someone else."

"Maybe, but he spends his time with me, and time equals

relationship." Shannon folded her arms and stepped closer to Shay.

Shay looked her up and down. "Giving you a ride to church doesn't count."

Shannon wouldn't let her win. "But what happens afterward does."

Shay was just as tenacious. "You are absolutely right, because that's when he calls me." Just then the limo arrived and Jason and Brian joined them.

"What time does your flight leave?" Brian asked Shay.

"One o'clock. I'm going to church for about an hour first."

Brian hugged her and quickly released her. "Have a safe trip." He turned to Jason. "I hope you have enjoyed your visit." He finally asked Shannon, "Are you ready?"

"Always for you." Her soft voice dripped with seduction.

Shay didn't find it necessary to respond. Shannon may get a ride home, but the kiss she and Brian shared earlier promised much more.

CHAPTER 36

Shay looked anxiously around the sanctuary one last time before leaving for the airport. Jason was already in the car with her uncle Mike. She hoped to see Brian before she left, but he was nowhere to be found. She gave up and left.

The ten-minute ride to the Oakland International Airport was long and quiet. Jason hadn't said much to her since she'd reminded him that she still didn't have any intentions of sleeping with him. Shay didn't mind his attitude, which only made it easier for her to end their bland relationship.

Her journey to rebuild her spiritual life had begun earlier that morning. Before she packed, she spent time on her knees praying and even read a few familiar scriptures. That, along with the talk she had with Reggie, made her optimistic about her relationship with Brian.

Reggie was just about to leave for service, when he knocked on her door.

"Mind if I come in?" he asked.

"Of course not." Shay lowered the volume on Donnie McClurkin singing about falling down and getting up again.

Reggie walked in and sat in the winged chair adjacent to Shay's bed. "Have you been reading?" Reggie gestured at the open Bible on Shay's bed.

Shay smiled and tilted her head. "Yes I have."

"I'm glad to hear that." Reggie tapped his fingers together. "Shay, did you ever have that talk with Brian?"

She tried to stall. "Reggie, you've been married to my mother too long."

"Are you saying that because I went straight to the point?"

"Exactly," Shay answered and continued looking through her drawers.

When she didn't say anything else, Reggie continued to say what was on his mind. "Shay, I hope you don't take what I'm about to say the wrong way or that I'm being partial because Brian's my son. I love the both of you and I want you to be happy."

"Reggie, I know you love me and I trust you. Now tell me what's on your mind." She faked a smile, knowing she didn't have a choice in the matter.

"Shay, I remember the night you told me you love Brian. Is that still the case?"

A genuine smile creased her face as she ran her index finger over the silver heart. She couldn't deny it if she wanted to. "Yes, Reggie, I love your son like crazy. Truth is I've always loved him."

"Then why have you been dating Jason for six months? The two of you are like oil and water. And why on earth did you bring him here?"

Shay didn't have a mature answer for him. She lowered her head. "I am—was only spending time with Jason because I couldn't be with Brian. I plan to break things off with him as soon as I get back."

"But why did you bring him here?" he asked again.

Shay sighed. "Because I thought Brian was seeing Shannon."

"What gave you that impression?"

Reggie listened to Shay replay the telephone incident for him. "I can see how you might have come to that conclusion, but the way you handled it was all wrong. You should have discussed it with Brian before dragging Jason across the country to make Brian jealous. Then, once you got here, you gave all of your attention to Brian. Please tell me, what were you thinking when you made Brian's plate and then held his hand while sitting right next to Jason? And don't think your mother and I didn't see the two of you slip out onto the patio."

Shay shrugged her shoulders. "When I left Massachusetts, the only thing on my mind was getting even with Brian. Once I saw him, all I wanted to do was be with him."

"Then why don't you tell him that?" Reggie asked. It was all simple to him.

Shay turned her back to him. "I can't right now."

Reggie stood to his feet. "Shay, the only thing you and Brian lack is communication. I'm not talking about your usual bickering or wisecracks, but real communication. The two of you need to sit down and have a heart-to-heart talk. If you don't do that soon, you're going to miss out on something really special." Reggie placed his hand on her shoulder. "Your mother and I didn't experience real love until we were both over forty, but you and Brian can enjoy fulfillment much sooner. Shay, tell him how you feel. The two of you aren't as far apart as you think, but you'll never know if you don't talk to him openly and honestly."

She turned around. "I know, but I need to settle things with Jason first."

"That's fair, but don't take too long and please no more games, like this weekend.

Do you know how hard I prayed nothing violent would happen between Brian and Jason?"

Shay smiled. "I thought you enjoyed the game."

"What gave you that idea?"

Shay raised an eyebrow. "The way you kept Jason out of the way, so I could watch the performance with Brian."

It was Reggie's turn to shrug his shoulders. "Someone had to keep him company after you deserted him."

"And you just so happened to be the one to save the day."

Reggie grinned. "I'm always here to help."

When he left the room a couple of minutes later, Shay felt good. She had an inner peace that things would work out, but now as she counted the hotels that lined Hegenberger Road she worried because Brian didn't say good-bye to her.

After receiving her boarding pass, Shay left Jason and went to the restroom. She had just finished drying her hands when her cell phone rang. She immediately smiled after reading the caller ID. It was Brian.

"I thought you forgot about me."

"I could never forget about you," Brian responded.

"Then why didn't you say good-bye to me before I left church?"

She heard him exhale into the phone. "Because I didn't want to see you leave with another man. I told you, I can't handle seeing you with any man besides me. I'm not ready for that, not now, not ever."

Tears welled in Shay's eyes. At that very moment she wanted to hold him and tell him that he was the only man for her. "It won't happen again," she said, her voice just above a whisper.

"So you did get the message," he mused, in what she perceived an effort to control his emotions.

"Loud and clear."

There was a brief pause, before he continued. "Shay, we need to talk about us."

"I agree."

"I don't think you understand. We need to *really* talk about us," Brian clarified.

"I do understand, Brian, and as soon as I tie up a loose end, we will."

"Does this *loose end* have locks?" Brian sounded hopeful.

"Yes."

Brian gave a sigh of relief. "Do what you have to do, but what I need to say to you, I want to say in person. I was thinking about coming out to Massachusetts after I break for the summer, near your birthday. Is that enough time?"

"It's more than enough time."

"I'll see you then, but before we disconnect, I'd like to say a word of prayer."

That surprised Shay. "You want to pray for me?"

"Why does that surprise you? It shouldn't, I always pray for you. You're always close to my heart"

She listened as he asked God to protect and help her. By the time he finished, tears rolled down her cheeks and gathered at her fingertips. The fact that he cared enough to pray for her deepened her love for him. "Thank you," she whispered.

"I'll see you near or on your birthday."

"I can't wait. Brian," she called into the phone.

"Yes, beautiful."

"Make sure your head is shaved. I love stroking your baldhead," she flirted.

"Anything for you."

When Shay joined Jason at the boarding gate, she was all smiles. July couldn't come soon enough.

CHAPTER 37

S hay finished unpacking and started the water for a hot bubble bath. For the first time since coming to Cambridge, she felt totally relaxed and free. She attributed her new serenity to the commitment she'd made in her spiritual life and her last conversation with Brian. She could tell by his tone that what he wanted to tell her was probably the same thing she wanted to tell him. And she didn't mind waiting two months to hear and say those three words. There was a lot of work she needed to do on herself before committing to Brian.

She had just poured the second capful of bubble bath into the hot water when the phone rang. She quickly ran and grabbed the cordless receiver from her nightstand. "Hello."

"Girl, I need to give you a Platinum Players Card for that stunt you pulled this weekend!"

"You know you were wrong for that!" It was her cousins Taylor and Leah on a three-way call.

"I don't know what you're talking about." Shay downplayed her childish behavior.

"I told you to handle your business, not commit suicide," Taylor teased. "Making Brian's plate right in front of Jason? You are crazy."

"But before that, you had the nerve to ship Jason off to Reggie and practically sit on Brian's lap," Leah exaggerated.

"That is not what happened and you know it," Shay defended.

"I wanted to bow down and call you Queen Shay, when

you sat between Jason and Brian and with all boldness held my boy's hand underneath the table!" Taylor hollered.

"I couldn't enjoy my food. I didn't know if I should eat or remove my earrings," Leah added.

"What are you talking about?" Shay turned the water off.

"Girl, stop playing. You know you wanted to beat Shannon down," Leah answered. "And if she would have raised her hand to you, you know we would've jumped in," Taylor added. "We would have torn the place up."

Shay laughed at her cousins.

"Justin and Craig removed their jackets when Jason walked back to the table and stood over Brian and asked him where he got his plate from," Leah exaggerated. "We were all praying neither Jason nor Shannon would notice what y'all were doing underneath that table," Leah screamed.

"We were only holding hands like always."

"You were trying to get yourself killed, or make Brian catch a case," Taylor corrected.

Shay conceded. "It was tacky."

"Correction, it was very tacky," Leah said. "What did your mother say?"

"Nothing," Shay answered.

"That doesn't sound like Auntie Julia," Taylor noted.

"She didn't say anything because she was too angry. However, if looks could kill, I'd be dead. All weekend, I felt like a dead woman walking."

"You were. Brian didn't know if he should strangle you or kiss you. Did you know he brought red roses to the airport for you, but threw them away when he saw Jason?" Leah asked.

"Really? How do you know?" Shay was surprised.

"Sure did. Your mother told us," Taylor answered for Leah.

"That won't happen again, I'm breaking up with Jason."

"Are you finally going to have that talk with my boy?" Taylor questioned.

"Yes. He's coming here for my birthday."

"Girl, you had better start praying right now, so you'll have enough prayers stored up to keep you from jumping his bones. You know when you're alone with him intercessory prayer will be the last thing on your mind," Leah teased.

"I don't think nothing will happen, now that I've made up my mind. I will not have sex again until I'm married," Shay firmly stated.

Taylor grew serious. "Do you regret it, you know, having sex with Brian?"

Shay took her time and analyzed the question. "Yes and no."

"Explain," Leah asked.

"Yes, I regret that I was not married and I do feel guilty about that. I felt guilty the second after I did it, however, I enjoyed it. I don't regret that my first time was with Brian. No, I love him and I can't imagine my first or one-hundredth time with anyone else."

"He's right, he does own you," Taylor teased.

"Forget you," Shay snapped.

"Trust me, cousin, the feeling's mutual. A harem could parade in front of Brian and he wouldn't touch one of them. He's saving himself for Queen Shay."

"Do you really think so?"

Leah smacked her lips. "Shay, why are you at Harvard if you insist on being stupid? You have to know that Brian is in love with you."

Shay reflected on the night they first had sex. He told her he loved her, but she knew better than to hold someone accountable for the words spoken at their sexual peak. He could actually love her, but as a friend and not as his woman. She'd have to wait until July to know for sure. "You're right, Leah, what Brian and I have is special."

"When are you going to break up with Jason?" Taylor wanted to know.

"Tomorrow."

"You move fast once you make up your mind. How do you think he's going to handle it?"

"I honestly don't know."

"Be careful, girl, you're a long way from home," Leah warned. "And he looks kind of shady to me."

"I know, but he's harmless." Shay told her cousins good night and climbed into the tub under a blanket of fragrant bubbles. As her stiff muscles relaxed, Taylor's question replayed in her mind. She really didn't know what to expect from Jason. He didn't speak to her on the plane ride home, but he did say good night before her cab pulled away. After her late class tomorrow, she planned to meet him at Chevys and break the news to him.

Her thoughts switched to Brian. Leah was right; she had a lot of work ahead of her if she was going to be strong enough to control her desire for Brian once it was just the two of them. He would most definitely have to stay at a hotel and absolutely no swimming.

No sooner had she pulled the drain plug, the cordless telephone sounded again. By the time she stepped from the tub and wrapped a towel around her, it was the seventh ring. She didn't look at the caller ID.

"Hello," she answered breathlessly.

"What took you so long to answer the phone?"

"Hi, Brian, I wasn't expecting a call from you tonight."

"You didn't answer my question."

"What question?"

"What are you doing?" he asked again.

Shay squeezed the towel tighter around her. She didn't think it was a good idea to give Brian a mental picture of her dripping wet in her birthday suit. "Right now I'm talking on the phone to you."

"Are you alone?" Brian asked impatiently.

"What kind of question is that?" Shay raised her voice as if she were insulted.

"The kind that needs to be answered," Brian pushed. "Stop stalling."

Shay understood now. "You think Jason's here, don't you?"

186

"The thought did occur to me," he admitted to jealousy.

"Brian, I told you I was going to resolve that situation."

Brian's sigh came through as static on the line. "I know what you said, but sometimes a person can speak louder when they're quiet. Like how you remained quiet about Jason for six months."

"You don't trust me, do you?" After all they'd shared the idea that she didn't have Brian's trust never occurred to her.

"Shay, I trust you, but sometimes you drive me crazy. Case in point, the stunt you pulled this weekend."

"If I drove you crazy before, you're going to be insane by the time we end this call."

"Shay, I don't want to argue with you. I just—"

She interrupted him. "Brian, since you insist on knowing, I'll tell you exactly what I'm doing and with whom I'm doing it with."

"I hate when you act like this."

Shay spoke as soft and seductive as possible. "Brian, when you called I was sitting inside of a hot, steamy, bubble bath thinking about you. This very second, I'm standing in my bedroom, dripping wet, wearing nothing but the skin I was born with and a towel." She paused. "Am I driving you crazy yet?" Then she laughed in his ear.

It took Brian a minute to respond. "You were wrong for that. How am I supposed to go to sleep after that visual?"

"You wanted to know."

"Next time just say it's personal."

"Next time trust what I tell you." She was serious again.

"I'm sorry, sweetheart."

"Apology accepted." Shay giggled, but Brian bade her good night. "You're dismissing me so fast?"

"Yeah. I need to take a shower, before I jump on a plane and fly to Massachusetts to dry you off," he flirted then she heard the dial tone.

Shay set the phone on her nightstand and skipped back to the bathroom. Her life was definitely taking a turn for the better.

CHAPTER 38

Shay waited nervously inside the booth at Chevys for Jason. Ending relationships was new territory. The casual dates in high school and college didn't reach this magnitude. She'd been practicing how to break up with Jason most of the day. She needed to be honest and straightforward, but she didn't want to be brutal. This morning she prayed for the right words to soften the blow. She still liked Jason as a person and didn't see why they couldn't remain friends.

She'd just taken a bite of the warm tortilla chip dipped in the fresh salsa when Jason slid into the booth. She'd expected for him to be distant with her, like he'd been in class a few hours ago, but he wasn't. He actually smiled and reached for her hand.

"Hey, sweetheart." He pushed his luck by kissing her hand.

"Hello, Jason," she said and slowly withdrew her hand. She ignored the flicker of hurt she recognized in Jason's dark-brown eyes.

"Have you ordered yet?"

"No, I was waiting for you."

Jason raised his hand to signal for the waiter, but Shay stopped him. "Jason, we need to talk."

Jason appeared to contemplate where this conversation was headed. "What do you want to talk about?"

"Us."

Before he bit into his third chip, he asked, "What about us, LaShay?"

Shay swallowed hard. "Jason, this past weekend I made some major decisions about my life."

"Decisions like what?"

Shay maintained eye contact. "I'm getting my spiritual life back in order. I have been away from God far too long. I've also decided to end our relationship, but I would like for us to remain friends." She quickly took a sip of water.

Jason looked at her incredulously. "You want to end our relationship, so you can be closer to God? We haven't done anything that's ungodly. The only token you offer me is an occasional kiss on the lips and you've made it perfectly clear that we're not going to have sex. How much more godly do you want?"

"It's not just the sex issue, Jason. I told you in the beginning you weren't really my type," she explained.

"Then why have you been leading me on for six months? And why did you invite me to meet your family?"

Shay lowered her head and sighed. "Jason, I told you in the beginning that we would take it slow and see what develops. So far nothing has changed for me and last weekend helped me to come to this decision."

Jason sat back and stared at her, then looked down at the silver heart around her wrist. "Is there someone else?"

"Huh?" She wasn't prepared for that question.

"Is there someone else at home that helped you come to this decision?"

"Why do you ask that?" She wanted to be honest with him, but didn't want to tell him about Brian.

"Because you were a different person in California."

"What are you talking about?" she asked, although she knew.

Jason took a sip of water. "LaShay, I've never seen you as relaxed and happy as you were in California."

"That's because I was at home and in familiar surroundings."

"Or was it because you were with the person who gave you that silver heart around your wrist?" he asked flatly.

Shay nearly choked on a tortilla chip. She drank some water and tried to come up with an excuse, but changed her mind. She had rededicated her life to God and now she needed to take responsibility for her actions.

She looked him in the eyes. "Jason, there is someone that I have cared about for a very long time. But until last weekend I wasn't sure anything would come of it."

Jason looked hurt and angry. "Then what were you doing with me?"

"Like I said, I didn't think anything would come of it. I'm still not sure, but I have to give it a fair try."

Jason laughed in her face. "Now you want to be fair. What about me? Have you been fair with me?"

"No I haven't, but remember you're the one who insisted on this relationship. I am sorry, I shouldn't have agreed knowing my heart is with someone else."

Jason glared at her. "Sorry, I bet you are. Like I said before, I'm a grown man; I don't need you to feel sorry for me."

Shay turned away from his hot stare. Her head snapped back at his next question.

"Who is it?"

"Excuse me?"

"What's the name of this person that you can't let go of?" Jason clarified.

"That's not important," Shay answered, shaking her head.

"To me it is. I want to know who owns the deed to your heart. I want to know who I have been competing with all this time."

"I am not going to answer that," she answered with finality.

Without warning, Jason reached for her arm and snatched the silver heart from her wrist.

"What are you doing? Give that back," Shay screamed, ignoring the stares from the restaurant patrons.

Jason read the inscription on the back of the heart. His concentrated facial expression left no doubt for Shay that mentally he was replaying the names of everyone he'd met over the weekend. There was only one that started with the letter "B".

"Brian? You are in a relationship with Brian?" Jason threw the heart across the table at her. It slid off the table and landed in her lap. Shay sat speechless, looking at everything but Jason.

"It all makes sense now. He's perfect for you, tall and dark. What kind of game were you playing with me in front of Brian? Were you using me to make him jealous? Hanging on to me while wearing his heart around your wrist?"

"Jason, I—" Jason cut her off and raised his hand as if he wanted to strike her. He slowly lowered it and clinched his fist. "You have worn this heart every day since Christmas. You could have told me then about you and Brian instead of parading me around like the village idiot to your family! This explains why your own mother didn't know we were dating, but I guess we really weren't dating. You were just using me."

Shay wiped the tears that rolled down her cheeks at a steady pace. She wasn't afraid of him hitting her, just sorry that she'd hurt him.

He looked at her with so much disgust; Shay figured he had more regard for a two-day-old wad of gum than for her. "I bet you're not pure as the driven snow either. I bet you've slept with him. As deceitful as you are, you probably had sex with him while I was asleep in the guest room."

"No I didn't. Jason, I never told you I was a virgin, you assumed that."

Jason shook his head and smirked. "I'm glad you've decided it's time for you to have a relationship with God, because you definitely need Him." Jason stormed out of the restaurant and left her holding the broken chain.

With heavy steps, Shay returned to her apartment and phoned Taylor and Leah on three-way and gave them a recap. They'd texted her three times already wanting updates.

"No he didn't snatch the chain from your wrist!" Taylor exclaimed.

"What else did he do?" Leah asked.

"He told me I needed God and left," Shay answered, still remorseful for the unnecessary hurt she'd caused Jason.

"If he put his hands on you, he's going to need the father, son and Holy Ghost to save his life." Taylor smirked.

"If I tell Brian about Jason breaking the chain he gave you and raising his hand to you, he'd be on the next plane to Boston," Leah added. "I should text him."

"Don't you dare!" Shay warned. There was no way Brian and her male family members would let Jason get away with what he'd done, even if she was the one in the wrong.

"Please don't tell Brian. I got myself into this and I can get myself out of it. Besides, Jason is right, I do need God." Shay attempted to extinguish the fire.

"I agree, but that doesn't give him the right to destroy your property," Leah instigated.

"He was angry and hurt. I can buy another chain," Shay rationalized.

"True, but—" The rest of Taylor's words evaporated once her father bellowed behind her. "Uh—Shay, my dad wants to speak to you," Taylor said cautiously.

Uh-oh, Shay thought. Before she could respond to Taylor, her uncle, Attorney Jonathan Simone cross-examined her like she was on the witness stand in a case he was defending.

"What happened with Jason? Did he put his hands on you? Is he there with you?"

Shay quickly told her uncle what had transpired and prayed he wouldn't pursue anything. There weren't any gray areas for the Simone men on the subject of disrespecting and abusing women.

"Is that all?" Jonathan Simone didn't sound convinced.

"Uncle, I promise everything is fine. If anything changes, I promise you'll be the first to know," Shay reassured him.

"I don't like the fact that he raised his hand to you. It doesn't matter that he didn't hit you this time, he might the next time."

"Uncle, there won't be a next time. I'm not going to see him outside of classes."

"Make sure you don't."

Shay acknowledged the statement for what it was, an order and not a mere suggestion, and quickly complied. "Yes, sir." She hung up the phone without saying good-bye to Leah or Taylor.

Before the night was over, she received calls from three uncles and five of her male cousins. Each of them assured her they were only a telephone call away. Reggie called the next morning, after Julia left to take Josiah to preschool.

"Thank you for not telling my mother," she said to Reggie.

"Shay, if this escalates any further, I'll have to tell her and Brian. Someone will have to bail me out of jail."

Shay laughed. "I love you, Reggie."

"I love you, too. Be careful and young lady, no more games."

Shay left for class a short time later, feeling really blessed. She enjoyed her morning prayer time and although she'd created a mess, God showed his love for her through her family and because of that she knew everything would be just fine.

CHAPTER 39

Brian's palm lingered on the horn longer than normal. Shannon had better hurry; he only had twenty minutes to make it to Wednesday night Bible Study on time. Less than a week ago, he'd told Shannon to drive herself to church, but this afternoon she'd called and said her car had broken down and asked him to pick her up. He didn't feel good about resending so quickly, but he didn't want to be the reason she missed a word from God, so he agreed this one time. By Sunday her car should be fixed.

* * *

Inside of her apartment, Shannon practiced her damsel-in-distress act. Her Ford Focus had broken down numerous times, but today it was running just fine, except for the knocking noise underneath the hood. She'd deal with that later. Tonight she needed Brian's company.

After meeting the infamous Shay, Shannon realized the only way she was going to win Brian's affection was to escalate her plan. That was the only way to get Shay to back off. After watching Shay ignore her boyfriend and cater to Brian, Shannon's intuition told her Shay held the same feelings for Brian as he had for her.

Shannon had been carefully calculating a plan for two days. Before leaving out, she checked her bedroom one last time. She laid the black satin and lace camisole on her bed and turned out the lights. Game time was over; tonight she would not be denied.

* * *

"Thanks for giving me a lift," Shannon said, after climbing into the RAV4.

He waited for her to fasten her seatbelt before pulling off. "No problem."

The small SUV soon filled with a familiar fragrance. Brian sniffed. "Are you wearing a new perfume?"

Shannon smiled. "Do you like it?"

On Shay I do, he wanted to say, but instead Brian shrugged his shoulders and answered, "It's familiar, that's all."

"Fond memories I hope." Shannon began to casually stroke Brian's arm, but stopped when he gave her a warning stare. With her long acrylic nail she brushed a lock of hair from her face. "Nice song," she said and bobbed her head to the CD the rest of the ride to True Worship.

During Bible class, Brian sat in the front and took notes as usual. Since reconnecting with God, he'd acquired a thirst for the Word that could not be quenched. At times he wondered if the hunger was God's way of calling him into the ministry. He placed that thought on the backburner, for now his desire was to learn more of the Word and how to incorporate it into his daily life.

Shannon paid close attention to Pastor Reggie's teaching on the book of Esther. For her it was confirmation of her next move. Her mind went into overdrive planning the event that was sure to change her life. If Esther could beautify herself to entice the king for a good cause, then so could she. Tonight she was going to seduce Brian and even if she didn't get pregnant, she would make him think she was long enough for him to marry her. Brian, a noble man, would marry her even if he didn't love her to keep his child from growing up without a father like he'd done.

Shannon's irritation became noticeable after Bible class while Brian conversed with Pastor Reggie.

Julia noticed Shannon's fidgeting. "Shannon, is everything all right?"

"Yes, Pastor Julia. I'm just tired."

"Maybe you should head on home," Julia suggested.

"I'm trying to, but I have to wait for Brian. He's my ride," Shannon answered matter-of-factly.

Reggie gave his son a disapproving look. "Brian, maybe you should take Shannon home before it gets too late. Call me later."

Brian knew he would get a speech from his father later so he ended the conversation and left. Shannon followed close behind.

Brian pulled in front of Shannon's apartment building and waited for her to get out.

She gave him an innocent smile. "Thanks for the ride."

"No problem." He never looked in her direction. He heard the latch open, and then he heard her scream.

"Oh, my ankle! My ankle!"

Brian turned the engine off and ran around to the passenger side. "What happened?"

Shannon lay on the ground clutching her right ankle. "I tripped and twisted my ankle."

Brian tried to touch her ankle, but she screamed, "Ouch!"

"Do you want me to take you to the emergency room?"

"No! I'll be there all night. If you could carry me up to my apartment so I can put some ice on it, I'll be fine."

Brian had never been inside of her apartment and didn't feel like it now, but he couldn't leave her outside on the ground. He helped Shannon to her feet and carried her to her second-floor one-bedroom apartment. She wrapped her arms around his neck and laid her head on his shoulders. At the front door she resisted his attempt to set her on her feet by squeezing his biceps and squealing.

"Shannon, how are you going to open the door if you won't let me go?" Before Brian blinked Shannon produced a silver key.

"Could you open the door for me?" she whimpered and snuggled closer. "I don't think I can walk."

Brian shook his head in disbelief at her sudden helplessness. Since he felt partially responsible for the fall for not assisting her out of the vehicle, he obliged. Balancing

Shannon in one arm, he freed the other and unlocked the door. After kicking the door closed with his foot, Brian walked inside and sat Shannon down on the sofa.

"See you later."

"Brian," she whined. "Can you please get me some ice from the freezer? There's a plastic bag in the top right drawer." Shannon pointed toward the kitchen.

Brian didn't say anything, but hurried into the kitchen and grabbed some ice. He looked at his watch; he wanted to get home in time to call Shay before midnight on the East Coast. He returned to the living room area to find Shannon stretched out on the sofa.

"Here's the ice. Good night," he said, then started for the door.

Shannon threw her head back and moaned, "Brian, I don't think I'll be able to walk on my own until morning. Would you mind carrying me into my bedroom? Otherwise, I'll have to crawl." She winced in pain.

Brian stopped midstride at the request and slowly turned around. He didn't want to step foot into her bedroom, but she looked so helpless. Once again he obliged and quickly gathered her in his arms. That's when he noticed her blouse was unbuttoned. She pointed toward the bedroom and arched her back, giving him a clear view of her cleavage.

Brian walked into her bedroom and nearly dropped her on the floor. The red-and- black décor with unburned candles strategically placed around the room was a sure invitation to something he didn't want to partake in. He hurried and laid her on her bed and turned to leave. Brian stopped in his tracks at her next request.

"Brian, would you please help me get undressed before you go?"

When Brian turned around, Shannon was leaning back against the pillows with the hem of her skirt up past her thighs. Her blouse practically hung off her shoulders. Her blonde locks fanned her shoulders.

"Shannon, I can't do that."

Shannon lowered her voice to a seductive tone. "Please, Brian, I just need a little help." Her legs opened and closed to every syllable.

Brian closed his eyes and ran both hands over his baldhead. The cinnamon fragrance wafted from the candles and flooded his senses. At that moment, he understood his father's warnings.

"Shannon, I can't give you the kind of help you're looking for." His cell phone rang.

"But, Brian, I just need you to assist me in removing my skirt and nylons, then you can leave." She lowered her eyelids and pouted.

He looked at the caller ID and held his hand up for Shannon to be quiet. "Hi, Mom." Brian turned his back to Shannon and she pounded her fists on the bed.

"Hey, baby, how are you doing?" Alysse asked.

"I'm fine, Mama."

"I know you're fine," she giggled, "I heard Shay was in town over the weekend."

"Brian," Shannon whined from behind.

"Hold on a minute, Mama."

Brian pressed the mute button on his phone. When he faced Shannon again her blouse lay crumpled on the floor. "Look, Shannon, I'm sorry about your ankle, but I'm not going to help you undress. You'll be fine until morning, if not, call one of your family members to help you." Then he left.

Back inside the Rav4, Brian continued his conversation with his mother. "How's Mark doing?"

"He's fine, we're going for our yearly checkups tomorrow."

He activated the hands-free device and merged into traffic. "Mama, I've never known you to see a doctor regularly."

"Well, it's time for me to start. Back up," she said as if suddenly remembering something. "Tell me how things are going with you and Shay." Alysse was excited. "Are the two of you a couple yet?"

"Not yet, but I'm working on it," Brian answered honestly.

"What do you mean, you're working on it? All you have to do is tell her how you feel. That's not hard."

"I'm flying out to Massachusetts for her birthday. I'll talk to her then."

"Boy, you have two speeds: slow and stop. You get that from your daddy's side."

Brian laughed at his mother. "Mom, I know you like Shay, but some things can't be rushed. If it's meant to be, Shay and I will be together when the time is right."

"I hope the time is right before I lose my eyesight and my hearing."

"Mama, you've always looked out for me, but this time I think you're being selfish."

His reference to her having grown up in the foster care system was common, but she asked anyway, "Boy, what are you talking about?"

"Mama, I know it's important for you to have grandchildren and when the time is right, I will give you as many as Shay will allow."

Alysse gasped. "So you have decided you want to marry her? I knew it! I tried to pry it out of your daddy, but he won't tell me anything."

Brian considered his mother's question. In his heart, he'd always believed he would marry Shay, but this was the first time he verbally expressed his desire to anyone.

"I guess I have, but, Mama, please don't tell anyone. Give me the chance to tell her myself."

"Brian, you know I would never stick my nose into your business." Alysse found her attempt to sound innocent comical and said as much.

"Of course, you wouldn't butt into your only child's business," Brian said sarcastically.

"How's law school?"

Brian talked to his mother all the way home and even after he got settled. He couldn't remember when she sounded so relaxed and stress-free. Before he disconnected, he reminded her to call him after her checkup. He checked his watch once again. It was too late to phone Shay.

CHAPTER 40

Shay listened intently to the professor's lecture. Although she used a tape recorder, she still took handwritten notes, mainly to distract her from Jason's cold stares. She'd ended their relationship over two months ago, but he still treated her with resentment every time he glimpsed the silver heart around her wrist. Every chance he got, Jason would make nasty comments either to her or about her to anyone who would listen. She prayed Jason would eventually forget about her and concentrate on passing his final exams. She even hoped Rhonda would start spending time with him. Actually, the two had much in common.

She'd settled back into her spiritual routine. Every morning she prayed and read scripture and every day Brian called and left a prayer on her voicemail while she was in class. She'd celebrate her twenty-fifth birthday the following Tuesday. Brian was scheduled to land at Logan International Airport tomorrow evening. Shay had the entire weekend planned right down to the minute, dividing the four-day trip between Boston and Cambridge. Her list of non-stop activities included visiting historical museums and sites, a dinner cruise, a stage play and a carnival.

She scheduled every activity in public places. Except for the time they'd spend driving, they would never be alone. They agreed that it wasn't a good idea to have Brian in Shay's apartment or for Shay to hang out in Brian's hotel room. He would meet Shay in the hotel lobby for their daily excursions.

It was like old times. The two of them had grown closer since the CD recording. They talked on the phone three times a week and for the first time since they'd known each other, they didn't argue about trivial matters.

Outside of school, most of their conversations were of a spiritual nature. She was impressed with how well he could explain scriptures and how dedicated he was to the Lord. Last month for his twenty-fourth birthday, she sent him a black leather study Bible with his name engraved in gold letters. On the dedication page she wrote: *To a wonderful man whom I will respect and cherish forever*

"That's sweet, thank you," is what he told her. They both knew there was more to be said, but wanted to wait until they were face-to-face.

As was her routine now, Shay checked her voicemail for Brian's daily prayer on the drive back to her apartment. Today he didn't leave one. She was disappointed, but guessed he was too busy getting ready to come see her. She tried to push him to the back of her mind, but it proved futile. Something wasn't right; he always found time for her. After she dropped her books on the sofa and grabbed a root beer from the refrigerator, she called him.

"Hi, sweetheart."

She could tell he had been crying. She set her bottle of root beer down on the table without a coaster. "Brian, what's wrong?" Her voice filled with urgency.

Brian sniffled and cleared his throat. "I'm sorry, but I won't be able to make it out to see you this weekend."

She was more concerned about him than she was about herself. "Honey, what's going on, why are you crying?"

She waited while Brian blew his nose then sniffled some more. "My mother's having surgery on Monday. I'm leaving for Phoenix tomorrow."

The announcement left her puzzled. "What's wrong with Alysse? What kind of surgery is she having?"

Brian's voice broke again. "My mother has breast cancer, she's having a mastectomy."

Shay was stunned. The last time she saw Alysse, she looked fine. She didn't look like someone with cancer. "When was she diagnosed with breast cancer?"

Shay listened patiently as Brian told her about the doctor discovering a lump at Alysse's annual exam two months ago and the subsequent mammogram and biopsy that confirmed their suspicions. "Why didn't you tell me about this before?"

"I didn't know until last night. You know my mother, she doesn't like for me to worry about her. She only told me about the surgery because Mark insisted."

"Brian, I am so sorry. But you have to believe that they'll be able to remove the cancer and keep it from spreading."

"After the surgery she might have to start chemotherapy and that's going to be very hard on her." His voice broke again.

Shay stood and paced the length of the couch. "I know, but, honey, your mother is a very strong woman."

"But, Shay, why does she have to suffer this? She's suffered most of her life, why this too?"

Shay cried too because she didn't have an answer for him. "Honey, I don't know." Her voice was just above a whisper. She couldn't stand to hear him cry, especially since she wasn't there to comfort him, so for the first time, she prayed for him. She prayed hard until he regained control of his emotions.

"Shay, I'm really sorry about this weekend. I really wanted to see you."

"You will," she said softly. Like always she would be there for him.

Shay ended the call with Brian and with record speed called the airlines and booked a flight to Phoenix for Saturday morning. She then called Rhonda and asked her to email the class lecture notes to her until she returned.

"How long are you going to be gone?" Rhonda asked.

"I'll be there as long as Brian needs me to be," Shay

answered. The last call she made was home to her mother. "Mama, did you know Alysse is having surgery?"

"Yes, Mark called us last night right before he and Alysse told Brian."

"Brian doesn't sound good. I'm really concerned about him. Maybe Reggie should stay at the house in Oakland with Brian tonight."

Shay's genuine concern for Brian pleased Julia and she said as much. "You still have some common sense left, but I don't think that will be necessary. Brian came over last night and hasn't left. He's upstairs lying down. Reggie is with him most of the time."

"That's good." Knowing Brian wasn't alone only comforted Shay a little. She wanted to be there for him. "Are the two of you going to Phoenix?"

"We're flying out Sunday afternoon after Sunday service. Angie's going to keep Josiah for a few days." Julia paused then posed the question deliberately. "Are you coming to Phoenix? I can arrange for the family plane, if you'd like."

"That's not necessary. I already used your credit card to pay for a flight. I'll be there Saturday afternoon."

Julia heaved a sigh into the phone. "I'm so glad your common sense has returned. You had me worried the last time I saw you."

"Mama, on my craziest day, Brian's well-being is a priority." The last words staggered as their power flooded her being and settled in her heart.

CHAPTER 41

Sleep eluded Brian as his body yielded to another bout of tossing and turning. The words, *My mother has cancer*, kept invading his mind. It didn't make sense to him. His mother was only forty-six years old, much too young to have cancer. She had just begun to really enjoy her life and see the fruit of her sacrifices. "This is not fair," he said when he had tried to pray before Shay called. After Shay prayed for him, he did feel better, but worry over his mother's health stressed him to the point of a near nervous breakdown.

He needed to see Shay. She always knew how to make him feel better without doing anything besides being there. Just hearing her voice comforted him and he did notice that she referred to him as "honey" more than once. That surprised him and he didn't think she even realized it. This weekend he had planned to officially ask her to be his girl, but right now he needed her friendship.

He turned onto his back and stared up at the ceiling. His phone vibrated and he groggily answered without checking the caller ID.

"Hey, I didn't see you on campus today." It was Shannon.

Brian had limited his communication with her since the night she supposedly twisted her ankle. Yet she made it a point to hunt him down at school and at church. Her continued attendance at Sunday service and Wednesday night Bible Study after he stopped chauffeuring her around surprised him. Maybe she'd grown in her spiritual life, but today he was not in the mood for games and cut to the chase.

"Look, Shannon, this is not a good time. I'm leaving town for a few days on a family emergency. I don't have time for idle chit-chat."

"What's wrong, is someone sick?" Shannon sounded concerned.

Brian sighed. "My mother is having surgery for breast cancer on Monday and I'm going to Phoenix to be with her."

"Brian, I'm so sorry."

She was either really sorry or a very good actress, he thought. Her voice quivered and he heard a sniffle. "Thank you, Shannon."

"Are you going by yourself? Do you need me to come with you?" Shannon offered.

The last thing Brian wanted was for Alysse to have an assault case on her hands before going into surgery. Alysse detested Shannon and reminded Brian of her feelings every chance she got. "That won't be necessary, my family will be there."

Shannon cleared her throat. "Will Shay be there?"

Brian didn't see any need to conceal anything from her. "Yes," he answered plainly.

"What about her boyfriend? Will he be there as well?"

Brian made things perfectly clear for Shannon. "If you're referring to Jason, she's not seeing him anymore. She's coming to be with me and I don't consider myself to be her boyfriend. I'm her man and hers alone."

"Well. Um. I see." Shannon seemed to search for a response. "I didn't realize you two were a couple. I wonder if that little bit of information went over Shay's head as well. At any rate, I hope things work out with your mother. I'll still be here when you return—alone."

Brian shook his head and pressed the red end call button on his cell phone then turned the phone off. He turned onto his side and within minutes was sound asleep.

CHAPTER 42

"Brian!" Alysse called out.

Brian came running into the kitchen ready to put out a fire. "Are you all right, Mama? Are you in pain? Do you need any medicine?"

Alysse waved away her son's concern. "Boy, I'm fine. I just need your long arms to hand me that box up there." Alysse pointed above her head.

Brian handed her the box and went back into the living room and sulked on the couch. He was trying hard to contain his emotions, but Alysee's nonchalant attitude wasn't making it easy. Since arriving the previous night and seeing his mother, he wanted to fall apart, but she wouldn't let him. She told him she needed him to be strong, so she wouldn't have to worry about him. The more he looked at her, the harder it was for him to contain himself. He knew it was only a matter of time before the levee would break and Alysse would be furious. Fifteen minutes later, the doorbell chimed.

"I'll get it." Brian jumped up and sprinted to the door. He swung the front door open and smiled, then welcomed Shay into his arms.

"Hey, you," she said softly when he loosened his grip.

"Hey, sweetheart," he responded back as he stroked her hair. He stepped back and allowed room for her to enter the house. Shay strolled through the foyer and into the living room with familiarity. No sooner had she set her purse down on the copper leather sofa, he embraced her again. This time he squeezed her tighter than before and when he released her there were tears rolling down his cheeks and gathering at his chin.

She reached and half-cupped his wet cheeks. "Honey, it's all right? Alysse will be fine."

Without verbally responding, Brian took her hand and led her down the narrow hallway and into his old bedroom. He closed the door and sat down on the bed then motioned for her to join him.

***

Shay stared at the comforter covered with major-league-baseball-team logos. Hesitantly, her eyes traveled to Brian, starting at the long muscular dark-chocolate legs the khaki walking shorts revealed and ending at his long-outstretched arm. She felt his need pull her heartstrings and draw her to him. Fueled by his urgency, Shay hurried to him and planted her body next to his. Words weren't necessary as she placed her arms around him and he rested his head against her shoulder.

His cries were light at first. Then they turned into gut-wrenching sobs that shook them both and caused them to fall back into the center of the bed. When he finished releasing himself, they remained on his bed with her holding him and stroking his head. She laid there with him, whispering words of prayer, until he fell asleep.

Careful not to wake him, Shay retrieved a clean T-shirt from his drawer to replace the now-wet one she had on. She slipped the size 2X Cal Berkeley shirt over her smaller frame and kissed him on the forehead.

When she returned to the living room Alysse and Mark were watching television.

"Hello, Shay!" Alysse's face lit up. "I didn't know you were here."

"I arrived a little while ago." Shay hugged Mark and Alysse then sat on the loveseat.

"I knew she was here," Mark said, giving Shay a knowing nod. "Brian was showing her something in his room."

210

"What's he doing in there now?" Alysse asked.

"He's sleeping," Shay answered, careful not to give any indication of Brian's emotional state.

"I'm glad, because he's been getting on my nerves. Following me around like I'm going to keel over at any moment," Alysse complained.

"He's just concerned about you, and so am I." Shay reiterated the reason for her visit. "How are you doing, Ms. Alysse?"

"Shay, I'm fine. I'm not in any pain. I'm not worried about this surgery. Sure, I'll lose a breast, but I really don't need two of them anymore, considering I only have one husband." Both Shay and Mark laughed at Alysse's reasoning. "I'll probably lose my hair, but a good wig will fix that."

"Ms. Alysse, you are too funny."

"Seriously," Alysse continued, "I've found my peace with God and I know He's going to see me through this. No matter what happens, I'm going to be all right."

"Amen," Shay agreed. She believed in Alysse's full recovery; if she could only transfer that confidence to Brian. "Is there anything you need me to do? I have a couple of hours before I check into the hotel."

"I'm fine." Alysse leaned against Mark and propped her feet on the couch. "Just try to make yourself comfortable in this desert heat." A few minutes later Alysse abruptly sat up, as if she'd suddenly remembered something. "Shay, there is something I need you to do."

"What's that, Ms. Alysse?"

Alysse's expression turned serious. "Be good to my son, whether I'm around or not."

Shay swallowed hard. Did Alysse know something she didn't? "I'll do my best."

"Good." Alysse smiled. "My son deserves the best."

Shay spent the remainder of the afternoon laughing and talking with Mark and Alysse. Although she categorized Alysse as rough around the edges, Shay genuinely enjoyed

Alysse's straightforwardness. She reminded her so much of her mother. Like Reggie, Mark was the head of the household and served his position with a quiet yet strong presence. Alysse and Mark weren't as openly affectionate as Reggie and Julia, but their love for one another was evident.

Shay's thoughts drifted and she began to wonder how she and Brian would interact as a married couple. Would they kiss every morning? Would Brian's eyes sparkle at her presence the way Reggie's did at the sight of Julia? Would they openly express their love or be conservative? Shay preferred openness. She shook her head in an effort to remove those thoughts from her mind. *Slow down, girl. Brian and I aren't an official couple yet and here I am thinking about marriage.*

Shay excused herself and went into the kitchen for something to drink. Her throat was parched from the dry desert heat. Halfway through her Arnold Palmer, Brian walked in and kissed her from behind on the cheek.

"Thank you."

"Anytime." She smiled and offered him some of her drink. She didn't ask him what he was thanking her for; she knew he was referring to the intimate time they shared earlier.

Brian finished off the Arnold Palmer and refilled the glass for her. He looked at his watch. "It's almost four o'clock; you must be tired."

"I am starting to feel the effects of the time difference. I'd better go and check into the hotel before it gets too late."

Brian placed his hands on her shoulders. "Shay, why don't you stay here with us?"

"That's a good idea. That way you won't have to drive back and forth," Mark added from the archway.

Shay would have refused, but the pleading look on both Brian and Mark's faces wouldn't let her. "Where will I sleep?"

"You can sleep in my old room," Brian offered.

Shay tilted her head to the side. "And where will you sleep?"

"He can squeeze his oversized body on the couch." Shay looked over Brian's shoulder to see Alysse standing next to Mark.

"Please," Brian asked again, stroking her cheek. He didn't say the words with his mouth, but his eyes told her that he needed her close to him.

"I guess I'd better get my things from the rental car and call the hotel," Shay finally agreed.

"Give me the key; I'll take care of it," Brian offered.

Keeping her eyes locked with his, Shay slid her hand into the front pocket of her white walking shorts then held the key out to Brian. When their hands met, Brian expressed his gratitude by squeezing her firmer and longer than usual.

Alysse sat down at the kitchen table. "I don't know why you resisted. You know that boy can't function without you," she said when Brian was out of earshot. "My baby lost twenty pounds after you left for school. I had to stay with him nearly a whole month to get him eating properly again."

Shay poised a neutral position. "Ms. Alysse, what are you talking about?"

"You know exactly what I'm talking about. You know my baby's in love with you."

Shay blushed and joined her at the table. "Do you really think so?"

"I know so. Brian's not interested in anyone but you."

"Did he tell you that?" Shay asked hopeful.

"I'm not going to tell you what he told me, because I'm not one to gossip. But trust me, I know my son."

Shay placed her right hand over her heart and prayed Alysse knew her son as well as she thought she did. Her stomach growled. "Do you want me to help you with dinner, Ms. Alysse?"

"It's too hot to cook. I'd planned to send Mark out for Chinese, but you and Brian can go instead."

"Shay and I can go where?" Brian asked, returning from the car. He turned to Shay. "Your luggage is in my room."

213

"You two can drive into town and pick up dinner," Alysse answered.

"I don't want to leave you," Brian firmly replied. "I'm not going anywhere."

Brian's declaration infuriated Alysse. "I've had enough of your overprotective attitude. Boy, I told you I'm fine. You've been in this hot house all day, you need to get some fresh air and I need some space before I kill you."

"You don't need space, you need to sit down and take it easy!" Brian snapped back.

Alysse stood and pointed her index finger at Brian. "This is exactly why I didn't want to tell you anything. You worry too much."

Brian stood and yelled in his mother's face, "I'm allowed to worry; I am your son. Now sit down!"

Mark stepped into the kitchen.

Shay reached for Brian's arm before things got out of hand. "Brian, we'll only be gone for a short period of time. Mark's here, she'll be fine."

Brian's sudden cold eyes bore into her. "You're supposed to be on my side. But you don't understand."

It was out of his character to yell at her and she didn't take it personally. Shay kept her voice low and steady. "Brian, I am on your side. I do understand, but I agree with your mother: You need a break."

"You'd better listen to her, before you find yourself in the hospital. Just because you're a twenty-four-year-old man, doesn't give you the right to raise your voice at me!" Alysse yelled back.

Brian glared at both of them and stormed out without saying another word. Shay found him outside sitting in her rental car.

"I'm scared," he said after she closed the driver's side door.

She turned and faced him. She wasn't used to seeing this vulnerable side of him, her giant afraid. She ran her fingertips along his jaw line. "I know you're scared. I felt the same way when my mother had her emergency surgery."

214

"I almost forgot about you running and screaming through the hospital ward and then collapsing on the floor outside of Mama J's door."

"Do you want to know who helped me get through that the most?" she asked.

"Your uncle Jonathan," he assumed.

She moved closer to him and held his face steadily with her hands. "No, Brian, it was you." She worked hard to keep her voice from breaking; her emotions threatening to pour out like a gushing river. "It was the words, the promise you made to me in the nursery that gave me the assurance I needed. Do you remember those words?"

Brian nodded his head. "Yes."

"And just like you told me that I'll always have you; you'll always have me, Brian. I'll always be here for you."

Brian had to pull away from her like he'd suddenly been scorched.

The heat from his inward inferno leaked outward and grabbed Shay. Too much for her to handle, Shay turned away from him and looked out the window. At that very moment she wanted to take him into her arms and love him. She wanted to be the vehicle that drove his pain away, but she couldn't.

"We'd better get going, if we're going to beat the crowds," he said after a long silence.

She drove all the way to the restaurant without saying a word and very little on the return trip.

CHAPTER 43

Alysse held Sunday dinner late to allow time for Reggie and Julia to arrive from California. Mark and Brian tried to convince Alysse to rest and let them prepare dinner, but she insisted on cooking dinner herself. To keep Brian off Alysse's case, Shay helped her prepare a traditional backyard barbeque with all the trimmings and helped her pack for her three-day hospital stay.

The four of them were playing Monopoly when Reggie and Julia arrived. Shay noticed when Brian greeted his dad, he held onto him longer and tighter than normal; he did the same thing to Julia.

Alysse stood back and watched as Julia and Shay then Reggie and Shay then Reggie and Mark, and finally Mark and Julia exchanged hugs. "I hate to interrupt ya'll little hug-a-thon, but it's time to eat," she fussed.

Julia planted her hands on her hips. "Girl, shut up and give us a hug. You know you want one."

Alysse smiled as Julia and Reggie gave her a group hug.

At dinner, Brian sat between his mother and Shay. The non-traditional family enjoyed good food and good conversation. They had come a long way in five years. Julia and Alysse were friends. It didn't bother Alysse at all that Brian referred to Julia, as Mama J. Mark and Reggie were also friends, but Brian still chose to address Mark by his name. And of course, Alysse loved Shay like she was the daughter she never had.

Reggie, Julia and Alysse watched how their children

217

interacted over dinner. Every time Shay called Brian "honey", Reggie and Julia exchanged glances. And when Brian wiped barbeque sauce from the corner of Shay's mouth, Alysse nearly fell out of her chair.

When she finished eating, Alysse got up the nerve to verbalize the thoughts parading through her mind ever since receiving the breast cancer diagnosis. Things she may have never said if not faced with a life-threatening illness.

"I have something I'd like to say," she announced, rising from her chair. "There are a few things actually."

Brian expressed his immediate concern. "Is something wrong, Mom?"

Alysse scolded her son. "I told you, I'm fine," she paused, "but I do have some things I want to say. Actually, I need to say them."

The room silently sat on pins and needles, because Alysse was known to say whatever came to her mind with little regard for one's feelings. Finally, Mark encouraged her, "Say what's on your mind."

Alysse surveyed the table and took a deep breath. "First, I want to thank you, Reggie, Julia and Shay, for coming to support me through this little crisis. As you know, I don't have any blood relatives outside of Brian and I really appreciate you for extending yourselves."

"It's not a problem," Reggie interrupted.

Alysse huffed and put her hand on her hip. "Look, Reggie, this is hard for me, so don't interrupt me or else I'll change my mind. Just because you're a preacher doesn't mean you always have to talk."

Reggie held up both hands in surrender. "Go ahead." He was used to Alysse's defensive and offensive behavior. That's just who she was.

She continued. "Like I was saying, Julia, I've never told you how much I appreciate you and your family for accepting Brian and treating him as your own. I have watched you and Brian together and I know you love him. It's comforting to know that if something does go wrong and I'm no longer around, that Brian will have someone to mother him."

Brian opened his mouth to speak, but Alysse stopped him with a raised open hand.

"Also, you're the first female friend I've had in years. The last female friend I had ended up sleeping with my trifling fiancé." She paused to glare momentarily at Reggie then softened her expression for Julia. "Thank you for being a good friend to me. I'm eternally grateful to you for taking the time to find me. I can honestly say my life has truly changed for the better as a result of knowing you."

Julia patted her hand. "Thank you, Alysse. It means a lot to me to hear you say that."

Alysse inhaled deeply and turned to Reggie. "Now as for you, motor-mouth. I spent over seventeen years hating you, but today I can honestly say I have nothing but absolute respect for you. You were a lousy boyfriend, but you're a great father to Brian. I have forgiven you for what you did to me, but now I need to ask you to forgive me for what I did to you."

"What are you talking about?" Reggie asked, guardedly.

"I'm sorry for taking Brian away from you and for depriving you and your parents of being a part of his life."

Reggie swallowed hard and Julia placed her hand on his. "Alysse, I forgave you a long time ago."

"Thank you." Alysse walked around to Reggie and hugged him then continued with her speech.

"Shay, I told you what I wanted to say earlier. Mark, I'll talk to you in private. Now, as for you, Brian. Boy, you have gotten on my last nerve from the moment you entered this house two days ago. And you know what, I've enjoyed every minute." Alysse kissed Brian's forehead. "When I look at you, I see my past, present and future. You're the one thing in my life that I'm most proud of and the only thing I've done right. I love you, son, and I'm so proud of the man you've become. You've worked hard and overcome obstacles others would have walked away from."

When Alysse finished hugging Brian, he left the kitchen in tears. Reggie stood to follow him, but Shay stopped him. "I'll go."

Shay found Brian sitting on the side of his bed, crying with his head in his hands. Shay hunched on her knees in front of him. After seeing Alysse, who never showed her true emotions, so open and transparent, Shay felt it was time for her to come clean with her own feelings. Maybe it would help ease Brian's pain.

She gently removed his hands from his face and lifted his chin. "Honey, I have something to tell you."

His mouth didn't move, but Brian's wet eyes told her to continue.

She swallowed hard and exhaled. "I love you."

"I know." He lowered his head again.

She lifted his head again and held his face steadily in her hands. "You don't understand. I'm trying to tell you that I not only love you as my best friend, but I'm in love with you and have been for a long time. Do you think I could've made love with you if I didn't love you?"

The tears subsided and a faint smile creased his face when she removed her hands. He remained silent and she sat back on her legs and continued speaking. "When you asked me over the phone, if I meant what I said at Emery Bay, I lied to you. I do love you. I love everything about you, even the things that irk me. You were right; I can never give my heart to another man, because it really does belong to you. It has since the day I met you."

She let out a deep breath, closed her eyes and leaned her head back. She felt so much lighter now that she'd voiced what she'd been hiding and trying to suppress.

She felt his fingertips encase the back of her neck, but kept her eyes closed as he pulled her closer to him. His lips touched hers just as her eyelids fluttered. His kiss was soft and sweet, gentle, but void of passion. He waited for her to open her eyes fully and for her breathing to return to a normal pace before continuing. He then kissed both cheeks and her forehead, before returning to her lips for a deeper kiss.

"My Shay," he whispered, the warmth of his breath fanning her face. "I love you, too. That's what I've been waiting months to tell you. I was going to tell you when I came to Cambridge. I loved you long before I gave you my virginity and I've loved you every day since. Truth be told, since we met, I can't remember a single day I haven't loved you."

"For real?" Her voice cracked.

"Sweetheart, I love you so much, it hurts." The quivers lacing his voice sent tremors surging through her. "I've agonized every day not being able to share the depth of my feelings."

Her eyes watered and she swallowed the lump that formed in her throat. "So what happens now?"

He drew her closer and rested his arms around her waist. "We grow up and stop playing games and start building our relationship and planning for our future."

His answer sounded like a glorious song to her. "Are you sure that's what you want?"

"Absolutely." Brian offered the goofy grin she loved so much. "Blondie, will you go with me? Blink once for yes, twice for no."

Shay giggled and cried all at once. "Only if you promise to keep your head shaved."

"Do you promise to keep your hair blonde?"

"Anything for you, handsome." She wrapped her arms around his neck. "I got a boyfriend," she sang until laughter poured from him. They shared another kiss then Brian maneuvered away from her.

"I love you, LaShay Hampton, but right now being this close to you is deadly, if you know what I mean."

Shay nodded in agreement and he assisted her to her feet. She took a step backward toward the door. "I understand and I don't want to mess up things again either." She blew him a kiss. "I love you; meet you in the living room."

Inside the bathroom Shay danced and leaped for joy. Brian didn't just consider her his best friend. The man she loved, loved her back.

The blended family spent the rest of the evening looking at old pictures and taking new ones. Their parents took note of how giddy and relaxed Brian and Shay were with one another. They were so comfortable that Brian actually put his arms around Shay and kissed her cheek a few times. He whispered something in her ear that made her blush uncontrollably.

"What?" Shay and Brian asked simultaneously when they finally noticed the four adults staring at them.

"Is there something you'd like to tell us?" Reggie asked.

Shay giggled and Brian grinned from ear to ear.

"Shay and I are dating," Brian answered proudly.

Julia gasped and put her hand over her mouth.

Alysse waved her hand in Brian's face. "Boy, you're slower than I thought if you're just now figuring that out."

"Mom, I'm serious," Brian continued talking to his mother, but focused his eyes on Shay. "I love Shay and she loves me. We're a couple."

Reggie gave his smile of approval, but Julia, who was so ecstatic the game-playing was over, stood to her feet and lifted her arms in the air then looked toward heaven and yelled, "Thank ya!"

Alysse laughed so hard, she cried. "Now I'm ready to have this surgery," she said when Mark handed her a tissue.

CHAPTER 44

At 6:00 a.m. Alysse and her family entered through the dual-sliding automatic hospital doors. Just before the orderly wheeled Alysse back for the life-altering surgery, the family held hands and Reggie led them in prayer.

"Gracious Father," he began after Alysse's warning to keep it short, "we thank you for being a great and magnificent God who's capable of doing more than we can ask or think. We thank you for giving us this opportunity to experience how powerful you are. We ask that you be with Alysse and safely guide the hands of the surgeon and allow her to come through this procedure successfully and give her a speedy recovery. And, Father, through this crisis, draw Alysse closer to you. Amen."

"Amen," everyone echoed and kissed Alysse.

Brian didn't want to let her go. She snatched her hand away from him, but did so with a smile. Long after she disappeared through the double doors, Brian continued to stare in that direction.

Julia placed her arm around him. "She's in God's hands, and no matter what happens in the operating room, she'll be fine."

Brian looked down at his stepmother and asked the question that plagued him. "What if the cancer has spread?"

She looked up at him with a question of her own. "What if it hasn't?"

"Mama is right, you have to stop thinking the worst and start speaking positive words," Shay added. "The Bible tells us that we can decree a thing and it shall be established and that life and death are in the power of our tongue. Brian, you need to speak healing over your mother's life and when you say it, believe it."

Julia's mouth gaped at Shay using the Word of God with bold confidence. "That's right, Brian, say it until you see the manifestation," she added, still staring at Shay in astonishment.

Brian sat down, closed his eyes and inwardly prayed. An hour later, he still sat in the same position.

"Since he's asleep, I'm going to the cafeteria," Shay whispered to Reggie.

She hadn't taken two steps before she felt his cold hand on her wrist.

"Where are you going?"

"To get some coffee; want me to bring you back a cup?"

"No, I'll go with you. I could use some breakfast." He stood and stretched his stiff muscles.

Shay entwined her arm with his. "Now that's the Brian I know." She offered to bring Reggie and Mark something back, but they both refused.

The cafeteria's offerings didn't appeal to Brian. He suggested they walk the three blocks to a nearby restaurant and Shay obliged. Inside the family-style diner, Shay placed her elbow on the table and propped her hand underneath her chin and watched Brian eat a plate of steak and eggs. She'd finished a light breakfast of fruit and yogurt before his meal arrived. After washing down the hearty meal with a glass of apple juice, he invited her to move closer to him in the booth.

"Can a brother get a little warmth from his girlfriend?"

Shay's cheeks reddened as she scooted into his opened arm. "I'm glad you're feeling better," she said when his arm made contact with her shoulder.

"Thanks to you, I'm feeling much better." He squeezed her shoulder. "I'm still concerned about my mother, but I'm not worried."

She gazed up at him. "What did I do?"

The softness of her hazel eyes almost made him lose his train of thought. "You helped me to remember the power I have as a believer," he stammered.

"Glad I could help you out. Spiritually, you've helped me so much since we've started talking again. I really look forward to our talks about the Word"

When she finished speaking, Brian was dumbfounded. He hadn't heard one word Shay said. Watching the movement of her full lips so close to his distracted him.

"Um, maybe you should move back over to the other side."

Shay looked confused. "Why, did I say something wrong?"

Brian gulped down a half-glass of water. "No, you didn't say anything wrong, but if you remain this close to me, I might do something wrong."

Shay's eyes narrowed. "Something like what?"

"Like kiss you."

She dismissed his statement with a wave of the hand. "Brian, you kissed me three times last night."

He lifted her chin. His voice deepened, making his desire crystal clear. "That's not the kind of kiss I'm talking about. What I want to do to you right now would earn us a trip to the altar for a month."

Shay moved away so fast to the opposite side of the booth, she knocked over her glass of water and her cold coffee. She and Brian laughed while the waitress cleaned up the mess.

Between chuckles, Brian said, "It's going to be a long two years."

"Why two years?"

"That's when I finish law school."

"What happens then?"

Brian sat back and folded his arms. "You'll see."

CHAPTER 45

Brian and Shay returned to the waiting room to find Reggie and Mark matching wits over a game of chess. Brian pulled a chair up next to his dad and watched. Julia and Shay left the men in the waiting room and went to visit the patient education center. There, they gathered information on breast cancer and treatment options. Julia picked up some pamphlets for local support groups.

"Do you really think Alysse will attend a support group?" Shay asked. "It's going to be hard enough getting her through the six-to-eight-week recovery period and chemotherapy. And it'll be a miracle if she allows the homecare nurse to help her."

"I know, but she's changing. I didn't think I would ever hear her say what she said last night." Julia waited a moment before adding, "Neither did I think I'd hear Brian say what he said before all my hair turned gray."

Shay faked innocence. "Come on, Mama, you knew eventually we'd get together."

"True, but I didn't think it would be this soon, considering the little stunt you played the last time you were home."

"People change, Mama; I've grown up."

Julia took a long hard look at her daughter. Shay was saying all the right words and doing the right things, but Julia's doubts remained. "Are you sure you're ready for a serious relationship, because Brian is in it for the long haul, if you know what I mean?" Julia arched her eyebrows.

"Mama, I really love Brian. I know Brian is serious about us, so am I," Shay answered sincerely.

"I know you love Brian, but are you mature enough to handle a relationship that could possibly lead to marriage?"

"Mama, I'm in love, I can handle anything," Shay declared.

"O Lord, I have some more praying to do," her mother responded. "I can see it now; the first sign of trouble and, girl, you're going to run Forest run."

***

Back in the waiting room it was Brian's turn to try and defeat his father. After Reggie had beaten him, Mark took a walk to the cafeteria and left father and son alone.

Reggie watched Brian make his first move. "Tell me, when did things escalate between you and Shay?" Reggie didn't try to conceal his smile.

Neither did Brian. "Things started budding after her last visit and last night it all came to a head."

Reggie played a counter move. "So how do you feel?"

Brian looked up from the game board. "I've never felt better. If Moms wasn't sick I'd be doing back flips."

Reggie shared a laugh with his son. "What timeframe are we looking at?"

"You know me so well, Dad. I plan to make my move the day after I graduate law school," Brian answered unwavering.

"You have it all planned, don't you? How does Shay feel about that?"

"I haven't exactly told her, but I'm sure she won't object."

Reggie stopped looking at the board and focused on Brian. "Two years is a long time when you're young and dating. The temptation will be great, especially since the two of you have been intimate. Are you sure you can handle that?"

Brian looked his father in the eyes. "Dad, I have to handle it. If I don't, I won't do it. I won't marry her just so I can have sex. I won't marry Shay until I can financially provide for her. I want to marry her when the time is right because

228

she's the one God has chosen for me. This in-between time will give us a chance to have a real courtship without the bickering and game-playing."

Brian's insight and maturity impressed Reggie. "Son, you don't need my advice. I wish I was as knowledgeable as you are when I was your age."

"Dad, this might sound strange, but I'm glad Shay and I committed fornication." Reggie frowned at that statement. "What I mean is, the process to restoration has taught me a lot about myself and even more about God. The lessons I've learned will help me in my relationship with Shay."

Reggie moved his pawn. "How so?"

"It took me months to understand that God loved me and was still committed to me when I made the wrong choice. He never turned His back on me. While I was sulking and feeling ashamed, He was waiting with open arms, ready to love me unconditionally. He never gave up on me, even after I did it again. I admit He scared the black off me with that pregnancy scare."

The game piece fell from Reggie's hand and toppled half the board. "Pregnancy scare?"

Brian shrugged off his father's shock. As he reset the board, he briefly explained the event that nearly altered his life.

Reggie shook his head. "No wonder you were so miserable after she left. If she was pregnant you would have married her, and not just for the sake of the baby, but because you love her."

"Isn't that the same kind of love a husband should have for his wife— unconditional and sacrificial. Dad, that's the kind of love I have for Shay. When she brought Jason here two months ago, I was devastated. But that didn't stop me from loving her and reaching out to her. I still loved her just like God loved me when I took her into my bed. God waited for me, because I belong to Him and I can wait for Shay, because I know she was created just for me. The next time I'm intimate with her, it will be the way God intended."

"Son, you've come a long way. I'm proud of you. However, I do think you should share your plans with Shay. The ride will be much smoother if both of you know where you're headed."

Before Brian responded, Julia, Shay and Mark returned to the waiting room. As always when she returned from being away from her husband, Julia kissed Reggie softly on the lips then sat down beside him. Shay stood behind Brian and began massaging his shoulders.

"We should hear something soon," Mark said after he checked his watch then walked over to the window.

Beneath Shay's fingers Brian's shoulders tensed slightly. She instructed him to lean his head back against her. As her fingers worked on his head, neck and shoulders, she softly sang "His Eye Is on the Sparrow".

"Shay, I didn't know you could sing?" Mark said.

She turned to Mark. "I can't. I'm just making noise."

"Sounds beautiful to me. She sounds the same way she looks," Brian offered.

Shay looked down to see Brian's upside-down face smiling at her.

"Is there a time when this man doesn't think you're beautiful?" Mark teased.

Shay blushed, but didn't verbally respond because at that moment Dr. Consorti stepped into the waiting room.

The middle-aged Caucasian gentleman in green scrubs and a surgical mask approached Mark. Brian immediately walked over and joined them.

"Mr. Green." Dr. Consorti's voice was dry and raspy.

Brian didn't allow the man to finish his sentence. "How's my mother?"

"Your mother is doing fine; she's in recovery. We were able to perform the mastectomy and do the reconstruction as well. The cancer doesn't appear to have spread, but we'll have to wait a few days for the pathology report, to determine if she requires chemo or not."

Brian glanced upward. "Thank you, God," he whispered. Can we see her?"

"After she wakes up, one of the nurses will come out and get you." Mark shook the doctor's hand then, just as quietly as he appeared, Dr. Consorti disappeared.

Brian sat back down and Shay resumed his massage. The tension in his shoulders was gone. He didn't say a word; he held his head back against her body and accepted the therapy from her fingers.

For the rest of the afternoon, the family took turns visiting Alysse. She slept most of the time, but Mark and Brian sat by her bedside nonetheless. A few hours later, Reggie and Julia left for their hotel, but Shay stayed with Brian. Finally, at the close of visiting hours, Brian decided it was time to go home.

Shay was asleep in the backseat when Mark pulled into his driveway. Instead of awakening her, Brian lifted her from the backseat and carried her into his old room, laid her on his old bed and removed her shoes.

"Thank you," he whispered before kissing her cheek and turning the lights off.

CHAPTER 46

Tuesday morning when Shay opened her eyes she thought she was dreaming. She rubbed her eyes twice to make sure she wasn't hallucinating. There were balloons of various colors everywhere. On the nightstand, a clear crystal vase filled with a dozen red roses. There was another one on the dresser. Loose petals were strewn on her and over the bed. On the pillow next to her she found a stroll enclosed by a red ribbon.

She sat up and with her hand brushed her hair from her face. She unrolled the stroll and laughed when she recognized Brian's handwriting. When she started reading, her laughter turned into crying.

My Shay,

I hope this day brings you half as much joy as you have given me. You are my fresh fragrance after the rain and the strength that has carried me through this storm.

To some, roses are extraordinary and beautiful. But to me, the most splendid rose fails in comparison to you. Shay, you are an extraordinary young woman. Nothing compares to your natural beauty, both inside and out.

When I prayed this morning, I thanked God for creating you for me and asked that He would protect you and provide you with everything you need on this day. I prayed for Him to show me how to express my love and appreciation for you, not just today but every day.

Sweetheart, today I don't want you to worry about anything. If

*you need anything, just ask and I'll take care of it. I love you and
I'll always be here for you.*

Happy Birthday, My Love,

B.

Shay placed her hand over her heart and read the words
again. She had been so focused on Alysse and Brian, she'd
forgotten today was her birthday. She was about to use her
shirt to wipe her face when Brian startled her.

"Here, sweetheart." He handed her a tissue and sat down
facing her on the bed.

After she wiped her face and blew her nose, she embraced
Brian and soaked his shirt with more tears.

"I guess this means you liked my note?"

She released him and cleaned her face again. "Brian,
everything is perfect: the roses, the balloons and this," she
picked up the scroll again, "this is beautiful."

"I mean every word." Brian's warm sincere tone massaged
her soul.

"I know you do." She stroked his cheek. "That's not why
I'm crying. I'm crying because I love you so much and I can
feel the love flowing from your heart to mine." She leaned
forward and gently kissed his full lips. When she sat back,
Brian's eyes were dark and his jaw muscles flexed almost
uncontrollably. He left the room without saying another
word.

After spending most of the day visiting with Alysse, Shay
enjoyed her twenty-fifth birthday dinner with her family at
PF Changs. Uncle Jonathan and his wife drove from
Scottsdale to celebrate with her.

It took some convincing from Alysse, but Mark agreed to
join them. "I can't be there, so you have to be my eyes and
ears," Alysse told him. She was hoping Brian would propose
to Shay on her birthday. Of course, that was the furthest
thing from Brian's mind.

During dinner, the older adults watched as Brian and
Shay took turns feeding each other and constantly flirting.

Julia looked up at her husband as she asked, "Do you remember what new love feels like?"

"I'm reminded every day," Reggie answered and kissed her.

"That's enough love talk," Mark announced. "Shay, maybe you should open your presents. You know I have to get back and give Alysse a play-by-play report."

"Whatever you say, Mr. Green." Shay giggled. "But Brian gave me his present this morning."

"I'm sure Brian's gift is the only one that matters, but your mother and I along with your Uncle Jonathan have something for you also," Reggie announced.

"Actually, it's a birthday and graduation present combined," Julia clarified.

"But, Mom, I don't graduate for another six weeks."

"I know, but I don't want you to think you're getting another gift. We shouldn't give you this; you're already spoiled rotten." Julia smiled and handed Shay a small white envelope.

Shay's eyes widened when she felt the outline of a key. She ripped the envelope open and screamed, "Oh, my God!" Inside was the key to a new Lexus. "Thank you! Thank you! Thank you!" She ran around the table to hug and kiss Reggie, her mother and Uncle Jonathan.

Brian sat back and folded his arms. "Hey, what about me? I picked out the floor mats and air freshener."

"I'll thank you later," she flirted, then turned to her mother. "Where is it? How did you know what I wanted? What color is it?" Excitement bubbled inside and gushed out.

"Slow down," Reggie said. "It's gold and it's at the house."

"Brian picked the color and told us exactly what you wanted," Julia added.

"Oh, that was sweet of you." Shay hugged Brian. "I love you," she whispered in his ear and he shared the sentiment.

Reggie cleared his throat, reminding them they were at the dinner table. "Shay, your mother and I are very proud of you for accomplishing so much at such a young age. It's our privilege to give you this."

"And I couldn't be more proud of you if you were my own daughter," Jonathan added.

As her mother and uncle sang a soulful rendition of "Happy Birthday", Shay laid her head against Brian. "This is the best birthday ever."

CHAPTER 47

A day after Alysse was discharged from the hospital, Reggie and Julia went back home, but Shay stayed in Arizona with Brian. She phoned Rhonda back in Massachusetts and had her email Shay's portion of their final assignment. By starting some of the work now, she could miss another week without jeopardizing her grade. Over the next few days, she divided her time between schoolwork and helping Mark and Brian care for Alysse.

To everyone's surprise, Alysse turned out to be a cooperative patient. She didn't argue or complain about anything, mainly because she was too tired and weak. She even obeyed Brian's orders. This morning while Shay helped her change the dressing on her incision, Alysse repeatedly told her how much she appreciated her for being there.

"Really, Ms. Alysse, it's not a problem."

Then Alysse said something Shay wasn't expecting. "I think it's time you started calling me 'Mom', don't you?"

The question flattered Shay. "Ms. Alysse, that's very sweet, but don't you think it's a little soon for that?"

A glimpse of the old Alysse returned. "Shay, are you trying to tell me you're as slow as Brian? You do know he's going to marry you, don't you?"

Shay didn't have an answer for her. "I-well-um; we'll have to talk about this later, Ms. Alysse," she said and assisted her back into bed.

Alysse shook her head. "Humph, between you and Brian, my grandchildren can't help but be mentally challenged."

"I love you too, Ms. Alysse." Shay laughed at her and quickly left before Alysse could get on a roll.

Later, as Shay worked on her laptop, Brian sat down next to her on the couch and watched. Occasionally, she would look up and find him staring at her and she'd blow him a kiss.

"Is there something I can help you with?" he offered.

"As a matter of fact there is, you can move away from me so I can concentrate," she said, pretending to be in serious thought.

Brian came even closer to her and looked deep into her eyes. "You're never going to get rid of me."

Shay felt that familiar tug in her heart and the need to be close to him. She closed her laptop and placed it on the square coffee table. "Brian, we need to talk."

"I'm listening." He moved even closer. "What's on your mind?"

She brushed her lips with the tip of her tongue. "You *know* what's on my mind, but that's not what I want to talk about. Now scoot back so I can stay focused."

A sheepish grin creased Brian's chocolate face, but he did move slightly away from her.

"Brian, what did you mean the other day when you said it's going to be a long two years? What would you like to have happen for us after that?"

Brian's flirty expression turned puzzled. "Shay, you really don't know?"

"From speaking to your mother and from the little hints I've gotten from you, I have an idea, but, honey, we've never discussed any short- or long-term plans concerning us."

His large fingers fanned his baldhead. "I didn't think we needed to. I thought after the other night we had an understanding."

"What understanding is that?" Shay asked earnestly. "The only thing I understand is that you love me."

"I thought we had an agreement to work on building a relationship until I finish law school," he answered.

She knew he had marriage on his mind, but she needed to

hear him say it. "And then what? What happens if we last through law school?"

His heat permeated from his eyes and singed her. He locked hands with her. "Shay, I love you and you're the only woman I want. I know in my heart that you're the one God created for me, but I don't want to rush things. Trust me on this, when the time is right, I'll get down on one knee and place a ring on this finger." He gently stroked her left ring finger.

Shay threw caution to the wind and wrapped her arms around Brian's neck and kissed him, enjoying a delectable feast. He didn't protest, instead he parted his lips and gave her what she wanted.

"Sorry, but I've wanted to do that since I got here," she said breathlessly. "I'll try not to let it happen again, but I can't promise you anything. Two years is a long time and we've shared much more than that."

Brian blushed for the first time. "Just don't let it happen too often," he teased.

"That was enough to hold me over for a while." She picked up her laptop and resumed working.

Brian stood on his feet. "Anytime you feel you need a shot in the arm, just say so. I can handle the kissing, but not the touching."

"Definitely, no touching!" she firmly agreed.

Three days later, Shay was getting all the shots she could handle as she waited in the security checkpoint line at Phoenix's Sky Harbor Airport.

"I miss you already," Brian whispered between planting kisses on her forehead and cheeks.

"Me too," she answered back.

Brian held her in his arms and spoke a quick prayer in her ear. When he released her, she saw a lone tear trailing down his face. "What's wrong?" she asked as she wiped his cheek.

He leaned his forehead against hers. "Nothing is wrong, everything is just right. Perfect. I told you, I love you so much it hurts. I don't want to see you go."

There were only two people ahead of her so she had to hurry. "I love you," she said and gave him one last kiss. Now it was her turn to cry.

He watched her clear security and before she stepped onto the escalator that would take her to the departure gate, she turned and blew him a kiss. He caught the imaginary kiss in his palm and then placed his hand over his heart.

He's right, it's going to be a long two years, she thought waiting for the plane to take off.

CHAPTER 48

Shay hurried into her apartment, trying to catch the ringing cordless phone before the voicemail picked up. "Hello," she yelled breathlessly into the receiver.

"Hey, cousin?" It was Staci and Taylor. Shay knew exactly why they'd called so she dropped her remaining bags and plopped down on the couch.

"What's up?" she asked, trying to hide her enthusiasm.

"You, girl!" Taylor screamed. "My dad told me about you and Brian. You finally handled your business."

"Details, details," Staci insisted.

Careful to leave out the intimate parts, Shay gave them a recap of the past week.

"Ooh, that is so sweet. How do you feel?" Staci asked.

"How do I feel? Cuz, I feel like dancing and skipping and running all at the same time!" Shay laughed. "I feel alive!"

"So what's next? How long are you guys going to date?" Staci wanted to know.

Shay lost some of her excitement. "Well, Brian wants to wait until he finishes law school."

"When is that?" Taylor asked.

"Two years."

"Two years! There is no way you're going to last that long," Taylor declared.

"I don't think so either," Shay agreed. "But that's what he wants. I love him and I'm willing to wait—for everything."

"Listen to you, you're really in love," Staci teased.

"Yes, I am, and I'm so grateful to God for giving us

another chance. I'm not going to do anything to mess this up," Shay proclaimed. "I'm so serious. This time around I will love him without crossing the line."

"I'm really happy for you and I know things are going to work out for you."

Shay detected an unusual sadness in Staci's voice, but let it pass. She was in the middle of telling them about her new car when her cell phone rang.

"Got to go, my boo's calling." Shay hung up without waiting for Staci and Taylor to say good-bye.

"Hey, handsome." Shay covered her mouth and wondered where the giggle came from.

"You sound happy."

"I am now that I'm talking to you."

"How was your flight?"

"Lonely."

"I miss you too."

The flirting proved too much for her to handle, being so far away from him. Right now she wanted to reach out and touch him. She changed the subject. "How's your mom?"

They laughed as Brian told her about Alysse faking a heart attack when she found out he didn't propose to Shay yet.

"Don't forget to email me a picture of my new car. It's a shame I won't get to drive it for another month and a half."

"Exactly when are you moving back?" he inquired.

"I might not. I might stay here for another year, that way I won't have to torture myself every day."

"If you don't come back, I'll come there. One way or another, you'll be with me," he stated, jokingly, but with enough seriousness for her to know he meant the statement.

"What makes you so sure of that?" Shay teased.

This time when he spoke, he wasn't laughing. She knew for certain that he meant what he said. "You're my woman and one day you'll be my wife."

How am I supposed to last two years without losing my mind?

"Baby, have you considered taking summer classes?" she voiced.

"No, but if you keep calling me 'baby' I might?"

"Oh really? Tell me what do I need to call you in order to get you to take night and weekend classes?"

He gave her a haughty laugh. "Sweetheart, you're crazy. You just keep being you and there's no telling what I'll do for you."

They talked for a few minutes longer then Shay unpacked and started studying for her finals.

***

Shay sat working on her laptop inside the café waiting for Jason and Rhonda. Once again she'd been paired with them for her final project. She'd just finished retrieving her daily prayer message from Brian when Jason pulled up a chair. He hadn't said much to her lately and his snide remarks, made within hearing range, seemed to be subsiding.

"LaShay." He nodded and opened his backpack.

"Hello, Jason, how are you?" She thought she read a smirk on his face and inwardly prayed Jason wouldn't give her a hard time.

"I'm fine. How are you?"

"I'm fine. Thanks for asking." Determined to limit their conversation to schoolwork, she proceeded, "How's the research coming?"

He pulled out a stack of papers from his book bag and handed them over to her. As she scanned the documents her peripheral vision caught sight of him staring intently at the silver heart that was once again around her wrist. Shay was halfway through the stack when his voice sounded, "How are things working out with Brian?"

She unsuccessfully tried to prevent the smile that instantly rested on her face. She only offered him a one-word answer though. "Good."

"I can tell by that cheesy grin on your face that you're happy. There's no chance of getting back together, is there?"

The slow movement of her head from side to side confirmed his assessment.

"Look, LaShay, I'm sorry about the way I've been treating

243

you these last couple of months. I've said some things about you that I'm not proud of, but at the time I felt justified. I really hope everything works out for you."

She felt his sincerity. "Thank you, Jason." She paused. "And, Jason, I'm really sorry for how I treated you. I shouldn't have entered into a relationship with you knowing I loved Brian. I definitely shouldn't have taken you home to meet the family to make him jealous."

Jason stared at her long and hard, then finally gave her a half-smile. "Apology accepted." He turned away and booted up his laptop. They worked in silence until Rhonda joined them ten minutes later.

CHAPTER 49

Brian checked the cell phone caller ID and reflectively motioned to throw the phone down, then withdrew his arm. It was Shannon—again. She'd called him numerous times while he was in Arizona, but he chose not to answer any of her calls. He wasn't avoiding Shannon; he just didn't have time for all the games she played. Accompanying Alysse to her chemo treatments for the six weeks following her surgery left him with little time for foolishness. Thankfully, for Brian, outside of the nausea and hair loss, his mother was handling her treatments well. He believed in his heart that any day now, Alysse would be cancer-free. But as for Shannon, he didn't know what he would have to do to be free of Shannon. The woman didn't understand English or sign language.

Even after he told her that he and Shay were officially dating, Shannon wouldn't let go.

"You said you were in love with her, but you still continued to see me," was what she told him during their last phone conversation.

"But I wasn't in a relationship with you. I was trying to be your friend."

"I'm trying to be yours too, but you keep pushing me away. I don't think that's fair. I was there when your precious Shay was running around with someone else, remember?" Shannon snapped.

Brian couldn't stand to hear anything negative about

Shay, particularly coming from Shannon. Shay wasn't perfect, but that didn't make her open game for Shannon.

"Look, Shannon, I'm sorry you got the wrong idea, but I doubt seriously that you and I can be friends, so let's end this mess right now."

"So you think I'm a mess? I wasn't a mess when you didn't have anyone else to talk to!" Shannon yelled so loud, Brian pulled the phone away and massaged his ear.

As irritating as Shannon was, he had to concede. In the beginning he did in fact use her to fill the space vacated by Shay. He acknowledged the error in doing so.

"Shannon, you're right. I did use you to feel the loneliness I felt when Shay left. For that I am sorry. But the fact still remains, Shay and I are in a relationship. I love her and one day I am going to marry her."

"Whatever, Brian!" she screamed and slammed the phone in his ear.

That was two days ago, now she was bugging him again. Against his better judgment, he answered, "What, Shannon?"

"Hey, Brian!" She sounded as if everything was perfect. "When are you returning home? I have something I want to give you."

"You have something for me?" he questioned.

"Yes, I do, just to prove that there aren't any hard feelings. So when are you coming home? I want to make sure I have everything ready."

His inner conscience told him not to give her an answer, but once again he went against his better judgment. He felt that little piece of information couldn't hurt. It wasn't like he was planning to invite her over for a visit. "I'll be home late Saturday afternoon," he finally answered.

"Good. Call me after you get settled," Shannon said cheerfully.

"What do you have for me, Shannon? I don't want any drama."

Her voice shifted from cheery to low and sultry. "I'm not

246

going to tell you, but trust me, it's something you'll never forget."

"Shannon—" she ended the call before he could finish his next question.

That evening, Brian skipped dinner, unable to shake the wave of nausea that settled on him since speaking with Shannon.

* * *

Shannon hung up on Brian and danced around her small living room. Victory was so close she could taste it. At first she'd considered giving up and walking away after Brian told her about his new *relationship*. But the more she thought about it, the more she realized this would be the perfect time to turn his focus back on her.

Last Sunday at church she'd overheard First Lady Pennington telling some of the members that Shay would be home in a couple weeks. Shannon had to move fast, if her plan was going to work. For three days straight, she'd parked her car down the block and watched Todd's in-and-out patterns. He was rarely there, which was a good thing.

This morning, she took a chance and checked under the huge potted plant near the front door and found exactly what she was looking for. No obstacle could stop her now. "Shannon Yates never gives up without a fight," she said to the reflection in the mirror.

CHAPTER 50

S hay paid the taxi driver and scurried upstairs to her apartment. She'd just finished returning the SUV her mother had leased for her. Now all she had to do was finish packing her personal items in the furnished apartment then she'd be headed back home to sunny California, her family and Brian. She looked around the small apartment and mentally reflected on the last twelve months of her life.

Overall, Massachusetts had been good to her. Just like she'd planned, she finished the credentialing program in twelve months in the top five percent of her class. She was excited and well-prepared to enter the wonderful world of educating young minds. She had gained a good friend in Rhonda. She didn't think it was possible for her and Jason to maintain a friendship considering how she treated him, but he vowed he'd send her an occasional e-mail.

When she arrived in Massachusetts, she was running away from God and her feelings for Brian. Now twelve months later, she was running to Brian and her relationship with God was stronger than she could ever remember.

Just thinking of Brian made her cheeks warm and her heart flutter. She missed him so much at night sleep eluded her as images of him collaged through her mind. The seven weeks since she'd left Arizona felt more like seven years. They talked every day and his voice was the last sound she heard before drifting off to sleep. Not a day went by that he didn't leave a prayer on her voice mail, but it wasn't the same as having him near and accessible.

It was nearly impossible, but she'd kept her return date a secret from him. She wanted to surprise him with a welcome home dinner on Saturday. She went into her bedroom and held the picture of Brian from his graduation. "Three more days, sweetheart," she said out loud then packed the picture away.

* * *

In the middle of doing laundry on Saturday morning, Shay's cell phone rang. Brian called again. A millisecond before she pressed the green answer call button, little Josiah burst into the laundry room. She let the call go to voicemail. Halfway through the mound of clothing, she went into the privacy of her bedroom and returned his call.

"Hey, beautiful," he answered.

"How are you, my semi-sweet chocolate drop?"

"Lonely for you, when are you coming home?" he whined.

She covered the mouthpiece in an effort to conceal the giggle from her voice. "You'll see me soon," she answered evasively.

"That's still too long," he whined again.

"If you think that's too long, waiting for you to finish law school will seem like an eternity."

Brian's heavy sigh sounded like static. "Don't remind me."

"What are you doing tonight?" Shay inquired, innocently.

"Nothing. My flight gets in at three o'clock. I was thinking about driving out to Blackhawk to see the folks, but that's about it."

"Oh." She had to convince him not to come to the house without arousing his curiosity. "Brian, I don't think it's a good idea for you to drive that far after your flight. I'm sure you're going to be exhausted."

"It's only a two-hour flight and the drive is only forty-five minutes."

"I know, but you have been working nonstop with your mother and I know you're mentally drained. Besides, I would feel better if you waited until you've had a chance to rest." Shay hoped she was persuasive enough.

"You win. I'll do what I'm told and go straight home. My stomach has been a little queasy and I do miss sleeping in my own bed."

"Now that's a good boy," Shay teased.

"You mean man, don't you?"

"Oh, most definitely."

CHAPTER 51

Brian walked into his home and exhaled his relief. Home at last. He'd been gone for eight weeks and although his mother needed him, he missed his space. He'd gotten used to the three-bedroom two-bath ranch-style house his father allowed him and Todd to live in while they attended school. After dropping his bags in the den, he went into the kitchen and opened the refrigerator and smiled when he saw it was fully stocked. "Thanks, Todd," he said, although he was there alone.

After pouring a glass of orange juice, he sat at the kitchen table and sorted through the pile of mail. Most of it he considered junk mail. He opened the utility bills and placed them in the accounting book he and Todd shared. He then went into the garage and started the washer. He unpacked the rest of his things while waiting for his clothes to complete the wash cycle.

On the way back to his room he noticed the box from the post office bearing his name and address, but no return address, in the den. He assumed the package was what Shannon referenced earlier in the week and decided he'd open it later. Inside his room, he prepared to take a long hot shower. Before undressing, he sat on the side of his bed and admired the framed picture he kept of Shay on the nightstand. He picked up the picture and outlined her face with his fingers. He instantly felt the familiar longing in his heart. "I love you so much," he whispered at the image.

He hadn't told her yet, but lately he'd been rethinking his two-year plan.

Every day he realized it was unrealistic to wait that long to take their relationship to the next level. But with him being a student, he didn't know what else to do. As a law student, he couldn't handle the financial responsibility of a wife. Shay was accustomed to the finer things in life and he wanted to continue to give her the best. He felt Shay deserved that. Shay never spent a day in her life wondering how her financial needs would be met and Brian didn't want her to start now. And what about children? He couldn't afford a child now anymore than he could have a year ago when they had the pregnancy scare. Letting the dilemma rest for now, Brian set the picture down and made a mental note to talk to his father about his predicament.

From his dresser drawer, he pulled out a pair of black boxers. He walked out into the hallway and grabbed a towel from the linen closet. Two steps back into his bedroom, Brian decided to retreat to the den and turned on the surround sound system, filling the house with a medley of his favorite gospel artists.

***

Shay drove her new Lexus down Interstate 580 like the piece of machinery was made just for her. With the V6 engine and more than 300 horsepower under the hood, she practically floated down the highway. She glanced down at the clock. It was five-thirty; right on schedule. She'd planned to have Brian's favorite Mexican meal of chicken enchiladas with Spanish rice and black beans, ready by six-thirty. She even baked him a lemon pound cake, which she tried unsuccessfully to hide from Reggie. "I'll bake you one tomorrow," she vowed to Reggie.

Reggie wasn't buying it. She had to cut him a slice to keep him from calling to tell Brian she was home. Just before she left the house, Reggie reminded her that she was expected to be home by midnight. That was part of the accountability system she worked out with Reggie and her mom to help her monitor how much time she and Brian spent alone.

Shay's heart fluttered when her exit came into view.

***

Shannon parked her car in the driveway then retrieved the spare key from under the potted plant and quietly entered the house. She had expected to see Brian as soon as she entered, but didn't. She knew he was there because the music was on and there was a light coming from a back room. She had never been inside so she took the opportunity to inspect the front of the house.

Although she couldn't cook, she was impressed with the large size of the kitchen and loved the bay window overlooking the city from the living room. She looked at the picture of Reggie and Julia on their wedding day sitting on the mantle and again wondered what was it about Julia Simone that made a man like Reginald Pennington love her so much. She really admired Julia, but she knew after tonight, Julia wouldn't like her at all. She would probably be banned from the church. That thought saddened her a bit, but she quickly pushed it to the back of her mind. Shannon loosened the belt on her trench coat and started down the hallway.

The closer she got to the light coming from the back of the house, she heard the shower. "This will be easier than I thought," she said and stepped inside of what she figured was Brian's room. The picture of Shay on the nightstand was a dead giveaway.

She rolled her eyes at the picture and proceeded to pull back Brian's bed covers. She had just finished unbuttoning her coat when the shower stopped.

***

Brian causally dried himself and dressed in his boxers while humming the words to the song playing. He stayed inside the bathroom and trimmed his goatee before stepping into his room. He took two steps and his heart nearly stopped.

CHAPTER 52

The driveway was full so Shay parked on the street in front of the house. She assumed the Ford Focus parked next to Brian's RAV4 belonged to Todd. She grabbed the two grocery bags and the cake from the trunk, then used her key to let herself into the house.

When she saw that the house was dark with the sound system blaring, she knew Brian was probably in his room asleep. He often slept to loud music. She decided to set things up in the kitchen before disturbing him.

***

"Shannon, what are you doing here?" Brian demanded.

Shannon didn't seem worried at all. She seductively let the trench coat fall to her feet revealing the black lace and satin camisole. Before she answered him, she climbed onto his bed.

"I'm waiting for you. I told you I had something for you." She licked her lips.

"Shannon, put your clothes on and get out!" he yelled.

"But, Brian, I've been a good friend to you." She crawled on her knees on his bed to him and ran her hand across his chest. "Don't you think it's time for you to be a good friend to me?"

Brian jumped away from her at her touch. His jaws flexed and his chest heaved rapidly. He felt the nausea returning, he was going to be sick and Shannon perched there grinning.

"Shannon, I'm only going to tell you once more. Put your clothes on and get out!"

"Brian, please, just make love to me this one time and I won't bother you again. You owe me that much," she said and lay on her back waiting for him to join her.

His nostrils flared and his eye twitched. "If you're not going to leave on your own, I'll throw you out." Brian picked her up just as Shay entered the room. At the sound of Shay's gasp, he turned around.

***

Time stood still as Shay looked from Brian's horrified expression to Shannon's smirk. There Brian stood nearly naked and in his arms was an equally undressed woman. The woman who Shay knew wanted Brian all to herself.

To Shay, it took her brain an eternity to tell her lungs to breathe again. "Br-Br-Brian?" she finally stuttered his name.

His mouth moved up and down, but no sound was made. When he didn't respond, tears streamed down Shay's face. Shay could only look at them a second longer before she felt like she was going to be sick. She turned and ran from the room.

Watching Shay run out on him unfroze Brian's faculties. He literally dropped Shannon on the floor, stepped over her and ran after Shay. When he caught up with her, she was running out the front door. "Shay, wait!" he called after her.

She didn't stop. Brian ran outside in his boxers and bare feet. He caught up with her at the end of the driveway.

"Shay, wait! It's not what you think!"

She pushed him against the bushes. "Don't touch me!" she screamed through tears and continued on to her car.

"Shay, please wait. Give me a minute to explain." He ran around to the driver's side.

Shay started the engine. "There is nothing to talk about! Stay away from me!"

Brian tried to open the car door, but she sped off, leaving him standing in the middle of the Campus Drive in nothing but his boxers.

Brian ran back inside. Shannon sat on his bed, like her actions hadn't turned his world upside down. Brian hurriedly threw on sweats and a pair of Nikes. Before he ran out, he glared at Shannon. This time his tone and his eyes were deadly. "When I get back you had better be gone!"

CHAPTER 53

Shay made it home safely only by the grace of God. The entire drive hot and heavy tears obstructed her vision. Wave after wave of nausea constantly rushed through her body as thoughts of Brian and Shannon being intimate flashed before her. She had to pull over twice on Interstate 680 to empty her stomach. When she pulled into the circular driveway at Blackhawk, she barely stopped the car before she opened the door and jumped out.

Reggie and Julia were sitting in the den watching television when Shay slammed the door and ran up the stairs wailing.

Julia stood to follow after her, but then Brian burst through the door.

"Where's Shay?" He was breathless.

Julia recognized the fear in Brian's eyes and knew something was very wrong. "What happened?"

Brian ignored the question. "Where did Shay go?"

"She's upstairs, but—" Julia started, but Brian couldn't wait.

In no time, he hiked the winding staircase two steps at a time and entered Shay's room. He found her in the adjourning bathroom leaning over the toilet bowl. He watched as she finished emptying the last of her stomach contents and for the heaving to stop. He waited for her to rinse her mouth and handed her a wet towel for her face.

"Brian, get out!" she finally yelled, without looking at him.

When he stepped out of the bathroom the crying started

261

all over again. This time tremors shook her body. When she finally stepped into her bedroom, he was still there; sitting on her bed.

"Brian, I told you to leave," she screamed.

He stood up. "Shay, I'm not leaving until you talk to me."

Shay turned to face him. "I don't have anything to say to you, not now, not ever!" He stepped toward her and reached for her arm. She snatched it away. "How could you do this to me?"

"Shay, sweetheart, I didn't do anything. I promise."

"I may have been stupid and naïve to fall in love with you, but I'm certainly not blind," she yelled.c"And don't call me 'sweetheart'."

Her words hurt, but he couldn't let it show, not now. "I know what it looked like, but, Shay, all you saw was me trying to take Shannon out of the house."

"What I saw was you carrying half-naked Shannon to your bed." Her voice quivered. "To the same bed that you shared with me." She pounded his chest repeatedly. "How could you? How could you even think of doing the same things to her that you did to me in the same bed?"

He didn't stop her from hitting him, but absorbed the blows without resistance. She inflicted more pain on her fist than she did to his steel-like torso. Frustrated and exhausted, she gave up and gave way to more tears. If she noticed the drops trailing down Brian's cheeks, she didn't show it.

"I dated Jason for six months and not one time did I remotely consider sharing my body with him." She held her index finger up for emphasis. "Not one time did I allow him to touch me intimately, because I didn't desire anyone but you. I can't believe I was so stupid." Then the thought came to her, "Is this your way of getting back at me for Jason? Is this the real reason why you wanted me to wait two years for you? So you could continue messing around with her? Have you been sleeping with Shannon the entire time?"

Brian shook his head as if to clear it. "Sweetheart, I—"

"I told you not to call me 'sweetheart' ever again," she snarled. "I hate you!"

Brian heaved and wiped his face. "Shay, I swear I have never slept with Shannon. I have never even had the desire to."

She stepped back and folded her arms. "So what were the two of you doing half-naked in your room?"

"When I came from the shower she was there. I don't even know how she got inside the house. When she wouldn't leave on her own, I picked her up, but only to put her out, not take to her to bed. Shay, I promise that's what happened."

Brian's gentle and sincere tone tore into her resolve, but she hid the effect.

Brian's lips moved as if he were praying as he stepped closer to her. "Shay, you know me. I love you and I would never hurt you like this. I have never lied to you."

Shay lowered her head so she couldn't see the tears in Brian's eyes.

"You're the only woman I want and the only woman I desire. Please, you have to believe me." He held his arms open to her as he'd done countless times in the past.

Shay felt that familiar tug in her heart. She wanted to believe him. She wanted to run into his arms and forgive him. She would have if an image of Brian and Shannon in bed together and the smirk on Shannon's face hadn't flashed before her eyes. She immediately stiffened.

"Get out!"

"Shay—" Brian tried to put his hands on her shoulders, but she pushed him away.

"Don't ever touch me again. Don't ever speak to me again."

"But—"

"Stay out of my life." She released the clasp on her wrist. "I don't want you and I don't want this!" she screamed and threw the silver heart he had given her at him. He caught it just before it hit him in the face. She quickly turned away from him, ignoring the hurt in his eyes.

***

Brian stood there for a moment praying she would change her mind. He waited for her to turn back around and tell him she really didn't mean what she had just said. He waited for her to yell or hit him again, anything that would make things go back to the way they were. Shay didn't do any of that.

Finally, he stepped close behind her and whispered in her ear. "No matter what you may think, I love you. I will always love you."

On his way out, Brian laid the silver chain on her dresser. When she heard the door close, Shay fell onto her bed and cried until she couldn't cry anymore.

On the other side of the door, Brian cried tears of his own. Between his sobs, he heard Shay's and that made him hurt more. But as long as she shut him out, there wasn't anything he could do about it. He couldn't comfort her against her will. Before he composed himself enough to go downstairs to face his father and Julia, he prayed for Shay's heart to soften and heal. He prayed she'd reopen her heart and let him back in.

Julia and Reggie waited anxiously in the kitchen. Both were pacing.

Julia didn't waste any time. "Brian, what's going on?"

Brian sat down at the table and rubbed his forehead and tried to calm the storm raging within him. He didn't speak.

"Brian, what happened tonight?" Reggie's voiced bordered on frustration and irritation.

Brian took a deep breath and began the horrid details. "Shay walked in on me in my bedroom—with Shannon." He hung his head down, not daring to look his father in the face.

Julia's cappuccino skin turned red and she fought with everything in her to keep from lashing out at Brian. Fighting to gain control of her anger, she stood and leaned over the sink.

In all the time he'd known his father, Brian had never

264

heard him yell outside of preaching. Tonight that would change.

"What was Shannon doing at the house and why on earth was she in your bedroom?" Reggie yelled.

Brian swallowed hard and summoned the strength to meet his father's gaze. "Dad, I honestly don't know how she got inside the house. All I know is when I came out of the shower there she was in my room, barely dressed."

Julia whirled around. "Exactly what did Shay walk in on?"

"I told Shannon to leave, but she wouldn't. I was going to physically put her out." Brian swallowed hard again. "When Shay walked in that's what I was trying to do. I had picked Shannon up and I was about to carry her outside. That's the truth."

Julia didn't say a word, just turned and faced the sink again.

Reggie had no problem voicing his anger. "How did Shannon know you were home?"

Brian thought back to the conversation he'd had with her earlier in the week. "I told her I would be home today."

Reggie banged his fists on the table and Brian and Julia jumped. "How many times have I told you to limit your communication with Shannon? How many times have I told you to watch her? Telling her when you will be home is like giving her an invitation!"

Brian hurt even more now because this was the first time he had disappointed his father. His whole world was crumbling right before his eyes. The woman he loved had just ended their relationship and now Mama J was so angry that she couldn't stand to look at him. Brian lowered his head again in an attempt to hide the tears he felt threatening to escape.

"Hold your head up!" Reggie ordered.

Finally, with much effort he looked his father in the eye. "Dad, I'm sorry. You're right I shouldn't have told her my plans. But the truth is, I didn't invite her in. She was there when I came out of the shower, barely dressed with my bed linens turned back. I had no intentions, and still don't, of sleeping with Shannon. Please, Dad, you have to believe me."

Reggie studied Brian's face as if searching for the truth. One thing Brian wasn't was a liar. But his disobedience may have cost him his relationship with Shay. "I take it Shay didn't believe you?"

Brian shook his head. "No, she didn't." He couldn't say anymore without breaking down.

CHAPTER 54

Julia knew Brian told the truth. She knew Brian and she knew Shannon. Julia was well aware Shannon only attended church for Brian's benefit and hadn't changed much. But that knowledge didn't remove the pain she felt for her daughter. Julia was smart and a woman, therefore, she knew how women thought. She listened as Reggie and Brian tried to figure out how Shannon gained access to the house. Todd wouldn't have let her in under any circumstances. She finally turned around and asked, "Brian, do you still keep an emergency key underneath the planter out front?"

Brian's facial expression answered her question. She unfolded her arms and walked over to Brian and placed her hand on his shoulder. She spoke friendly, but stern, "Brian, I love you, but you had better clean up this hot mess you've helped create—fast." Julia stormed from the kitchen to go check on her daughter.

She found Shay lying across her bed, shaking. She discarded the used tissues and lay down next to her. Shay didn't say a word; she just cuddled under her mother like she used to do when she was a little girl. Julia stroked her hair while Shay released a fresh batch of tears.

"Mama, how could he do this to me?" Shay asked between sniffles.

"Honey, are you sure he did something wrong?"

Shay raised her head and looked at her mother's face. "I know what I saw."

Julia was careful with her. "What did you see?"

"I saw Brian about to have sex with Shannon," Shay stated unequivocally

"Did you *see* them in bed together?"

"No, but he was carrying her to his bed."

This is just how the devil works, in illusion and delusion, Julia thought. It was pointless to try and convince Shay otherwise. Right now, Shay wasn't open to reason. Julia didn't ask any more questions. Instead she sang Shay's favorite song to her until she fell asleep.

The following morning after Julia finished her meditation time, she checked on Shay. "Baby, it's time to get up, if you're going to make service." Julia sat on the bed and brushed hair strands from Shay's face.

Shay moaned and stretched then frowned.

You look so much like your father when you do that."

Shay groaned. "Mama, you always say I act or look like my father when I act crazy or do something stupid."

Julia giggled softly. "Baby, every day and all day long, you look like Sean Hampton spat you out. I just provided the incubation. As for your craziness, I have to blame that on somebody, why not him?"

Shay grinned at her mother passing the buck, and then sobered. "Mom, I don't feel like going to church today. I want to stay here in this room forever."

"Shay, I think you should come to church with us. Praising God always makes me feel better when I'm burdened."

Shay turned away from her mother. Just the mention of God made Shay want to cry. How could she tell her mother she believed Brian's betrayal was God's way of punishing her for committing fornication? "Mama, if I feel better, I'll be there."

"I remember how it feels to have a broken heart so I won't push the issue." She did say a quick prayer before she left.

Shay tried to fall back to sleep, but the cell phone disturbed her solace. She looked at the numbers on her alarm clock and identified the caller. It was Brian. He always called her at eight o'clock to pray and wish her a good day. The beep sounded indicating she had a new message. She waited a few minutes before checking her voicemail.

Shay, I'm so sorry that you are hurting right now and that I'm the cause of that pain. If I could change the last twenty-four hours, I would. But I can't. Shay, I told you the truth, nothing happened. I don't want Shannon. I only want you. I love you, always.

Before erasing the message, Shay listened to the daily prayer he left for her.

***

Brian stared at the phone in his hand then placed it back on his nightstand. No surprise to him, Shay was avoiding him. He lay back on his bare mattress and tried to figure out how things took a turn for the worse so fast. He was angry with Shannon for her role in the whole mess. When he returned home last night, she was nowhere to be found. But he was also angry with himself for getting involved with her in the first place. His father was right; he should have ended his association with her long ago, especially after the stunt she'd pulled at her apartment. But he hadn't and now he would have to pay for it. By his calculation, the price was way too high for the offense.

Brian punched the pillow and reflected back to the conversation he'd had with his father in Arizona. *I can wait for Shay because I know she was created just for me.* In the weeks to come, those words would be his only consolation. He would find out if he really meant them or not.

CHAPTER 55

Julia stared out of the twenty-fifth-floor office window at the Golden Gate and Bay Bridges like she'd done countless times before, in hopes of finding an answer to her problems. The rolling movement of the sky-blue waves on the water always seemed to bring her peace, but not today. As founder and CEO of Pinnacle Developments, Julia was accustomed to handling problems with architects and building contractors and tenacious inspectors, but that was nothing compared to the problems she now faced at home.

It was hard, but she and Reggie had managed to keep Shannon's fiasco from Alysse and the rest of the family. If Alysse knew the stunt she'd pulled, Shannon would be on the run for the rest of her life.

Three weeks had passed since Shay and Brian's breakup and despite praying daily, sometimes three times a day, nothing appeared to be changing. With each passing day, maintaining a neutral position became more difficult. She couldn't understand why Shay was so bent on believing the worst about Brian. No matter what approach Julia took, Shay wouldn't listen to reason. In Julia's opinion, Shay knew Brian better than anyone. Shay knew Brian was not a devious and deceitful person. Brian had always been honest. True, he was a little naïve when it came to women and relationships. To be honest, Brian was just plain ignorant when it came to any female besides Shay. But he was always honest. Besides that, he loved the very ground Shay walked on.

Lately, Julia could barely stand to look at Brian, he was so pitiful. He didn't have his bright smile anymore and she hadn't seen his trademark left dimple in days. Even his laughter had vanished. Nowadays, when Brian bothered to visit the house, he moped around, looking defeated and depressed. It was just a matter of time before his personal life would start to affect his school performance.

Shay didn't fare any better. Most of the time she moped around the house like a zombie or hibernated inside her bedroom. The other day she was washing dishes, but was too distracted to pay attention to what she was doing. She absentmindedly picked up the roast Julia had cooked for dinner and started washing it. When Reggie and Julia finally got her attention, she threw the Angus beef down and ran upstairs crying. She spent the rest of the evening in her room.

However, Shay did go to church. She didn't sit in the front like Reggie and Julia wanted because she didn't want to look at or be next to Brian. She sat in the back and didn't participate in the service, but at least she was there.

Yesterday when Brian came over for Sunday dinner, Shay wouldn't even look at him, let alone speak to him. He brought her flowers, which she promptly threw in the trash. During dinner, if Brian asked her to pass him a dish, she ignored him. When she wanted something, even if Brian was the closest one to it, she'd ask her mother or Reggie. She even asked Josiah for the pitcher of lemonade, knowing he'd probably spill it.

Halfway through dinner, Reggie grew tired of dancing around them and pushed his plate back. "I've had enough of this," he said before he left the table. Julia, feeling his frustration, followed after him.

Inside their bedroom, Julia snuggled against Reggie on their bed. She was determined not to let the lives of their children create a wedge between her and her husband. Eventually, Brian and Shay would move on with their lives, but what Julia shared with Reggie was solid, stable and satisfying.

The intercom buzz brought her thoughts back to the business at hand.

"Ms. Julia, there's someone here to see you," her assistant, Michelle, said.

Julia glanced down at her appointment schedule; she didn't have anyone scheduled until the afternoon. "Who is it, Michelle?"

"The young lady says she attends your church."

True Worship currently had over three thousand members on the roll. Julia had no idea who the young lady could be, but if she was a member of True Worship, Julia would definitely make time for her. "Go ahead and send her in." Julia sat at her desk and waited.

Nothing could have prepared Julia for her surprise visitor. The welcoming smile disappeared from her face and she quickly had to pray for control over her temper. She remained quiet as the young lady adjusted herself in one of the guest chairs and took note of her grim demeanor. The young lady looked like she hadn't slept in days and her usual sophisticated conceit had vanished.

"Hello, Pastor Julia," the young lady said, with her head lowered and in a voice barely audible.

"Shannon," Julia responded dryly, not moved by her humble demeanor. "What are you doing here?"

"I know you don't want to see me, but I really need to talk to you." Shannon's voice shook. Her entire body shook.

Julia leaned back in her executive chair and folded her arms. "Shannon, what could you possibly have to say to me after the way you've hurt my family?"

Unexpected tears and whimpers poured from Shannon. "That's why I'm here. I'm so sorry for what I did. I didn't mean to do it."

Once again, her tears didn't move Julia. "Didn't mean to do what? You didn't mean to break into my house? Or, you didn't mean to fail at seducing Brian?" Julia asked sarcastically.

"Ms. Julia, I'm so sorry for everything."

Julia stood and planted her palms on her mahogany desk. "Look, Shannon, you may be sorry, and you very well should be, but I still don't want you in my office. Now leave."

The whimpers escalated into sobs with pleading. "Please, Ms. Julia, I need you to help me. I don't have anyone else to turn to."

For whatever reason Julia began to feel sorry for the girl. The sight before her gave new definition to the word pitiful. She slid the box of tissue across the desk to Shannon. "Lord, I really don't need this drama," Julia grumbled while she waited for Shannon to compose herself. "What's really going on, Shannon?" Julia asked and sat down, not really caring about the answer.

Shannon sniffled a few times and blew her nose once more. "Ms. Julia, I'm here because you're the only person I know who can help me."

"Shannon, I am not a psychiatrist," Julia said flatly.

"But you are everything I want to be."

Her answer caught Julia by surprise and left her speechless. After using her hand to close her gaping mouth, Julia leaned forward with her chin resting on her fist.

Shannon continued talking, but kept her eyes glued to the floor. "Pastor Julia, I knew from the beginning that going after Brian was a mistake. He never liked me and to be honest, I never really wanted him. I only wanted the things I thought he could give me. It didn't matter to me that he constantly turned me down, because I'm used to that. Rejection is normal for me. All my life I have been trained to use and manipulate people in order to get what I want. But now I want more."

Julia leaned back, still resistant. "Shannon, what does that have to do with me?"

Shannon finally looked her in the eye. "Everything. I've watched how your presence demands respect. I like how you carry yourself, with respect. You've figured out a way to get what you need without using your body or people. That's what I want to learn. I've seen how Pastor Pennington's face lights up when he sees you. He cherishes you. I had never seen love in a positive light until I saw the two of you together. At first I wanted Brian for financial and material reasons, but after watching you, I wanted Brian to do for me what Pastor Pennington does for you. I thought tricking him into getting me pregnant was the way to accomplish that."

"I watched your family at Marcus's CD recording and I was dumbfounded by the way everyone accepted each other, no matter the color of their skin and it didn't matter if they were skinny or fat. My family has always made me feel inferior because of my dark skin and my kinky short hair. That's why I wear so much makeup and all this hair." She pulled on her blonde tresses, then took a deep breath before she continued. "Do you remember that day you approached me after service? You know the day after I met Brian's mother?"

It didn't take much effort for Julia to remember because she recalled telling the Lord that day also that she didn't want to deal with Shannon's drama. "Yes, I do."

"Well, that day," Shannon continued, "was the first time anyone, including my mother, had given me advice that didn't involve being deceitful or taking advantage of another person. That was also the first time anyone had ever said a kind word to me after I had offended them. That gesture alone showed me that it's possible for people to still care for one another after they'd done something wrong. To this day, my family holds everything I've ever done wrong over my head."

Shannon played with the used tissue in her hand. "Pastor Julia, I'm here because I realize that I need help. I don't like the person I have become. I'm tired of spinning my wheels and getting nowhere. I'm tired of hiding behind makeup and tracks. I don't know who I am or what I like anymore. Please,

Pastor Julia, you've got to show me how to change. I promise, I'm for real this time."

Julia watched Shannon cry with tears in her own eyes. For the first time she saw the real Shannon. She wasn't some evil person, but a wounded little girl trying to find her way. The anger she felt earlier dissipated and all she now felt was compassion. It wasn't going to be easy and it would take a while, but she had to help Shannon.

"Shannon, let's pray," Julia said and walked around to where Shannon sat. She was about to take her hands in hers, but at the last second took Shannon in her arms. Julia sensed her need for comfort and acceptance. *Lord, what am I getting myself into?* Julia wondered when Shannon gripped her firmly.

CHAPTER 56

Shay rolled over and punched the off button on her alarm clock. It was six-thirty in the morning, time to get up. Although she tossed and turned all night, she was determined to restart her daily exercise routine today. Since her breakup with Brian, she had not been in the mood to do much of anything. The decline in her appetite was the only thing that kept her a size-ten.

Last night she made a decision: It was time for her to move on with her life without Brian. She wasn't going to spend another day crying over Brian Pennington. He represented the past. She was ready for the future. As an attractive twenty-five-year-old woman, with a Master's degree in education, her whole life was ahead of her. It was time for her to start living her life. After her workout she would look for a job.

By nine o'clock Shay had completed a vigorous workout, showered and was dressed. She didn't bother to check her voicemail, knowing Brian had made his daily call to her. She didn't trust him anymore, but his tenacity impressed her. In the two months since the demise of their short courtship, not one day went by that he didn't call her and pray for her and he never ended the call without declaring his love for her. Today she didn't want to hear that. She still loved him very much, but it was time for her to move on.

She rummaged through her jewelry box in search of her gold-studded earrings. She almost lost her newfound liberation when her hands touched the silver heart Brian had given her last Christmas. "Why can't I throw this in the trash?" she grumbled and instantly felt the empty space she had for Brian in her heart. No matter how hard she tried, she couldn't bring herself to throw the heart or anything else he had given her away. She held the heart in the palm of her hand, remembering the good times, until her cell phone rang.

She put on her happy voice after reading the caller ID. "Hey, cousin." It was her cousin, Staci.

"What are you doing?"

"Getting dressed then I'm going to look for a job."

"It's about time, you spoiled brat," Staci teased.

Shay rolled her eyes as if Staci could see her. "Now isn't that the cat calling the kettle black. Stop acting like your daddy didn't buy you a new Mercedes when you graduated, then sent you on a trip to Europe."

"Don't be hatin'. Anyway, I was wondering if you wanted to go shopping with me this weekend."

Shay twisted her mouth as she weighed the invitation. Maybe a shopping trip would do her some good. Besides, she planned on starting work soon and could use some career clothes. "That sounds good. Where did you have in mind?"

"Union Square."

"I'm in. Let's meet at my mother's office building at nine o'clock. You can leave your car in the garage."

"Sounds good to me," Staci agreed.

The first cousins talked for a few minutes longer about nothing in particular. After she hung up, Shay went online and looked for a job. She inquired about a few positions then checked her e-mail.

"Leave me alone!" Shay screamed at the computer after she opened a message from Brian with an attached picture of them taken the night before Alysse's surgery. The message said he missed her and couldn't wait until they would share more good times together. Shay didn't want any more good times with Brian, however, she didn't delete the picture.

Saturday afternoon Shay laughed and cracked jokes with

her cousin as they went from store to store collecting bags. It was the first time she'd been out of the house, except to go to church and it felt good. It was nice to enjoy life again without Brian's presence. If she could remove him from her thoughts, life would be great.

"Thanks," Shay said to Staci while they sat in a booth at the Cheesecake Factory for lunch.

Staci gave her a half-smile. "For what?"

"For reminding me what it feels like to live," Shay answered.

***

Staci studied her cousin. Shay was two years younger, but they were alike in many ways. Staci knew about her and Brian's breakup; she didn't know the all the details, but she knew Shay was devastated. She also knew that Shay loved Brian with all of her heart.

Staci had been trying to summon up the nerve to talk to Shay since the night of Marcus's CD recording. She had put their talk off because of how painful it would be for both of them. But after hearing of the breakup, Staci knew she had to speak up. Watching Shay all afternoon solidified her decision to have a heart-to-heart talk with her cousin and friend.

Sure, on the outside, Shay appeared happy as she tried on numerous outfits and endless pairs of shoes. Shay tried to hide her emptiness, but Staci didn't miss the sadness that adorned Shay's face every time they passed by a couple shopping together or when they passed by a men's clothing store.

"Shay, that's why I asked you to come with me today," Staci started, "I want to talk to you."

The look in Staci's eyes told Shay this was going to be a serious discussion. She leaned forward and gave Staci her undivided attention. "What's going on?"

Staci took a deep breath. "Shay, why are you and Brian no longer together?"

Shay sat back against the booth. "Because he's a liar and

a cheat and I don't trust him," Shay answered defensively, rolling her eyes and neck. "Is there anything else you would like to know?"

Staci would not be deterred by Shay's attitude. "Shay, I know Brian and so do you. One thing he's not is a liar and he loves you too much to cheat on you."

Shay rolled her eyes again. "What's love got to do with it?"

"Did you actually catch him cheating?"

"Not exactly, but he was about to."

"How do you know that for sure?" Staci pressed.

Shay remained quiet, momentarily. She really didn't know for sure. "All I know is I caught him undressed in his bedroom with Shannon who was just as naked as he was. He wasn't expecting me, so for all I know they could have been sleeping together for months."

Staci placed her arms on the table and interlocked her hands. "Shay, I have something I want to share with you. I should have told you this earlier, but I didn't have the courage. What I'm about to tell you, I have only told to one other person. That person is my mother and I didn't tell her until long after it happened."

"I'm listening." Shay's voice was so soft, Staci wasn't sure if she had heard her.

"I understand why you ran off to Harvard after you and Brian had been intimate and I understand why you now feel you can't trust him."

Staci expected Shay to interrupt, but she didn't. Staci took another deep breath and continued. "Before Derrick and I broke up last year, we had been intimate also. After the first time, I felt so guilty that I vowed never to do it again, but I couldn't stop myself. I loved Derrick and still do. Having sex with him felt so wonderful, but it destroyed my spirit. Not only that, I lost confidence in myself to make sound decisions. I lost trust in myself and because of that I couldn't trust anyone else, not even Derrick. The worst part being that I thought God wouldn't forgive me."

Shay's eyes instantly began to water. Staci was speaking

what she had been feeling for over a year. "How did you handle it?"

Staci took a sip of water and swallowed hard. "Shay, that's my point. I didn't handle it. I made a complete mess of the situation and lost Derrick in the process."

"What happened?"

Staci's eyes misted. "I got pregnant."

Shay's eyes bulged, but Staci continued talking. "When I found out I was pregnant, I was so ashamed and angry. I was ashamed because the evidence of my hidden sin was about to be thrust into full view. I was angry with myself because I wasn't able to control my reckless behavior. I felt the pregnancy was God's way of punishing me for repeatedly having sex with Derrick and breaking my vow to Him."

"There were so many emotions I felt like I was being tossed in every direction. Anger, guilt, shame and resentment controlled me. Unfortunately, I allowed those emotions to cloud my sound judgment." Staci wiped her cheeks before continuing. "Shay, I made the biggest mistake of my life. I had an abortion." Staci's voice quivered. "I didn't even tell Derrick about it until after the procedure."

"Derrick didn't know about the baby?" Shay questioned.

"Oh no, he knew about the baby, but he didn't know about the abortion. In fact, he was excited about the baby. He said he wanted to get married right away, but because I didn't trust myself, I couldn't trust him. Oh, I believed he loved me, but in my eyes, he broke the commitment he made to God by sleeping with me. If he could do that, there was nothing to prevent him from breaking a promise to me."

"When I told him about the abortion, he was devastated. That's why we broke up. He couldn't get over the fact that I ended the life of our child." Staci paused and cried softly. "He was willing to do whatever he had to in order to support me and his child, but I couldn't trust him. I didn't understand that he was carrying just as much guilt as me."

"Shay, the reason I couldn't trust him was because I hadn't

forgiven myself for yielding to temptation. God had forgiven me, but I didn't receive God's forgiveness. I avoided God as if I could really hide from Him. The few times I did communicate with the Lord, I treated Him as if He were a stranger, instead of the loving father that He is. It was only after I was able to accept God's forgiveness and forgive myself that I was able to heal. I am healed now, but I lost Derrick and I ended the life of my unborn child before I was able to let go of the shame and guilt."

Shay looked as if she would keel over any moment, so Staci moved closer to her.

"Shay, as soon as you forgive yourself and get back into real fellowship with God, you'll see things differently. You'll understand that God is loving and merciful. He doesn't hold our mistakes over our heads like we do one another. He loves us no matter what. Shay, God loved you before you got into Brian's bed. While you were enjoying the way Brian made you feel, God still loved you. And after you finished, God still loved you. He didn't like what you did, but that didn't change His love for you. Now, He's just waiting for you to bring Him your guilt and shame. He can handle it, but you can't."

Staci watched as tears flowed down Shay's face. "And do you know what?"

Shay couldn't speak so she just shook her head from side to side.

"God knew I was going to mess up before I did. He knew I wasn't as strong as I had professed to be. He knew that when the moment presented itself, I would yield. Even knowing that, God didn't give up on me. When I messed up, He didn't give up on me. He just waited for me to ask for forgiveness and to realize how much I really need Him."

Shay couldn't take any more; she leaned on Staci's shoulder and cried hard sobs. Staci had managed to speak everything Shay had been holding inside of her for the past year. She had been using the episode with Brian and Shannon to cover up her inner struggles. It wasn't that she didn't trust Brian, she didn't trust herself. Deep down, she felt she deserved to have Brian cheat on her since she had cheated on God. But Brian didn't cheat on her; in her heart she knew that. Even if he had, she loved him enough to forgive him. Brian loved her. He proved that to her every day, even though she wouldn't speak to him or acknowledge his presence.

Shay finished crying then made the most important decision in her life. She was going back to her first love: God—wholeheartedly. This time it would be different. She would open up to Him completely. She'd been praying and reading her Bible, but she wasn't completely in fellowship with Him. To be honest, she'd been afraid to walk in true fellowship with Him since the night she gave her virtue away. Shay had been walking on eggshells, expecting His wrath to fall. Things will be different now. She was different.

Back at the garage, before Staci got out of the car, Shay gave her one of those, girl-you-know-you-just-saved-my-life hugs.

"I love you, cuz," they almost said in unison.

"Do you think you and Derrick will get back together?"

"I don't know," Staci answered sullenly. "We haven't talked in a while."

"You know, every gone is not good-bye." Shay smiled.

Staci narrowed her eyes. "You remember that when it comes to Brian."

CHAPTER 57

S hay was dressed and ready for church before both Reggie and her mother. She decided to wear one of the new suits she had purchased the day before since she was starting a new life. After lightly applying her makeup and inserting a pair of small silver hoop earrings, she clasped the silver heart around her wrist without a second thought.

Like clockwork, her cell phone sounded at eight o'clock sharp. Today, she smiled when she heard Brian's ringtone, but she didn't answer the phone. She had more important business to take care of first.

"There's no need for us to take two cars. Why don't you ride with us?" Reggie suggested as the family prepared to leave for church.

To Reggie and Julia's surprise, Shay quickly agreed and climbed into the backseat of Reggie's Mercedes. Shay hummed all the way to church.

Reggie and Julia exchanged hopeful glances, but neither commented.

This Sunday morning Shay walked straight to the front center row where she belonged. As the Praise and Worship ministry went forth, Shay stood with her hands raised and her eyes closed. The congregation went forth in song, but Shay held a private talk with Jesus. As the tears began to flow, she got down on her knees with her hands still raised. It didn't matter to her that she was a member of the leading family or that she was in the front where everyone could see her. She was completely unashamed in her worship.

Shay felt God's presence deep down in her being. She felt God's love fill her heart with peace like she'd never known. God's presence overwhelmed her to the point all she could do was lie there and allow Him to heal her in every place she hurt.

When Shay was finally able to stand and walk back to her seat, she felt an abundance of joy. She sat on her front row seat smiling and laughing for reasons unbeknownst to everyone, but her. It was like her and God were sharing an inside joke.

The choir finished singing "I'm Healed" and Shay did something she had never done before. She danced in the spirit.

Shay practically ran onto the dais after the benediction and nearly knocked Reggie off balance when she hugged him and kissed his cheek.

"Thanks, Dad, for everything. I enjoyed the message so much, I took two pages of notes."

"Wow, I'm glad to see you're excited again," Reggie responded, displaying his left dimple.

Shay then embraced her mother so tightly that Julia was winded. "I love you, Mama," she whispered in Julia's ear. "Did I look like my daddy today, while I was dancing and praising?"

"No, baby, that was all my genes."

Shay would have held onto her longer, but Josiah pulled her skirt. "What about me?" He held his little arms out to her.

She laughed at her little brother. "I can never forget about you." She squatted and gave him a bear hug.

"Where's Brian?" Shay asked as her eyes scanned the crowded sanctuary.

"Check in my office," Reggie suggested and continued greeting his congregants, but Shay read his optimism about them reconciling.

Brian was just about to put on his suit jacket when Shay

walked into Reggie's office. A smile instantly creased his face and he laid his jacket across a chair.

She matched his smile with one of her own as she walked over to him. When she was directly in front of him and about two feet separated them, he reached his arms out to embrace her, but she prevented him and caught his hands in hers.

She looked deep into his eyes and spoke sincerely. "Brian, I am so sorry for not trusting you. Please forgive me. I love you."

He responded by wrapping his arms around her and pressing her close to him. She laid her head against his chest and listened to his heartbeat. She began to cry when she felt his tears graze her forehead and slide down her face.

"My Shay, I love you so much," he said repeatedly as he held her and stroked her hair.

Reggie stepped into his office then quietly retreated when he saw the two of them.

***

Brian and Shay walked through the church's parking lot hand in hand. Neither of them could stop smiling.

"Brian, Shay, can I speak to you for a moment?"

They turned around to find a young lady of dark complexion, about five-foot-two-inches tall and very petite. Her eyes were dark brown and she wore her black hair in a short sassy flip cut. Her modest makeup complimented her natural features well. She was conservatively dressed in a dark-gray pantsuit.

"Please, it'll only take a minute," the young lady pressed.

Both Brian and Shay looked at each other with puzzled expressions.

"I'm sorry, Miss, but you must have us mixed up with someone else," Brian said and turned to walk away, but Shay kept her eyes on the young lady. She knew her from somewhere.

"Brian, it's me, Shannon."

Brian turned around and looked at her with amazement. "Shannon? That's you?"

"I knew you looked familiar!" Shay exclaimed.

Shannon lowered her head. "Yes, it's me. This is the *real* me without the makeup, tracks, long decorative nails and colored contacts."

"You look nice," Shay said sincerely.

Shannon fidgeted, like she felt uncomfortable when the two kept gawking at her. "Look, guys, I wanted to apologize to the both of you for-um-my-um-I want to apologize for all of the problems I caused between the two of you. Shay, nothing happened between Brian and me. He really loves you and I hope things work out for you guys."

Brian was speechless.

"Thank you, Shannon," Shay said. "I accept your apology. I know it took a lot for you to say that."

Then as quickly as she appeared, Shannon disappeared.

"Talk about the difference between night and day," Brian said, shaking his head as he continued toward his vehicle.

Brian closed his car door then gave Shay a soft gentle peck on her lips.

"Why did you do that?"

"It's been three months, ten days and eighteen hours since I've been this close to you. I need a shot in the arm." He smiled.

She tilted her head, and asked, "How are those night and weekend classes coming?" She then kissed him back.

Back at the house, Reggie was so happy to see Brian and Shay together again that he offered to do the Sunday dinner dishes. Brian and Shay took advantage of the free time and did something they should have done a long time ago. They talked—really talked.

As they walked around the lake behind the Blackhawk estate, they learned a lot about each other. They were surprised to learn that they both struggled with the same guilt-ridden feelings about their sexual impurity. They expressed their fears and their ambitions. She told him the things she liked about him and the things she felt he needed to work on. He did the same for her. At the top of his list was trust.

"Why didn't you trust me?" Brian stopped walking and collected Shay's hands in his. "Shay, you have been a constant fixture in my life since the day we met. You probably know me better than I know myself. You finish my sentences and speak my thoughts faster than I can voice them. We feel each other's pain. True, I should have leveled with you about really being in love with you," he pointed at her, "but you *know* me. Tell me you honestly didn't know I have loved you from the beginning. Tell me you didn't know it that first night we made love. Tell me you didn't feel it."

"I did feel it. Truth be told, I've always felt it," Shay admitted, blinking back tears. "Haven't you?"

Brian nodded. "Yes. Then why didn't you trust me when I told you nothing happened with Shannon? I believed you when you said nothing happened with Jason. You were over two-thousand miles away from me and all I had was your word. That was enough for me."

Shay used her hand, still encased by his, to wipe her cheek. "After committing fornication with you I didn't trust myself anymore. We traveled into forbidden territory together. Something we both vowed to God we would never do. I didn't trust my own judgment anymore. I couldn't trust you."

"I had the same struggle in the beginning, but my love for you never wavered. I do love you, Shay, and I would never purposefully hurt you. If I thought for a second that I desired another woman, I'd end our relationship before cheating on you."

The pure love radiating from Brian burned Shay's soul. It was at that moment she knew without a doubt, Brian would be hers forever. Resting her head against his chest and enjoying the feel of his immense arms enveloping her, Shay felt safe and secure. She felt blessed.

At the end of the three-mile walk, they had a clear

understanding of each other's feelings and expectations, something they never had before. They even set boundaries for themselves in regards to upholding biblical principles on premarital sex. They both agreed not to place themselves in situations that would leave them vulnerable to sexual sin again. Back at the house they continued talking in the den into the wee hours of the morning.

Julia came downstairs at six o'clock the next morning to find Shay stretched out on the couch asleep. Brian was asleep too, on the floor next to the couch. "Thank you, Jesus," she whispered and placed covers over them and went into her study for her daily meditation time.

CHAPTER 58

Thanksgiving Day found the Pennington house packed to capacity. Four of Julia's siblings and their families along with Reggie's family, plus Tyrone and Nikki joined them for the holiday. Alysse had completed her chemotherapy treatments and was well enough to travel. So when Brian called, she went and bought a new wig and made arrangements to come.

Shay was surprised when Taylor and Staci showed up at the front door. She'd just spoken to them the day before and neither of them mentioned coming over for dinner. Justin and Leah drove up from Los Angeles. She wondered why they didn't just stop at their grandparents' home in the San Fernando Valley, instead of driving four-hundred miles for a home-cooked meal. She wondered the same thing about her uncle Jonathan flying in from Arizona, but didn't bother mentioning it. The Simones were known for traveling at the drop of a dime.

Shay and her family mingled to the sounds of Ben Tankard. Everyone acted a little strange, especially her mother and Alysse. They wouldn't let her out of their sight and Reggie had a permanent smile on his face. Her aunts took turns asking what her plans were for the near future. Her uncle Carey, Marcus's father, kept hugging her and telling her how she wasn't his little Shay-Shay anymore. Auntie Nikki walked past her on several occasions and just shook her head, and said, "Girl, I remember the day you were born."

She didn't notice anything strange about Brian's behavior though. Since their reconciliation three weeks ago, a permanent grin branded his face. She hadn't seen much of him in the last two weeks because he was taking care of some business with his father, and of course there was school. She didn't mind his absence because she was still actively searching for employment and because she was now secure in their relationship. Today, he spent most of his time yelling at the flat screen television over the football game with her male cousins.

Shortly before dinner was served the doorbell chimed.

"Happy Thanksgiving," Shay said and invited Shannon in.

"Your mother invited me," Shannon explained. "I hope you don't mind me being here?"

Shay waved Shannon's apprehension away. "Of course I don't mind. I left all that mess in the past. Come on in, I'll introduce you to everyone." Shay went around the room and formally introduced Shannon to her family members she hadn't met.

Brian spotted Shannon and Shay together. He hurriedly left his boys and joined Shay.

"Happy Thanksgiving, Shannon."

She held her head down. "Happy Thanksgiving, Brian," Shannon said in an unfamiliar soft voice.

Brian could tell she was uncomfortable by the fidgeting. He bent down and gave her a light hug. "I told you everything was all right. I've forgiven you."

"Thank you." Shannon smiled slightly just as Marcus joined them with a Henry Wienhard's root beer in hand.

"Hey, cuz, why didn't you introduce me to this lovely young lady?" Marcus asked, while smiling at Shannon.

Shay looked at him sideways. "Marcus, what are you talking about?"

"How come I haven't had the pleasure of meeting your beautiful friend?" Marcus's eyes remained on Shannon.

Shannon looked up at Marcus and rolled her eyes.

Brian stood there with his mouth open.

"Marcus, you know you've met her before," Shay snapped. Then it occurred to her that Marcus hadn't seen Shannon since her transformation.

Marcus stepped closer to Shannon. "You'll have to excuse my cousin and her bad manners. She really does have better home training. Let me introduce myself, I'm Marcus Simone," he said then took a swig of root beer.

Shannon put her hand on her hip and rolled her neck. "Marcus, it's me, Shannon."

Before he could stop himself, Marcus spit out his root beer, right into Shannon's face.

Brian and Shay fell over with laughter.

Embarrassed, Marcus stammered, "I'm so sorry-I...Let-me-"

Shannon held up her hands. "Forget it, Marcus!"

"Come on, Shannon, I'll show you where the bathroom is." Shay giggled.

After the ladies were gone, Marcus looked at Brian with amazement. "That's Shannon? What happened to her?"

"It sure is and from where I stand, it looks like you liked what you saw," Brian teased.

"Man....I...What....How?" Marcus couldn't even form a sentence.

Brian left Marcus standing there trying to remember how to put more than two words together in a sentence. A moment later, Marcus turned to see Justin and Craig pointing and laughing along with Brian.

When Shannon returned from cleaning herself up, Marcus approached her again. She saw him coming and held up both hands. "Hold on, let me get an umbrella."

He laughed, but she didn't, so he turned serious. "Look, Shannon, I'm sorry, but I didn't recognize you. You look so, so different. You sound different too. I didn't know it was you."

Shannon cowered her shoulders and spoke so low he

barely heard her. "Marcus, I know I look different, but this is the real me."

Marcus watched her for a moment, as if he were making an assessment. She nervously folded her arms around her midsection. "Shannon," he said finally. "Keep up the new look. The real you is very nice." He turned and walked away just as Julia announced dinner was served.

Reggie gave the traditional Thanksgiving prayer. The family and guests then took turns expressing what each of them was thankful for before everyone dug in. On more than one occasion, Shay looked up from enjoying her food to find at least one person smiling at her. That one person was Brian.

Completely stuffed, everyone congregated into the living room. Shay wondered why everyone chose to crowd into one room when there were other rooms available. Then she spotted Marcus's keyboard on a pedestal in the corner and assumed he was going to entertain the Thanksgiving crowd with his music. She went back into the dining room and helped Leah, Taylor and Staci with the dishes. It was a tradition at every family gathering, the grandchildren handled clean-up duty.

"Shay, why don't you go into the living room and let us tackle this mountain?" Taylor suggested.

Shay walked by her and placed the stack of used plates on the center island. "I don't mind helping with the dishes. Anyway, I can hear Marcus play anytime."

When she left for the dining room again, Julia came into the kitchen. "Where is she?" Julia asked excitedly.

"She's in there collecting dishes." Staci pointed toward the dining room. Julia left without another word.

Uncle Jonathan was waiting for Shay when she dropped off the second load of dishes. "Can I see you in the living room for a minute?" he asked seriously.

"Well, sure," she answered, more confused than ever.

Her cousins snickered amongst themselves while Shay

washed and dried her hands. As soon as she walked out the threshold, they laughed then raced to the living room.

Inside the crowded living room, Shay immediately knew something was up and that she was at the center of it all. All eyes were on her as she followed her uncle Jonathan to the only vacant seat in front right next to the fireplace. Julia and Alysse were standing on opposite sides of the empty chair just smiling like they needed a trip to the county psyche ward. Reggie stood behind them with a handheld camcorder.

Shay finally sat down and Brian appeared out of nowhere with a dozen long-stemmed red roses. At that moment, Shay realized this would be a Thanksgiving she would never forget.

"These are for you." He squatted down in front of her and placed the roses across her lap.

"Thank you," she said softly, trying to keep her emotions in tack. Julia passed her a tissue, because it was just a matter of time before Shay would lose control. The Simone women were known for shedding sentimental tears.

"Shay," Brian continued, "I love you more than I know how to say."

"You're doing all right to me," Mark said from behind Alysse. Several others agreed.

"If I could sing, I would sing you a song. But since I can't sing, I wrote these words." He placed a scroll in her hand. She motioned to open and read it, but he restrained her.

"You can read it later. I gave the words to Marcus and he has put them to music."

Shay looked over Brian's shoulder at Marcus, who was grinning, then back at Brian.

"As you listen to Marcus sing the words, remember you're listening to my heart."

Shay started to cry and so did most of the other females. Even Shannon dabbed at her eyes.

When the music started, Brian stood and extended his hand to her. "May I have this dance?" She handed the flowers to her mother and yielded to him. They slow-danced as Marcus serenaded them. As they moved in perfect rhythm she allowed the words of the song to resonate in her heart. She loved the song. Shay laid her head against his chest and cried some more. Brian held her even tighter to emphasize what the words meant.

"Whew," Alysse used her hand to fan herself. "I can't take too much more of this."

"Neither can I," Nikki added.

When the song ended the crowded room erupted with cheers as Brian knelt down on one knee and took Shay's left hand into his.

Shay didn't think she had any tears left, but a fresh batch came quickly and effortlessly. "Oh, my God! Oh, my God!" she screamed when Brian reached into his pocket and came out with an engagement ring.

"LaShay Seana Hampton, will you marry me?"

"Yes!" Both Julia and Alysse yelled before Shay could answer. The audience laughed. "Trust me, she will," Julia added.

When she finished laughing, Shay used her thumb to still Brian's lower lip. "Yes, Brian Deshawn Pennington, I will marry you."

Everyone celebrated with hugs and high-fives as Brian placed the engagement ring on her finger. Brian was about to plant a kiss on her lips when his mother and the rest of the family interrupted his flow.

Alysse put her arm around him. "Boy, you're a little slow, but you come through. You come through big too. I didn't know you were this romantic."

The newly engaged couple was bombarded with congratulations until Alysse asked the question, "When's the wedding?"

"Not until Brian finishes law school," Shay answered from over her shoulder.

Alysse was not happy. "What? That's nearly two years away."

Reggie and Julia looked at each other.

Shay wrapped her arms around Brian's waist. "I'm sorry, Ms. Alysse, but that's what my boo wants."

"Humph, boy, I guess I can't expect too much from you, considering who your daddy is." Alysse glared at Brian and folded her arms.

Reggie surprised everyone in the room when he said, "Alysse, shut up."

Brian spoke up before his mother let loose. "I hear June weddings are nice. I checked the calendar and guess what?"

"What?" Shay tried to contain her excitement, but her bright eyes gave her away.

"My birthday falls on a Saturday next year. I can't think of a better way to spend my birthday."

Shay wanted a clear understanding before she did her victory dance. "Brian," she began slowly, "are you saying that you want to get married on your twenty-fifth birthday? Are you saying that you want to get married eight months from now?"

"Yes." Shay jumped in the air.

"But on one condition."

Deflated, Shay's shoulders slumped. "What?"

He leaned down and whispered in her ear. "That we don't have any children until after I pass the Bar exam."

"Can we at least practice?" Shay asked out loud.

"As much as you want." Brian smiled then finally got his kiss.

AT LAST...

Brian waited anxiously in Reggie's office for the ceremony that would change his life forever to begin. So much had happened since he proposed to Shay eight months ago. It amazed him how everything had fallen into place for them. God had provided everything he needed to provide a comfortable living for his bride.

When Brian shared his financial dilemma with his father, he was surprised to learn that Reggie had money invested for him and was planning on giving it to him after he graduated law school. Since Brian had proven himself responsible, Reggie decided to give him control of the portfolio now. With proper budgeting, Brian wouldn't have any problems providing for him and Shay until he started practicing law.

Reggie had always planned on giving his parents' home to Brian one day, so for a wedding present he and Julia deeded the Oakland property over to Brian and Shay. Todd found an apartment closer to UCSF and Brian moved out to Blackhawk while Reggie and Julia had the house remodeled to Brian and Shay's specifications. This included adding a larger master bedroom suite and bathroom, plus a swimming pool. Shay's paternal grandparents furnished the house with new furniture and Mark and Alysse gave them a seven-day Caribbean cruise for their honeymoon.

As for his relationship with Shay, it was stronger than ever. Over the past eight months, they had gotten to know each other on a more intimate level. He didn't think it was possible, but he loved her more now than he did the day he proposed. Just the thought of her made his heart warm and his pulse soar.

"You must be thinking about Shay?" Best Man Todd said taking note of Brian's smile.

Before Brian could try to put up a front, his groomsmen answered for him.

"You know he is. She's the only thing on his mind," Craig answered.

"The other day I asked him what his name was and he answered, 'Shay'," Justin teased.

"One morning Shay left him standing in the doorway with tears in his eyes. She was only going to the grocery store!" Reggie enjoyed making fun of his son.

Brian didn't say a word while his boys and father continued poking fun at him. He didn't care what they said. He loved Shay and didn't care who knew how much.

Reggie looked down at his watch; the wedding was due to start in half an hour. "Can I have a moment alone with Brian?" he asked the group.

"Sure," the four groomsmen made their exit, but not before throwing a few more jabs at Brian.

Reggie walked over to Brian and straightened his bowtie. "How do you feel? Scared? Nervous? Anxious? Excited?"

Brian took a deep breath and answered, "All of the above."

"I felt the same way the day I married Julia."

Brian chuckled. "I remember you came in here yelling and screaming."

Reggie didn't deny his irrational behavior on his wedding day six years ago. He finished adjusting Brian's bowtie then stood face-to-face with his son. Reggie's facial expression grew serious. "Brian," he began, "I am so proud of you. I think you are going to make a very good husband and someday a great father."

"I know I am."

"What makes you so sure?"

"I have the best example," Brian said sincerely.

"Thank you," Reggie said right before he embraced his

son. Moments like this made the seventeen years he'd spent away from his son irrelevant.

* * *

Shay stared at her reflection in the mirror as her mother applied the finishing touches to her hair. In a short while she would stand next to the man whom she loved with all of her heart and vow before God and hundreds of witnesses to love him forever.

In the past eight months she learned so much about God and even more about herself. With prayer and perseverance, she remained faithful to God and to herself. She put her job search on hold until after the honeymoon and focused on serving God and planning the wedding. She spent what little free time she had tutoring the elementary children at True Worship's Community Center and on Sundays she taught the kindergarten Sunday school class.

On Thursday evenings, she and Brian attended the twelve-step pre-marriage counseling classes Reggie made mandatory for every couple that wanted him to marry them. In the classes Shay learned what it meant for a husband and wife to work together as a unit and not compete against one another. At the completion of the classes she and Brian had a new appreciation for their parents' relationship and for each other.

Shay placed her fingers on the silver heart around her wrist. She chose to wear it today for the traditional *something old* item.

"Thank you, God, for another chance," she said out loud.

Her cousin Staci stood to her right. "Amen, cuz!" she said, stifling a giggle.

Shay leaned in her direction. "What are you so happy about? I know it's not because of me and Brian."

"It's your wedding day, why shouldn't I be happy?"

"Girl, stop playin', that smile on your face has nothing to do with me," Shay insisted.

Staci couldn't contain her excitement any longer. "Derrick's coming!"

301

"When?"

"He's coming to the wedding."

"Does this mean you guys are getting back together?" Shay asked hopefully.

"We've been talking for the last month. We have a long way to go, but I think it's going to happen."

Shay placed her free hand on her cousin. "I'll be praying for you—as soon as I come back from my honeymoon, that is."

"I know that's right, your hands are going to be full for a while." Staci left Shay alone with her mother.

"Oh, Mama, I am so happy."

Done with styling Shay's freshly colored honey-blonde curls, Julia admired her daughter's reflection in the mirror. "I can tell. You better calm down before you pee on yourself," Julia teased.

"Mama, now I know how you felt that day when you ran around the airport over Reggie." Shay laughed.

"Baby, I love that man so much, I would chase a plane down the runway to get to him," Julia said with a straight face.

"That's how I feel about Brian. Mama, I love him so much."

Julia's expression turned serious. "Remember that, Shay. No matter what happens, always remember that you love him. If you can remember that, the tough times won't seem so hard."

Shay placed her hand on her mother's and held Julia's gaze. "Mama, I haven't told you this, but you are the best mother in the world. You are always there when I need you, even when I make a mess of things. You step back just far enough to allow me to make my own mistakes, but you never leave me."

Julia softly stroked Shay's cheek. "I am proud of how much you've matured over the past nine months. You have blossomed into an awesome young woman. You were always beautiful, but now you have some common sense to go along with that beauty." Julia reached into her robe pocket. "These are for you, for the *something new.*

Shay gasped. "Mama, these are beautiful!"

"I'm glad you like them," Julia said and inserted the tear-shaped diamond earrings into her daughter's ears.

Shay stood and embraced her mother. "Thank you, Mama, for everything. The house, the wedding, everything; thank you."

"Take care of yourself, baby," Julia whispered then scurried away before she broke down.

* * *

Brian stood majestic in his white tuxedo between his father and Todd. As hard as he tried, he couldn't stop smiling. He looked around the beautifully decorated sanctuary. The archway, under which he waited for his bride, was covered with red and white roses. Hanging from the pews and candelabras were more red and white roses and calla lilies. Above his head, the chandeliers were also draped with white netting. The lit candles gave the church an angelic ambiance.

Since Brian had such a small family and he and Shay were the products of blended families, he and Shay didn't see the point of separating the families for the ceremony. So instead of sitting on opposite sides, both families sat together in the center section. Julia and Alysse sat side by side on the front row with Mark and Brian's great aunt and uncle along with Shay's maternal and paternal grandparents.

When the aisle runner was laid, Julia stood and faced the door. The doors to the sanctuary opened and Brian's heart nearly stopped.

Shay waited in the vestibule while her bridesmaids marched into the crowded sanctuary. She could barely contain herself as she waited for the doors to the sanctuary to open for her entrance. This was her dream.

"You're not supposed to cry before you march down the aisle," her uncle Jonathan teased.

"I can't help it, Uncle Jon, I'm so happy," she shrieked.

303

"I'm happy for you." He kissed her on the cheek. "And you look simply beautiful."

"Thank you."

At that moment Shay heard the music to the song Brian had written for her when he proposed.

"Ready?" asked her uncle. Shay couldn't speak; she just nodded.

As Marcus sang the words written just for her, Shay slowly made her way down the aisle. She was glad her uncle was at her side, because it was his strong arm that kept her from running down the aisle to her man. To her, Brian was so handsome and perfect for her. His six-foot-four-inch, two-hundred-forty pounds was everything she wanted and his baldhead, an added bonus. Besides being satisfied with his physical attributes, she felt in her heart without a doubt he loved her with his whole heart and loved God even more.

On the front row Julia and Alysse were having a serious mommy moment that included tears and tissues.

"Girl, look at our babies," Julia started.

"Lord, where did the time go?"

"I hope I taught her everything."

"My baby boy is all grown up. Lord, what am I going to do?"

Waiting on the platform, Reggie in his white official clergy attire had a few tears of his own. But Brian had enough tears for everyone.

"I know why I'm crying; why is he crying?" Alysse asked Mark.

"He's in love."

"Does love make you cry like a wimp in front of everybody?"

Mark shook his head at his wife. "Alysse, I love you and sometimes you make me want to cry."

Alysse twisted her face at him. "I'll deal with you later." She turned her attention back to Brian. When she thought they'd made eye contact, she mouthed, "Man up."

Brian ignored his mother. Shay looked like an angel to

him, in the white off-the- shoulder beaded gown with extended train. With her blonde hair pinned up the way it was, she looked like royalty. To Brian she was simply beautiful. The best part was that she was his. "My Shay," he mouthed to her.

He took her hand from Uncle Jonathan and assisted her under the archway. Brian couldn't help himself and neither could she. They wrapped their arms around each other and held each other until Reggie whispered, "We're not there yet?"

They had written their own vows, but both were too excited to remember them. Instead Reggie had them recite the traditional vows.

When Reggie asked Shay if she took Brian as her husband, the audience laughed when Shay yelled, "I do," before Reggie could get the complete question out.

After Brian placed her wedding band on her finger, Shay made a fist in the air and yelled, "Yes!"

Reggie finally pronounced them husband and wife. When they kissed, Brian squeezed her so tight that he literally lifted her off of her feet.

"I love you," Shay whispered when their lips parted.

"I love you more." Brian kissed her again.

Halfway down the aisle, marching out, Shay looked up toward heaven, raised her hand and yelled, "Thank you, Jesus!"

* * *

Brian and Shay walked around the reception hall greeting their guests and handing out wedding favors. Every five minutes or so someone in the room would tap the glasses to get the bride and groom to kiss. The newlyweds didn't have any problems accommodating every request.

Brian and Shay gave Marcus a sideward stare when they saw that he was sitting next to Shannon. Marcus either didn't see them or pretended not to, and continued talking to her.

"I wonder where that's going to lead," Shay whispered to Brian.

"I have no idea, but I'm sure Marcus can handle it."

The traditional Father and Bride dance was another example of how far the blended family had grown together. Shay took turns dancing with her uncle Jonathan, Reggie and Mark. Brian did the same for Alysse and Julia.

"Mama J, I am forever indebted to you," Brian told Julia.

"What are you talking about, baby?"

"First, you gave me my dad and if it wasn't for you, I wouldn't have a beautiful wife."

Julia hugged him. "Just be good to my baby."

Brian looked over at Shay with his dad, and answered, "Always."

"I guess I can really call you 'Dad' now," Shay said to Reggie.

"If that's what you like," he answered, "I'd be honored."

Shay looked at him seriously. "You know, Dad, if Brian is half as good to me as you are to my mother, I know we will be happy. Thank you for being so good to my mother—and to me." Shay knew Reggie didn't know what to say; she kissed his cheek and continued dancing.

The DJ announced it was Simone family praise dance time and the dance floor flooded with the Simone family and friends. Brian and Shay led the group in the simple step similar to the Electric Slide. They were in the middle of the second song, when Shay took Brian by the hand and kissed him. "Happy Birthday, Mr. Pennington."

"Thank you, Mrs. Pennington." He returned the kiss. "Are you ready to leave? I'm ready for my present."

More Books

by Wanda B. Campbell

First Sunday in October (Simone Family Series #1)

Illusions

Right Package, Wrong Baggage

Silver Lining

Liberation (Simone Family Series #3)

Unresolved Issues (Simone Family Series #4)

Kayla's Redemption

Doin' Me

Back to Me

Under the Influence

EXCERPT FROM LIBERATION

Marcus and Shannon's story

CHAPTER 2

Marcus stood at the entrance of Shannon's workstation and watched her head bop as she sang to his CD and typed on the computer. She had her back turned so she didn't notice him standing there. As he studied her, he noted that he had never seen her so relaxed and natural. He had to admit he liked the new Shannon. The short dark brown sugar sassy young woman was simply beautiful in his eyes. She was insecure, but beautiful nonetheless. Every time he tried to talk to her, she hung her head down and nervously played with her hands. He had no doubt that if she knew he was observing her now, she would try to crawl underneath her desk and hide.

He had asked her out once before, but she turned him down and had avoided him since. He accepted her brush off as final, but now watching her, he changed his mind. He was up for a challenge and no doubt Shannon would prove to be a worthy opponent.

Marcus quietly and purposefully stepped to the front of her desk. "I'm glad you enjoy my music so much," he said when the song ended. He leaned against the door opening and observed her gasp then glanced downward and straighten her clothing before rubbing her tongue over her teeth to remove any lipstick. Something his sister, Staci used to do when meeting a guy she liked.

When she turned to face him the tables turned and he

became concerned about his appearance. His dark brown slacks and matching leather jacket seem inadequate for the woman before him. He opened the jacket, revealing a cream turtleneck that accentuated every muscle in his upper torso.

"Hello, Marcus. Ms. Julia is not here. She's at the Jack London Square worksite. Would you like to leave a message for her?"

To his surprise Shannon's voice was full of confidence. It's amazing what sitting behind a desk can do for a person, Marcus thought. "No, just tell her I came by, she'll know what it's about," he answered without taking his eyes away from her face. Five – four – three, Marcus mentally counted the seconds before she would start playing with her fingers.

"Would you like for me to autograph the CD for you?" he asked still focusing on her dark brown eyes.

Shannon turned her head and rubbed her hands together then removed papers from the printer and placed them in a company envelope. Her hands shook the entire time; she was about to lose control.

"Marcus, do I look like a groupie to you?"

Marcus recognized her tactic and smiled. "No, miss sassy, but you do look like someone who could use a break."

"Sorry, I don't have time for a break. I need to get this lease agreement over to the new tenant, MS Computers, before the end of the day." Shannon stood and reached for her jacket.

Marcus knew she was trying to brush him off again, so he decided to play along with her. He walked around her desk and assisted her with her coat "I'm headed in that direction, mind if I make the walk with you?"

Shannon wanted to scream NO, but answered, "As long as you can keep up." She grabbed the envelope and headed to the elevator without giving him a chance to respond. He followed behind with a big smile on his face.

Marcus studied her every move. Once they were outside in the plaza, Shannon's whole demeanor changed. The confidence and power that she had moments earlier were long gone. She held her head down and refused to make eye contact with Marcus or anyone else for that matter. He tried to entice her into stopping at a couple of stores, but she refused. He offered to buy her a drink or something to eat and again she declined.

When they passed by the flower shop, a young lady recognized Marcus and asked for his autograph. Shannon paused briefly, but when Marcus grinned at the tall, fair-complexioned model-type woman, she continued walking. He caught up with her just as she stepped under the ladder the workmen were using to put up the new MS Computers sign.

She reached for the door, but Marcus grabbed it and held it open for her.

"Thank you," she said without making eye contact. She stepped inside and Marcus followed.

"Marcus, I don't think it's a good idea for you to be inside, especially since the store hasn't officially opened yet."

Marcus pretended to look around. "I don't think the owner will mind."

"But-," Shannon didn't finish. A middle-aged gentleman wearing a light blue shirt with the MS Computers logo on the left front pocket approached them.

"I have the purchase orders for the new flat screens and laptops. They're on your desk."

"Thanks," Marcus answered. "'I'll sign them before I leave."

The confused expression on Shannon's face was enough to make Marcus bend over with laughter. Shannon stood stone-faced.

"Shannon, let me introduce myself," Marcus began. "I'm the MS in MS Computers." Shannon didn't respond so he continued. "MS: Marcus Simone."

"You own this store?" she asked, incredulously.

"Yes I do."

"But you're a musician."

"True, but before I became a musician I earned two

degrees. After graduation, my father helped me open my first store in the South Bay. I ran the business until my sister, Staci completed her Masters. Now she runs the business for me so I'm free to pursue my passion – music." Marcus held his arms out. "This store is our third expansion."

"You have two degrees? How old are you Marcus?"

Marcus shook his head. "Now, Shannon, if I were to ask you your age, you would call me rude, but I'll tell you anyway. I just made thirty."

She appeared impressed. "Wow, you've accomplished a lot in a short period of time."

"I double majored in undergrad," he said matter-of-factly.

Shannon folded her arms and narrowed her eyes at him. "So, Marcus, you're the owner of this company?"

"Yes."

"So you could have signed this agreement back at the office instead of having me walk all the way down here." She held the company envelope out.

He took the enveloped and gestured for her to follow him. "True, but then I wouldn't have the opportunity to spend time with you."

She reluctantly followed. "Marcus you didn't have to trick me to spend time with you."

He opened the door to his office and quickly cleared a space for her to sit in one of the chairs. After she was seated he replied, "Yes I did, because every time I try to talk to you, you brush me off, like I have some kind of disease."

Shannon lowered her head. "Sorry," she said softly.

"Don't worry about it. You can make it up to me by having dinner with me." He searched his congested desk for a pen and waited for her refusal, but her reply surprised him.

"Marcus, why do you want to go out with me?" Shannon lowered her head once again and started playing with her fingers as she waited for him to answer.

Marcus signed the last page of the documents before he walked over to her and squatted down in front of her. With his fingertips, he lifted her chin so he could look directly into her eyes. "Because I think you're a beautiful woman and I would like to get to know you better."

"No one has told me that before. You're joking, right?" she smirked.

"No, but even when I'm joking, I mean what I say. You have a beautiful face without all that crap you used to paint on it." Then as an afterthought he added, "Shannon you should hold your head up more often." He sensed how uncomfortable she was and tried to lighten the mood. "Woman, hold your head up and stop watching your feet; they are not going to run away."

It worked, Shannon smiled. "I'll try to remember that."

"Does that smile mean that you'll finally have dinner with me?"

Shannon hesitated before answering. "Marcus, I need to make sure we have a clear understanding before I accept your invitation."

"Okay," he said slowly.

"Marcus, you do know that I'm a Christian now and I don't, well, I don't sleep around."

"That's too bad," Marcus pretended to sound disappointed. "Not even if I buy you an expensive meal and jewelry?"

Shannon was serious. "No, not even if you bought me a house, car, and a dog."

"Good, because I don't do booty calls anymore either," he stated in a firmer tone than he anticipated. "I not only sing gospel music, I live it."

"In that case I will have dinner with you, just once."

Marcus started to correct her, but decided to wait until their fourth or fifth date to throw that statement in her face. What are you doing tomorrow?"

"Tomorrow's not good for me; it's my niece's birthday. Actually, Marcus, I have class every night except Wednesday and Friday. Or course Wednesday is Bible Study, so that leaves only Friday or Saturday."

"Saturdays I'm usually at the studio," he said. "That leaves Friday and today is Friday."

"So it is." Shannon rubbed her hands together.

Marcus stood upright. "What time and where do you want me to pick you up?"

"Today is not good. I usually don't get home until after seven, by the time I get dressed it will be well after eight and I really don't want you in my neighborhood that late on a Friday night."

She's making excuses again. "Why don't I pick you up when you get off at five and we can walk over to Chevy's. That is, if you like Mexican food?"

"It's my favorite," she admitted.

"That settles it. I'll see you at five and I promise I'll be on my best behavior."

"Okay," Shannon agreed and stood to her feet and followed Marcus out of the cluttered office. Just as they reached the front door, Marcus' sister, Staci, entered the store.

"Hey, big bro; hello, Shannon," Staci said. Her surprise at seeing Marcus and Shannon together was evident on her face.

"Hi ,Staci. I was just leaving," Shannon said.

"Don't leave on my account. You can stay around as long as you want, if you promise to keep Mr. Slave Driver smiling like that."

Marcus could tell Shannon was uncomfortable by the way she blinked rapidly, yet, when Shannon turned to say goodbye to Marcus, she held her head high. "I'll see you later," she said and left the store.

"Oh my." Staci turned to her brother. "What's going on Mr. Simone?"

"Nothing-yet," Marcus said and walked back to his office.